LABORS *of* THE HEART

ALSO BY CLAIRE DAVIS

Season of the Snake

Winter Range

LABORS *of* THE HEART

stories

CLAIRE DAVIS

ST. MARTIN'S PRESS
New York

LABORS OF THE HEART. Copyright © 2006 by Claire Davis.
All rights reserved. Printed in the United States of America.
No part of this book may be used or reproduced in any manner whatsoever without written permission except in the case of brief quotations embodied in critical articles or reviews.
For information, address St. Martin's Press, 175 Fifth Avenue, New York, N.Y. 10010.

www.stmartins.com

Design by Mary A. Wirth

These stories have appeared in slightly altered forms in the following publications: "Adultery," "Balance," and "Mouse Rampant," in *The Southern Review.* "The Same Sky" appeared in *Shenandoah.* A much earlier version of "Trash" was published in *CutBank.* "Grounded" appeared in *The Gettysburg Review,* as well as in the *Pushcart Prize Anthology XXI.* "Labors of the Heart" appeared in *Ploughshares* and *Best American Short Stories 2000.*

LIBRARY OF CONGRESS CATALOGING-IN-PUBLICATION DATA

Davis, Claire, 1949-
Labors of the heart : stories / Claire Davis.—1st ed.
p. cm.
ISBN-13: 978-0-312-33284-6
ISBN-10: 0-312-33284-X
I. Title

PS3554.A933414L33 2006

813'.6—dc22

2006040633

First Edition: October 2006

10 9 8 7 6 5 4 3 2 1

To my son,
Brian Wroblewski—the best part of
this heart's labor

And to my brother, Dale Davis, and
my sister, Mary Wolfgram

CONTENTS

ACKNOWLEDGMENTS

This collection has been a long while in the making, sandwiched between novels, essays, riding my horse, and walking the dogs, so, many thanks are forthcoming to those people who were so generous with friendship and talent. To Robert Wrigley and Kim Barnes, for their continuing love, support, and wisdom. To Mary Clearman Blew, who has always been gracious with her time and support. To Joy Passanante, for her raucous good humor and outstanding dinners. To Kimberly Verhines and Mark Sanders, good friends and colleagues. To Ellen Vieth, who keeps me sane, and Sean Cassidy, whose photos grace the jackets of my books. Thanks to friends Peggy Forman, Margo Maresca, Sandy Flowers, Becky Paull, and Virginia Fitzpatrick, all of whom have put up with me in the best of times (while writing) and the worst (when I wasn't). My thanks to David

Long, longtime friend, teacher, and mentor. My thanks to William Kittredge, who taught me to put flesh to the word. To Pattiann Rogers and Greg Pape, who bring celebration to the page. To Kent Nelson, Lynn Freed, James Galvin, and S. R. "Papa Rudy" Martin. In memory of James Welch, for his great kindness and help. My thanks to Phil Zweifel, my earliest mentor and teacher who remains one of the finest. Thanks to my colleagues at Lewis-Clark State College, especially division chair Mary Flores, academic dean Christine Pharr, and President Dene Thomas, for their continuing support. Thanks as well to the Idaho Commission on the Arts for its support. To my agent, Sally Wofford-Girand, who has so effortlessly steered me through the tangle—it's a joy working with you. Finally, my deepest thanks to my editor, George Witte, poet, friend, the first to believe, and the one who has made it all possible.

LABORS *of* THE HEART

ADULTERY

For twenty years Joe Earley encouraged his mother to divorce his father. They were no good together. Fought blow for blow. Not physically, understand, but sniping, from the bedroom, over the kitchen table, outdoors, in company. They battered each other with words. And then, just when he'd given up, his mother left his father after thirty-five years, and Joe discovered, despite his brave urgings, that his parents' divorce hurt, though by then he was himself married and had two children. Four months after the divorce, his mother married Harold, a wildlife artist—good God—who planned to make his career by winning the annual federal duck stamp competition. "Certain glory," Harold said. A pie-in-the-sky thing, just the sort Joe's mother always fell for.

To make matters worse, they all continued to live in the same small central Idaho town, Cordwood, where his parents had attended high school, gotten engaged, and raised their two children, and all the neighbors were the same neighbors, and everybody's business was everybody else's. And now this. Adultery. Especially with an ex-husband. His mother and father, and Harold—what an uncomely threesome that was. Enough to make a son pack his bags, wife, and children, flee the tiny town—two square blocks of one- and two-story business buildings, surrounded by single-family residences—whose only respite from boredom was gossip and the annual sausage feed. The only thing lacking? A town crier. Just beyond town were dairy farms and wheat fields interrupted by the occasional legumes, patch on patch of cultivation ending in the foothills of the Seven Devils on one side and the Gospel Range on the other.

The Devils were out today, their horned peaks white-capped and cheerful. Joe goosed his rig through the town's three stop signs and one light, past the West One Bank and the Log In Bar, the Lewis-Clark movie house whose owner, Harvey Manners, an ex-logger Christian fundamentalist, was bankrupting himself by limiting features to G and PG. Double bill—*Charlie the Lonesome Cougar* and *The Shaggy Dog*. Again. All these years later. Maggie, his five-year-old who squirmed through double features, would suffer doggish nightmares. And his son, Ted, a glutton at eight, would want more popcorn and candy than his stomach could hold. But they'd beg to be taken. He decided his wife, Grace, could do it, though he'd like to see *Charlie* again, watch the log drive down the Clearwater River, the part where the wannigan— the floating cookhouse—catches on fire in the Lenore eddy, a scant forty miles from home, a river he fished for steelhead.

Off Main Street he turned on Quackamore, and four houses

down pulled into the driveway. He flipped the air-conditioning off, waited before he cracked the door to the July heat that evaporated the spit in his mouth. The sprinkler was on. His son lay under it, hands crossed over his chest in imitation of the dead. Ted waved a weary hand, lifted his head to peer at his dad, and dropped it back down on the brown grass. Always brown. Just another losing battle.

He opened the screen door, called, "I'm home,"—no answer. He peeked in Maggie's room and she was asleep on the bed, shades drawn. She was naked, her small buttocks poked up in the air the way an infant sleeps. Joe was startled and mildly embarrassed. A wanton little thing—shedding clothes in the grocery store, outdoors, at the breakfast table. His wife, Grace, was at the kitchen table, reading the classifieds.

"If we bought a dog, there'd be someone to greet me," he said.

"Um-hmm," she said, not looking up.

"Nice to see you home, dear, I missed you, did you have a good day, dear, would you like dinner? *Some fathers* come home to children grabbing him around the knees. Our son's playing dead under the sprinkler. Our daughter's sleeping with her bare butt stuck up in the air for God and everyone to see—"

"If we bought a cat, you'd have something to kick," she said.

"Am I crabby?"

She crossed to him, ran her hand over his forehead, and kissed his cheek. "I've had a hellish day," she said.

"How about tomorrow, I come home, the kids spread rose petals in my path, then run out and play. I walk in the house and find you sleeping with your bare butt in the air?"

"You're right." She laughed. "We need a dog."

Stooping, he wrapped his arms around her. This was good, the feel of this small woman tucked in his arms, her hair smelling of strawberries, the way it mussed under his chin. In his own home. With a kitchen the color of slab butter. There might be better things in this world, but he wasn't convinced. He wanted to believe that this was all marriage was ever meant to be, that you could live happily ever after in the same pair of arms, but evidence to the contrary was tucked in his pocket—a picture of his mother he'd discovered while lunching at his father's house. Left out. Carelessly. Maybe purposefully—his mother in a chair, dressed in a scanty nightgown, a motel room painting behind her. And on the back, in his father's scrawling print: *Emmaline*. Dated three weeks ago.

Grace squirmed in his arms. "Woof," she said.

They took the kids to Becky's Burgers, stuffed their bellies before packing them into bed. Then Grace baked potatoes and grilled steaks; a bottle of Merlot was airing beside chilled peaches. He'd called his mother twice, hung up both times before she answered. He didn't mention anything of it to Grace, sneaking off like an adulterer himself to make the calls.

Grace had changed into a nightgown, the one with the thin straps that kept shrugging off her shoulders in a way he found ingenious. He loved hooking them back up, letting his thumb graze a moment longer than necessary where the little crease of skin at her armpit turned under neatly as a secret. This time the left strap had slipped. There was candlelight on the table, glass holders, and a hank of daisies. She cleared the plates before he had a chance to swab up the grease and blood with a slice of bread and detract from the mood. But after the steak, and especially after the wine, he felt compelled to tell her about his parents. Maybe his timing was off. Maybe this wasn't quite what Grace had in mind, because after he produced the picture she hiked her own straps up, sat brooding.

"She looks good in red," she finally said.

"That's it? My mother's running around with my father behind her husband's back, and you say she looks good in red?"

She looked confused. "Well, she does. The rest isn't my business."

He tipped the bottle of Merlot, and a crimson stream dribbled out. "Tell me that once the word gets out."

"You act like this is a new thing on the face of the earth. It happens all the time. Adultery."

"Not in Idaho. Not with my mother."

"He's her husband—was—whatever. It's sort of endearing. They must miss each other." She patted his hand as if he were a misdirected child.

She was so composed, and he knew how he must look, a man whose spreading paunch belied the child he still felt like, embarrassed at the thought of his parents' sexuality, his mother's infidelity. Grace had taken it well, better than he'd expected, and it was clear she was willing to condone more than he could. He was caught off-balance, not just by her reaction, but by his inability to foresee it. He wasn't so sure he knew his wife anymore. It was the wine, he decided, that made her more worldly than he, able to swallow the news like an unfortunate piece of gristle at the dinner table, then go on with the meal, with the rest of her life. "You're saying you understand this?"

She laughed, and the tip of her tongue wicked out between her lips like a small garden snake. "Because it's not *you* cheating on *me*." She got serious. "Haven't you ever thought about adultery?"

He felt the steak congeal in his stomach. He felt ill. She'd asked as if it was a familiar question, as if it was something she

tarried with on a hot summer day while the kids took naps. "No,"
he said, "I don't."

"Liar," she said.

So, all right, he was a small-town hick who loved his wife too
much to look at others. It had never occurred to him it might not
be the same for her. Did she think about other men, an old high
school love—Jake Bently at the hardware store—or someone he
didn't know, a newcomer to town, there were a few of them, or
worse yet, some packing boy at the grocer's? He'd believed he
knew her so well—the way she sat with her heels hooked beneath
her buttocks when her back hurt. The way she ground her teeth
to keep from making noise when they made love, or bit the
pillow—the children sleeping in the next room, the walls thin as
the chambers of a heart. He'd always believed himself an obser-
vant man with a certain acumen for reading women's needs, a skill
his father had refused to develop.

"You're really upset by this, aren't you?" she asked.

"I feel like a fool. All those years I told her to get out, she put
up with his drinking, his moods."

"Other women?" she asked.

He shrugged. His father had been a log-truck driver. A
rugged, good-looking man who came home with aching kidneys
and a well-used look, that Joe, in his teen years of awakening sexuality, had come to attribute to something other than long hours
behind the wheel. Curly looked used in a new way.

Joe laid his soiled napkin on the table. "And if there were
other women, what's it matter now, all these years later? She's
gone back for more."

"Your father's not the same person. He's been depressed.
She's probably worried about him." She blew out a candle.

"Worried, you check a person's temperature, send flowers, a get well card. That's worried."

She ignored him, licked two fingertips, and snuffed the smoking wick between them. "But poor Harold. Do you think he knows?"

And there was that. Harold. A tidy little man who used coasters under his drinks, who painted birds, and was willing to live with all the froufrou—doilies, patchwork pillows, the wreaths of dried flowers Emmaline was so fond of. A gentle man who must have thought he'd won it all when he snatched her from Curly. No. It would never occur to Harold unless someone trumpeted it in his ears. And in Cordwood, someone would.

She blew out the second candle, led him by the hand to their room. When she lifted the gown over her head, she was beautiful, her stomach mildly pooched from childbearing with small stretch marks shining like rain on a windowpane. He thought it utterly wonderful that her body could detail their lives together. And there she was, warm and inviting and his. He felt like crying. He excused himself and went into their bathroom, where he ran the water while looking in the mirror. He had his mother's gray eyes, full lips and narrow forehead. He felt betrayed. He wished he'd never brought any of it up, had never found the picture or visited his father that afternoon. He wished his wife were the woman he imagined her to be. He wished his parents were other than who they were.

The next morning was Saturday, a day off from his job as loan officer at the bank. He found his brother at Smitty's Auto Repair on Fifteenth Avenue, where Chuck worked as a grease monkey.

Their motto: *We'll fix your heap for a whole heap less.* There was an '84 Grand Prix on the lift. It belonged to Zack Garner, the prosecuting attorney, an avowed philanthropist without the means, who spent his salary maintaining his eight kids and the remainder on the arts—a significant need in Cordwood if you counted quilting, whittling, chain-saw sculpture. Tom Higgin's boy was manning the pumps. One gas station, full service; they had you by the balls in this town.

Chuck was under the rear axle with a trouble light. His coveralls were striped with grease where he wiped his hands, a habit he'd acquired doing dishes at home as a child. His hair was a black swatch he swiped back off his forehead and that, by the end of the day, obeyed under a shellac of motor oil. He wore his work like a lover. Chuck knew tools: ratchet wrench, torque wrench, spark plug socket, crimper, clamp, like Joe knew spreadsheets and numbers. He envied Chuck's down-to-earth competence, how he could listen to a motor's ping, diagnose it, tighten the bolt, replace the part, send the car humming to its befuddled owner. Where'd he gotten that? The same place he got his looks, his straight black hair—from their father, which had left the boys to wonder how their father'd gotten the nickname.

They'd asked him once, at home, at the picnic table on a hot summer day where he sat drinking with Erv Hastings, a wanna-be mountain man who lived in the foothills of the Gospel Range, trapping in season, poaching off. Curly said Erv was a man's man, coming down off the mountain for his monthly visit. Emmaline said Erv crawled out of the woodwork.

"Got the name from my long black curly eyelashes," their father teased.

Erv leaned into the boy's hearing. His breath smelled of beer and Fritos. "Don't you know? Your daddy's dick's as curly as a pig's tail. Drives women crazy."

And then Erv was flopping back off the bench, their father's fist still curving in a follow-through and Curly was on the man, leading him off their property like a bad dog on a short leash. And of course, they'd believed it, what Erv said, because why else would you thrash someone unless they'd given away your best secret. For months after, they'd marvel at the thought, try to get peeks of their father's privates, inspect their own for a hint of the miraculous, until one day their mother caught them at it, and they confessed. That night she made Curly show them his. "These fool boys will grow up twisting their dicks trying to live up to you," she said. Curly was drunk enough to be convinced. It was straight and moderately sized. But in that, at least, it wasn't his fault he was a disappointment.

Chuck took a break, walked with Joe around the back of the building, where Joe sat on upturned soda crates and Chuck perched atop an oil drum. They drank Cokes from cans. When Joe told Chuck about their mother and father's affair, Chuck kicked the drum with his heels, the sound poinging across the lot. "Goddamn," he said, "I'm never getting married."

Right now, handsome as he was, Chuck had the pick of girls, but Joe could warn him how in a town this small, someday he'd wake up to find them married away. All he'd get was older as the girls got younger. Then again, Joe thought of his mother. Wait a while and the girls would be single again, older, no wiser but readier. Enough to make a man dizzy. He thought about Grace, wished last night had been better.

"Cripes," Chuck said. "Mom's fifty-five. *Two* men?" He belched, sipped the Coke, and belched again. "What stamina. Maybe it's genetic?" He smiled at the thought.

"Get a handle," Joe said. But *maybe it was genetic.* Maybe they too were loose cannons knocking about in a small town just waiting to be damaged. He thought about his father, the handsome younger man hauling logs. How he stayed sober on runs—he had that much restraint, but afterward spent his weekends at home soured on beer. And there was some justification for it, after a week driving down mountain roads with twenty-five tons of logs chasing your heels. Joe's mother treated her husband's drinking like an occupational hazard—tiptoed around him, collected the checks, rang up the groceries, quarreled endlessly, sobered him, and always kissed him good-bye. Which brought up the picture of them in a motel—the bullheaded perversity of it all. "She's got a husband, Goddamn it. Whatever Curly used to be to her, it's different now. She's married to Harold."

"Harold," Chuck said. "That sap. Never could see what she saw."

"Like Dad's such a catch?"

"I mean, what do they talk about anyway?" There was a sequence of strangled barks from the Pomeranian chained to the fence in the neighboring yard. Small dust devils chalked funnels across the gravel lot and the sun spangled the fading chrome of a '52 Mercury gutted for parts.

"But Harold loves her, don't you think?" Joe asked. "And she married him. Shouldn't that count for something?"

"You could say the same for Dad." Chuck kicked off the oil drum. "He must have loved her once, long ago. They had good times, even I remember."

"Barely," Joe said.

"Remember the day we got dressed in our Sunday best on a Saturday for a picnic and Curly packed us all into his logging rig and we highballed it for the mountains?"

"I remember that bench road up into the woods, and Ma whimpering in the cab."

"And Dad singing the whole damn way. Wasn't he something? And once we got up there. Wasn't *that* something?" Chuck crushed the soda can under his heel and kicked it short of the Dumpster. "But since she left, it's crazy—he quits drinking and goes to hell. Sits around all day. Sleeps mostly." Chuck swiped at his hair. "Love will do that. Look at you." He poked a finger in Joe's stomach. "Put on ten pounds. Goddamn." He shook his head, turned back toward the garage. "I ain't never getting married."

Sunday mornings, Joe, Grace, and the kids attended St. Stanislaus. The town was unevenly divided between a minority of fundamentalists and a majority of Catholics, an unlikely pairing that got on well together. It wasn't that Joe so much believed in religion, but he believed in the effects of it. A certain moral culpability. Call it guilt. So he was religious about his attendance. Put up or shut up he believed, wrangled himself, Grace, and the children out of bed, hustled them in and out of the showers, warmed up the car, but no matter how hard he tried, how early he woke, it always seemed they barely made it, processing up the aisle just ahead of the priest and altar boys, Maggie chirping and waving to her friends in the pews as though in a parade.

Today was no different, except the small church was full, so they had to walk the full length and around the front before they could all clatter into a pew large enough to accommodate them. Bertha Wagner turned and shushed, flicking her rosary at them, beads like small bloody hearts. She was a genteel old lady with a body too small for her name, whose husband Albert died setting choker twenty-three years ago in the Selway National Forest. He was forty-three years old—too old they said after the accident. Setting choker took nerve and reflexes. "Nerves," the men said, "he had plenty of, but at forty-three—" and their voices would drift off, like it wasn't just a matter of when your number came up trimming, bucking, felling, hauling trees.

The priest faced the people, struck his breast, "Lord have mercy, Christ have mercy." Bertha's head bobbed on her scrawny neck, and her fist thumped her breastbone. Joe'd been ten when Albert died. At the wake, he sat in Albert's yard with Curly and the other men while the women kept to the house, fixed food, applied cold compresses to Bertha's neck. In the way of men, his father and friends drank, told jokes, stories about Albert, the great gallumping man who had two left feet and would have been better born a grocer's son than a logger's. "It's a wonder he made it this far," someone said. "A blessed miracle," said another. And they saluted the dead man again, and again, called him friend until the first stars turned from water to fire and crickets dirged in the weeds; then the house lights grew warm, the windows levitating in the dark, and the men sat entranced, basking in friendship and their unspoken relief to be the ones left alive to feel the whiskey sooty as damp earth on their tongues. And then, when they least expected it, from the stricken house came the sound of women's voices and laughter floating out into the night, and the men shuffled their feet, rolled their eyes at each other, and looked quickly away, as though the laughter of women had exposed them there, huddled in the dark, bolted to the earth with hob-nailed work shoes, and they took their leave, one by one melting into the dark, insubstantial as shadows.

The priest ascended the pulpit. Joe looked around and

thought of the legions of widows, found himself wondering if they lived celibate lives. The old ones, surely, surely. But what about Bertha, widowed at forty. It can't have been easy. What did she do? Hold a pillow to her stomach at night, pretend it was Albert, or did she quash her desire with bridge and the Cordwood Ladies' Garden Club? And he had the unfortunate picture of Bertha in mind, wrapped in sheets on a motel bed, waiting, watching the door. Expectant. Her hair straggling over scrawny shoulders.

Bertha turned to stare at him, and his cheeks heated. He sensed she knew what he'd been thinking, had caught him in church with her naked on his mind. But he could not let the picture go, Bertha strapping and lusting at forty, Bertha scrawny and still waiting in the motel at sixty-three. He thought to say something. Apologize. Undo the thing he'd thought. But his lips stuck together. She shooed at him with her hands, picked at his fingers as if it were her body he'd clamped on to instead of the bench, and then he realized he was still kneeling, his hands locked over the pew she was trying to sit against. He grunted an apology, slid back next to Grace, who was watching him carefully.

It was one of those Masses he didn't remember afterward. Except for that moment, when he'd looked into Bertha's eyes and he'd felt she'd read him like a confession. He drove home slowly, stopped at the baker so Grace could pick up sweetrolls for the kids—bribery for their tolerable behavior in church. Schumacher's Bakery. Emil, the son of German immigrants who brought the Old-World craft of brick-oven double-baked rolls, crullers, and kuchen to this Idaho backwater. His shop was manned by his four daughters, each as plump and sugared as the confections they fingered behind the glass-domed cabinets: their yeasty flesh kept rising wider and softer over the years. And unlike other Sundays, Joe stayed in the car, not wanting to face the girls, afraid of what visions they might produce.

Three blocks from home, Grace dipped into the bag. The car smelled of sticky fruit filling. Joe tugged at his tie, cracked the window. He couldn't breathe deeply enough. "If I died," he asked Grace, "would you remarry?"

She caught a dollop of raspberry in her palm from Maggie's roll, ran her tongue over the sweet concoction. "I hate this. This is one of those questions I can't win with. Next."

"Well, look. You're young. Beautiful. With two great kids. This is a small town, and pickings are slim." He wished the children were at friends' and it was just him and Grace in the car. He wanted to pull her shirt up over her breasts, spread them with the sweet jam from her palms, now, in daylight right out of church, say, *This is mine, and this.* Remind her and make her forget every other man she'd ever known or dreamed of. And he saw he'd been approaching this thing the wrong way. He should weigh her down with children, sail her into the great unwashed masses of grocery boys with a belly like a schooner that no man, save her husband, would find desirable. "What say," he whispered to her, "the kids go to the movies?"

"You're difficult to follow these days, Joe. What is it you want? You want to marry me off after you're dead or send the kids to a movie?"

Maggie perked up. "Movie," she said. Ted seconded.

"Who'll take them?" she asked, spit in a handkerchief, and scrubbed Ted's face while she had him captive.

"We'll get a babysitter," he said and winked. "I'll pay for them all." He felt generous. "Popcorn, soda, and jujubes."

The kids yelled hooray and would not be calmed. But it was Sunday and sitters were scarce, and by quarter to the movie hour the four stood outside the theater. Joe chafed in the sun while the children pressed their faces against the windows. There'd be some small comfort in this if he and Grace could snuggle in the dark. But the children would sit between them, as always, and Grace would not abide furtive groping within eyeshot of them. She'd dressed in shorts and a tank top; the air-conditioning in the old movie house hadn't worked since the summer of '92. A hot one that was.

Joe shuffled in his pants pocket for money, thought to beg out at the last moment, claim cramps, the onset of a cold, claustrophobia. But Grace would read through that, and he wondered if such insight was a quality inherent in wives and mothers. As a child he'd believed his own mother had eyes in the back of her head. They *were* more intuitive, women. And as if to prove it, Grace gripped his hand in hers to keep him from bolting. Men, he decided, didn't have a chance. None of them. Not he, Chuck, or Curly.

"By the way," Grace said, "it's Harold's birthday Wednesday. We're invited for cake and coffee. I told your mother we'd come." And he thought she smiled too widely, perhaps enjoying his discomfort.

Harvey was in the ticket booth. He greeted them effusively. "Plenty of seating," he said. "Does my heart good to see a family out together," he said. "Which movie would you like to see first?"

Joe liked to believe he knew his fellow employees as well as he knew his own family. Maybe better, he conceded, after thinking about the surprise his mother had turned out to be. He watched them for some sign. None gave any indication they knew about his parents. He listened to lunchroom conversations, lingered at the coffee and copying machines. He was embarrassed that he did it, that he felt compelled to mistrust, but his embarrassment had more to do with Grace than himself. Last night, before bed, he'd brought up the cake-and-coffee date on Wednesday. "Do we have to go?" he asked.

"Yes," she said. "I think so, don't you?"

"I don't know," he said. "They'd probably like an evening to themselves."

"Coward," she said.

He hated it when she nailed him like that. It drove him to defend himself, which he always did badly. "Hey," he said, "what am I supposed to think? Harold's got some lost ground to make up for."

She'd turned the light off then, left him standing in the bathroom door so that he had to feel his way to the bed. He didn't have to see her to know the stony stare fixed on her face. "You didn't used to be so cruel," she said. She let out a sigh. "And it was such a nice day, and all, at the movies with the kids."

He knocked his knee on one of the bed's four posters, sucked breath between his teeth, and muttered, "Shit."

"This way," she said. He heard a patting on the quilts. "Over here," and then she was tucking him in like she did the kids, and it was comforting, even though his knee still throbbed. "What's bothering you, hon?" she asked.

As if she didn't know. "I go to work tomorrow. Half the people there are friends of my mother, the other of my father. I'll be able to count those on my right hand who don't know about this. How do I face them?"

There was silence from her side, and she moved away from him. "If I really thought that's what was bothering you," she finally said, "I'd be sorely disappointed, Joe. I'm going Wednesday night, and so are the kids. If you're the man I think you are, you'll go, too."

And that was how women finally got you, believing you were more than you were. Joe rapped his pencil on the loan application folder sitting on his desk. Pete Fussel was coming in. He was an old-timer whose age was against him, except that Pete, a bachelor, had nothing and nobody but his farm and gave it the kind of smart love that always managed to pay off in the end. Collateral looked good, and everybody knew Pete would outlive any debt he'd set his mind to.

Pete smelled of barley and crankcase oil, but his clothes were meticulous and his hands scoured clean. "Fancy yourself a new tractor, Pete?" Joe asked, shoving the folder aside. He knew the contents by heart, and folks liked to believe it was their eyes and hearts you studied, not the numbers. And maybe that was true. Here. For a while yet.

Pete nodded, smiled. "Got a seat ain't sprung, and that's something to recommend a machine when you get my age." Then he paused and laughed. "It's a vanity," he said. "Saw it up in Haley's and had to have it. I'll put it to good use. You'll make your money."

Joe leaned back in his chair. He'd like to put his feet up, lace his hands behind his head, shoot the breeze with the old geezer. "You feeling well, Pete?"

"I'll make it another couple years," he said, nodding toward the folder. "It's a vanity," he repeated. "But sometimes it's all the excuse I need to keep these old bones together. I'm willing to risk it if you are," he said, and cocked his head at a jaunty angle that pierced Joe right through his permanent-pressed white shirt—this old man buying time on earth because he had no wife, no children to hold him in place, and Joe thought about Curly without so much as a farm. And Harold, who thought he had Emmaline. And himself, who as short as a week ago, believed he had it all.

Sunset this time of year was long in coming. They sat in the stretched shadows of cottonwoods and quaking aspen in Emmaline and Harold's backyard. The light slanted over the yard, the town, the fields beyond, and slipped from the face of the Gospels like a fading hallelujah. Joe wore one of Emmaline's damnable party hats. They all did, except Chuck, who, like his dad before him, refused on the grounds that he might become the fool he looked. Joe's hat had crepe paper streamers spewing from the top that kept wafting into his drink, tinting the Dickle a violent purple. Harold's hat looked like it came out of the HMS *Pinafore* wardrobe, but he struck less than a commanding pose, feet launched off the end of the chaise lounge. He wore black socks and bermuda shorts. There were blotches of color on his legs and hands: red, indigo, green. Joe wondered what duck he'd been painting before being yanked away and knew, before the evening was over, Harold would corner him for an opinion. He hated that. What did he know about art? Or ducks for that matter? It never failed; Joe would see one of the canvases and something would seem...not right. But he couldn't say what—a head too square, a wing too forward, the light too planned? And then there was Audubon, after all, who painted some pretty screwy-looking birds, but he did all right for himself, so who was Joe to judge?

He kept his distance from Harold, busied himself tracking down Maggie's shoes and socks and underwear. Maggie slumped, triumphant and naked yet again, in her mother's lap.

And then there was Emmaline, doting on her husband, perching small gifts in his hands: new sable brushes, crocheted slippers, a portable easel, a bottle of Canoe, a potted avocado. It would be amusing, Joe thought, if it weren't so reprehensible. Guilty conscience, no doubt. And then she was bringing out the cake, dazzling with sparklers instead of candles, and Harold ooohed and aaahed and slapped at the sparks swarming his legs like flaming bees, and then Joe was beating a path to the house, while behind him he could hear the first chorus of "Happy Birthday."

He entered through the kitchen, the most functional room and least cluttered, though the walls were frivolous with wooden ducks and rabbits, plaques and platters of tôle painting, and on a shelf that ran the length of one wall was a march of cookie jars Emmaline had painted in ceramics class years ago: a cat, a cow, a rocking horse. And most hideous of all, a clown, whose hand-painted face, tearful even in the best of times, was rickracked with seams and yellowing glue—salvaged after one of Emmaline and Curly's fights. Just another fight, another broken thing, except that this time, Joe remembered coming out into the kitchen late at night and seeing Curly at the table, bits of broken crockery between his lips like a seamstress with her pins, his fingers gummed with glue as he resurrected the clown in the quiet hours.

This house would never be home, he admitted, turning into the wrong doorway and into Harold and Emmaline's bedroom, though his mother had brought most of their old possessions over—Grandma's patchwork, the china knickknacks, a piping shepherd boy he'd bought her when he was thirteen that sat like a junkyard derelict on the bedside table. There were pictures of his children, of him and Grace and Chuck, on the dresser top. And over the bed, Harold's sole contribution: a framed portrait he'd painted of Emmaline, which might have been flattering, except something wasn't quite right—the jaw? the ear? the color?

A hand came to rest on his back, and he turned to see Emmaline looking at the picture with him. "Are you all right?" she asked.

"Fine," he said, moving away. "A little too much to drink. I've lost the bathroom again."

"Yes," she said, "I shouldn't worry about you anymore. You're all grown-up now." She seated herself on the bed, fiddled with the quilt. "You seen your dad lately?" she asked.

He wondered if Grace had sent her. "Last week. He looked good. Maybe he's getting over this." His hands swept around the room. "Maybe he's got someone of his own now, someone new."

Emmaline settled her chin on her fist, smiled. "That would be nice," she said. "He needs someone. He needs a good toss in the hay."

And that was the last straw. "You should know," he said.

She nodded. "I know more about that man than you'd ever dream. Spent a lot of years to get there. Sometimes—"

"What?"

"Don't get me wrong, but the best of it is knowing another person that well."

"I got to go," Joe said, not wanting to hear the sordid details.

"Joe." She twisted her hands in her lap.

And then he had the picture in his hand, and he flashed it in front of her face. "A good likeness, don't you think?" he asked, jerking a thumb at the portrait.

"It's not what you think," she said.

"That is so . . . trite."

"You're acting like a wounded husband."

"*Which one?*" he asked.

She sighed, plumped one of the frilly pillows on the bed. "How did you ever grow up to be so damned self-righteous?"

And he was out the door and down the hall and locked in

the bathroom. He waited until he heard the back door swing open and bang shut. He waited another minute, three. He stood over the toilet and watched the clean water flush once, twice. He ran the faucet, rumpled the towels, listened to his wife's footsteps approach, then fade back down the hall. He knew her walk.

Back in the yard, Joe studied the carnage: wads of wrapping paper, abandoned drinks, cranky children wired on sugar, and the two women reclining on lounge chairs, seeming to float there in the half-light of dusk, patiently biding their time until the children drifted to sleep. He sidestepped a slice of white cake with pink frosting marooned on the green grass.

Harold ambushed him on the back porch. He crooked his arm through Joe's, whispered, "Come on, I want to show you something," and so the new duck stamp effort was about to be unveiled.

Joe shrugged off the arm. "I'm not up for ducks right now," he said. "Nothing personal. But I got to go." He backed away. "Touch of flu." And fled through the house and out the front door. He circumnavigated family and sidewalks by cutting through yards, feeling young again, a whip of a kid making his way as the crows did, heedless of fence and arbor, straight as a prayer. It was getting on dark, late as it was, and the last of the twilight eclipsed distances so that the Apostles appeared just a yard away, a darker slash of gray in the blank gray air, and he looked down at his hands, his trousers and how the color had leached from them in this static time between sun and lamplight, and he could be anything, he thought, to those watching from windows, just another piece of the gray: a shrub, a dog, a quirk in their vision. He took the Rambolts' shrub, throwing himself at the three-foot hedge on wet grass in dress shoes with slick bottoms so that he landed with a skid, his torso twisting, his ankle bobbling and he stumbled down to a knee.

He stayed that way, listening to the nattering of a squirrel, someone's phone ringing. He waited for pain to ricochet from ankle to shin, but there was only the wet, green stain on his bended knee. He walked the remaining half block to where the street and alley convened at the side yard of his childhood home. He let himself in the back gate, fumbled with the latch Curly always *meant* to get to. He stood in the shadows of the ponderosa pine, a lofty veteran of three failed tree houses, the ground beneath it pillowed with duff and needles, redolent with pitch. Gnats drifted beneath the canopy, spun willy-nilly with the air currents, and from beneath the tree's umbrella, Joe watched the house. The curtains were drawn wide, glass glazed with twilight, the last hue of sky, slate now, unreadable, and he waited for the first lamp to light. But it was the back door that opened and there stood Curly.

Any minute now, Joe would call out. Call to his father, call him into account, flash the photo in front of his face, say, "This. This…"

What?

Should have been enough, years ago? Accountability was what was required for the mess Curly'd made of their lives, and continued to, even now, tapping into Emmaline's limitless capacity to be made the fool in the name of love. How much room did a heart have to afford? As if he heard those thoughts, Joe's father looked to the dark patch under the pine where Joe stood concealed, then his attention wandered to the far corner of the yard. Perhaps it was a function of distance, or poor lighting, but his father looked *smaller*. Joe felt startled that it should hurt so much. He wished he'd gone home. Wished he'd been there to greet Grace, tuck the children into bed. Better to view Harold's new canvas, some wedge-winged, off-kilter duck. Better to have stayed than to stand here an intruder on familiar grounds.

Crickets rustled in the weeds, taking up the first chirps of the evening. It felt as if they'd been standing here, he and his father, forever. Children were called indoors and dogs rallied to the rising moon; a clear blue light fell over the house, the house unmoored from the black of the yard. The neighboring yards settled into shadows while bats limbered in the eaves, and lights nipped on in kitchens and parlors. It was a grand shuffling indoors. Joe's favorite time of day, when chores were done and babies asleep, when his wife invited herself into his lap and talk was given over to the solace of familiar flesh. Joe's feet felt numb in his shoes, but still he held watch until he thought his blood would silt downward, and he would be rooted beneath this tree, to this yard as all his history had failed to do. There was a movement from the porch, and he heard his father sigh. He saw his father lean across the porch railing, lifting to his toes, suspended, as if he wished to ascend even as the moon did. The shank of black hair shone, catching the reflected light, and that all-forgiving moon made of his face a young man's again. Joe felt something in himself become buoyant, as though a space had opened in his chest, and even as he wished he could clamp his heart shut against what intruded, he could not. And then Curly was solid on his feet, and opening the door, he swung it wide and held it, as if to call in his wife or his lovely sons from the boughs of pines, as if to loose these vast regrets into the night.

BALANCE

There were enough consequences in life without looking for them. But some people made a fair living by it, and who was he to tell them they were wrong. Em sat across the desk from the court-appointed counselor, a heavyset woman with dewlaps and a pushed-in face, who favored the right side of the room to the left so that he was kept firmly in view, less so Judith, his wife of over ten years, who sat composed on the sofa. He'd chosen the chair for logistical reasons. Easier to get back out of than the sofa Judith had fallen into so gracefully. The counselor looked up at them after a brief perusal of their files.

She smiled at Em. It was disconcerting in the way it is to see a bulldog smile. "You're Emmett deSnoo?"

Em winced. She'd pronounced it snoo instead of snow; she'd called him Emmett instead of Em. Judith corrected her, as she had been prone to do all their married life—step in and set the record straight.

"When did you lose your arm, Emmett?"

He waved his hand, realized it was the one that wasn't there anymore. He hadn't done that in a while now. It brought home how nervous he was about this whole child custody business. "Two years ago, this past August," he said.

She got right down to business. "Has it affected your relationship with your child?"

He'd met better-dressed stupidity before. "It would have to, wouldn't it?"

Her eyebrow rose. "I mean," he went on, "I carry him in one arm. I cook and serve him breakfast with one hand."

"You hold it against him," Judith cut in.

"So *you* believe." He winced at the bitterness in his own voice, knew how it sounded in the confinement of the office, how it must sound to the woman behind the desk. He stopped himself from tucking the empty sleeve into his pants. Judith accused him of doing that every time he was in trouble—a way of calling attention to the fact that he was crippled. A way of shaming others. And perhaps she'd had something there, early on, in the first months; he didn't know. Now it was just something he found himself doing, like checking his fly, like listening for his boy Brad in the next room or out in the yard.

He had to be careful here. The counselor was watching them both closely though she made no apparent effort at it, sitting snug behind her desk, her elbows, pouched with skin, resting on the mahogany desktop as if for a comfortable conversation with friends. She had the look of someone who had seen it all and had

long since ceased to wear her concerns on the skin. That she was
smart he had no doubt. That she was practiced with people (as
Em had never been outside of his job), was obvious in the way
she moved the subject matter on to Judith, *her* history of their
early marriage—the rapid-fire courtship and the resulting no-trim
ceremony. He listened to Judith's recounting, her speech econom-
ical and precise, and he marveled, as he always did, at how she
could be so comfortable in such different situations. She could
mix with the mill hands at the bar or meet with a group of
lawyers. She was a woman for each occasion, her manner and voice
ranging from the clipped speech of reporting to the easy manner
of a chat over a fence. He thought about how liquid her voice had
been the time he was driving and she climbed from the front seat
into the back of his car to tease sweet obscenities into his ear until he became distracted enough to stop and join her—two years
married then and laughing at the awkwardness of elbows and
knees. Judith chronicled her rise from a clerk at the mill to a legal
clerk at a two-man law office, to legal secretary and researcher for
a team of four. She touched on their five childless years with
morning thermometers and afternoon doctors, their surprise
when they conceived Bradley right after they'd given up hope.

"How do you account for that, Judith?" the counselor asked.

"Resignation." Judith released a deep breath.

"And you, Emmett?"

He shrugged, not about to subject himself to that raised
brow again. He'd trashed the self-help books, pitched the thermometers, and spread her across the kitchen table still set with
the breakfast dishes. He wasn't about to tell a counselor the coffee cups rattled in the saucers, or that the table walked a good
two feet across the floor and the bacon was ground into Judith's
thighs, but damn it had been good. "Luck," he said.

"And so you were happy?"

"Yes," Judith said. "The baby filled our lives."

Behind the counselor was the only window in the room, looking out over the Bitteroot Range, Blue Mountain in the foreground. The room was spacious, matching teal wing-back chairs, a mahogany table with carnations pooled in the reflected surface, wainscoted walls—good craftsmanship, mahogany again, expensive, impressive but dark—where certificates ranged. He sat quietly in his seat, trying not to appear outlandish in the neat office, fearing the common grounds forming between these two professionals. They were women. They shared good taste. They were smart. He felt doomed.

What Judith didn't mention was that those first years the baby filled *her* life. He didn't begrudge it, too much. She'd given nine months, borne incredible pain; it was her investment. That was part of the consequences; you give that much, you reap the benefits. Anyway, he'd enjoyed watching her drop her gown to nurse the baby—her white breasts, nipples like new moons the baby latched on to with greed. But what did that leave him to offer the child? A finger to hold on to?

"I quit work to stay home with Brad," she said with a shy smile. She didn't mention what a sacrifice that had been. How she'd enjoyed her work and was good at it. But it was there between the women, Em knew, as obvious as if spoken out loud. "I was so clumsy at first with him," she admitted. Her legs crossed and uncrossed. "I dropped him once. He was seven months old, and I was leaning over with him in my arms." One of her arms cupped to her side as if she were holding the baby again. "And reached to pick something up with my other hand and he kicked."

The counselor nodded reassuringly.

"Out of my arm. It wasn't that far, but he fell. Right to the ground. God. I watched him for hours. I didn't sleep that whole night. I swore I would never lose him again. Do you understand?" Her knees were clamped together, and she was speaking to Em.

He admired Judith. For some women that story would have been a calculated move. For her it was an honest one. Yes. She was a good mother. But that left it up to him to bring home the money, in a job at the mill where layoffs were the practice and hires the exception. Promotion was a thing you scrabbled for, twelve- and fourteen-hour days, six-day weeks. He'd moved from the yard to the floor and saws. *Which made the whole business even crazier.* He'd come home tired, choke back some food, and crash. He didn't remember Bradley as a baby. He remembered Corky, the walleyed kid who, after one year, fled to college short two of the fingers he came on duty with. There was the sour smell of the mill and nights when the stacks spewed smoke in columns tamping out the stars, leveling the sky to a few hundred feet overhead, and the millpond burned with reflected fire so that he thought the whole world was being consumed as the men sat in small groups eating dinner out-of-doors, Ben and George trading sandwiches as they always did, just to keep it interesting. No, he didn't remember Bradley as a baby. If he hadn't been a good father back then, just maybe it came of her being a good mother. That was the trouble with studying consequences—it was endless. It led to blame.

"And was it that way for you, Emmett?"

Em foundered. "We got lost for a while, I think," he said.

"And how was that?"

Counselors were like shrinks. They didn't have a damned answer you didn't provide them with. But they had their fill of questions. He had to give them that. "I was busy. At work. Judith had the baby."

"So, you weren't happy?"

"It was different." He could see Judith looked hurt by his answer, still wanting to believe that, up until the accident, life had been good. And maybe it had been, things being relative and all. "But it was okay, you know, just different."

Em glanced away, wishing he could stand up, move around. He studied a large picture on the wall, as if he could move into it.

The counselor turned to see what he was looking at. She pushed off on the chair, casters rolling easily over the carpeting. Under the picture, she stood up. She was taller than Em had expected, all her height in her legs. She looked over her shoulder, and asked, "Do you hunt, Emmett?"

"Used to," Emmet answered.

"And you, Judith?"

Judith nodded her head toward Emmett. "He'd hunt, I'd gut. Em was never much good with blood."

It was an oil of a wooded scene at dusk. In the foreground stood a tree, oak maybe, Em thought, though he'd seen few enough of those. This was ponderosa pine country, cedars and larch and occasionally the black walnut—the big dollar tree—sweet-smelling with a grain so close and tight the wood came burnished off the saws.

She nosed close to the picture. "There's a deer in here, a sizeable buck." She pointed to a darker area in the picture and Em thought he could make out the shape of a rack among the branches. The counselor stood back a few feet. "My husband's work. One of his best." She dropped into the chair, whisked back behind her desk. "It's what Hank paints—pheasant, duck, elk, like a puzzle—find the animal in the picture. It's the mathematician in him, I think."

"He from the Midwest?" Em asked.

She looked up at him in interest. "Because he's a math teacher?"

Em smiled. "Because it's a third-generation forest." He was sure of it now. "Oaks."

She nodded. "He paints from memory. Says the clearest detail is the remembered detail. He's right, you know. Doesn't matter if it's true as long as it's accurate." She smiled over at Em, then glanced down again at the closed file. "How long have you been divorced?"

"One year," Judith said.

"And two months," Em added. He watched the brow rise again. Judith nodded from her seat on the sofa.

"And you were married almost eleven years. Your son is seven now?" They both nodded. "And four months," Judith threw in, looking pleased, always having enjoyed a good game of one-upmanship.

But this was no game and all this easy conversation did was lead you to believe it was so. And that was what came of trying to fit into a place you were never made for and pretending you could tell your story in an hour, letting yourself believe the story you told now would be better than the one you'd lived. Now, more than anytime in the last two years, he wanted his arm back. He wanted both hands. Still believing that if he had them, he could set her up on the counselor's desk like he had on the breakfast table, on the hood of the car, on the edge of their bed and make her believe in him again, in front of the puzzled deer, the counselor, God, and the snowcapped mountains just beyond the window. And if that wasn't the whole answer to their problems, it would have been a good start. But none of that was going to happen. He was going to sit there, with his arm a hole on his side, his wife good as gone and taking his boy with her.

"What happened, Emmett? You said marriage was different with Bradley there, but in your own words it was still 'okay.' "

The room smelled of beeswax, like the interior of a hollowed trunk when the cut in the wood was new and he *knew* what that felt like. The counselor pushed because it was her job. Because it was her nature. "What happened?" she asked again.

Em stretched his legs out, trying for a calmness he didn't feel. "Ask her," he said. "It was her idea to end it."

"Blame. You're good at that." Judith leaned toward the counselor, her own anger slipping out. "He blamed his son, a three-year-old baby, for the accident, and now he wants custody."

"Bullshit." Em tried to rise from the chair, hefted himself clear, then stood there, feeling clumsy and foolish. "Bullshit," he repeated softly. "I never blamed him."

"Why would you?" the counselor went on, as if she hadn't heard Em speak, as if she'd already chosen sides. He sank back into the chair. The counselor cut Judith off before she started. "I'd like to hear Emmett tell me."

He knew what she wanted. Judith looked smaller than she had before, her hands clasped together in her lap. She was worried. She was concerned about how much pity might be aroused by his story. He was embarrassed that Judith thought him capable of that. "About what?" Em asked.

"Would you like to tell me about the accident, Emmett?"

No. He didn't want to tell her. Out the window, over the counselor's head, on the far side of the valley and beyond the city's limits, Blue Mountain had grown larger overnight with the last evening's early snowfall. Snow did that—scratched every jag and peak clear against the blue sky, the breadth and distance revealed. But that was only illusion. Once you got up into the mountain, snow compressed the world, squeezed it into a tight space overhead and underfoot, swallowed everything—sound to your own hard breathing, smell to a slow burn, and touch to the end of your fingertips slowly going numb.

"Up near Deer Creek, I was getting some wood left over from a logging operation. One of the perks. Brad was with me." *The boy was dressed in a pair of rolled-cuff denim jeans, a quilted red-flannel jacket, and a brimmed cap. Em had taken pleasure in lacing up the child-sized hiking boots, the only ones Brad would wear when going to the mountains. One of those clean days, ponderosas like pitch in the air and the road rising evenly beneath the truck as the earth fell away at the side.* "We were up a ways when I saw a car stopped by some deadfall across the road." *He patted the boy's knees. A wet line from the corner of his mouth formed a moist patch on the jacket front. Em used his thumb to wipe away the drool. The boy's eyelids flickered briefly and remained closed. For the time it took Em to inhale he sat watching his son, wondering what young boys dream. Not what Brad dreamt, but what young boys dream. The truth was, he didn't know his son well enough to hazard a guess.*

"They needed some help, and Brad was asleep, so I put the truck in park," *the automatic being a concession to Judith, though he'd never laid that blame on her,* "put on the parking brake. It was on. They checked." *He left the door open, not wanting to awaken Brad just yet. Two men and himself, they'd have the tree, a fair-sized spruce eroded off the left bank, clear of the road in no time. The incline wasn't too steep, but he cranked the wheel, just in case.*

On his own, he probably could have walked over it with the four-wheel drive, but others had stopped, and it offended his sense of decency to leave a fallen tree across a road. A road was a clean thing you drove your family over, and he'd just nodded to the other men, gotten his fingers around the spruce, when he heard the noise of gravel grating beneath tires, the startled grunt from one of the men. At first he'd thought another vehicle was coming up the road. He turned to wave them back. "The truck was rolling. There was this drop-off—about a thirty-foot drop into ponderosas and scree—and the truck was rolling…" *So slowly that he didn't believe it at first, thinking it a trick of hearing, or like when he'd be stopped in a parking lot and the car next to him would start pulling away and he'd think it was his car, only now he thought it was the road maybe, that the truck was still parked and stationary, and the road and the mountainside itself had shifted strangely. It took him a moment to understand, to release the tree from his hands, nearly paused to wipe them on his jeans, then he was running, trying to catch up with the truck and every inch took it faster from him. He could hear the others behind him, felt a tug at his shirt as one of them tried to stop him. The windshield was a glaze of sunlight. As he ran he thought of other possibilities—he'd roused Bradley out of the truck and settled him safely on the roadside, Bradley had awakened, had gotten himself out of the truck, he had never brought Bradley along. As he came even with the door, he could see Bradley's head drooped sideways onto his shoulder, his lips open and the drool mark, crimson and growing on the jacket.*

"I caught up to the truck, just as it was hitting the shoulder of the road. And as the truck rolled down the ravine—" *this was the part he never let himself remember except in dreams, and then it would come up out of nowhere and jerk him awake* "—the door took my arm off." *At the time, he only knew his sleeve had been pulled free like some Hitchcock movie where, at the last moment, the cloth gives way and the arm slips out whole and safe. But it hadn't.*

"And Bradley?" the counselor asked, her fingers quietly drumming the desktop.

"About ten feet down, the truck hit an old ponderosa and stopped dead. Bradley had a bruised shoulder from the seat belt. One of the men put a tourniquet on me, laid me in the backseat,

Bradley up front, threw the arm in the trunk, and hauled ass to the hospital. End of story." *Which of course wasn't. There had been the long ride down the mountainside, his head in a stranger's lap who worked the tourniquet while another drove the car singing to Bradley to keep the child calm. Singing the only song he claimed he knew all the words to, "one hundred bottles of beer on the wall, one hundred bottles of beer."*

The counselor rocked back in her chair, her eyes shut. "If Bradley hadn't been there, would you have gone after the truck?"

He could feel the chair upholstery with both hands, the one that was there and the one that wasn't. He enjoyed the temporary sensation of believing what he knew was not so, as though he could lean on that phantom and it would sustain him, which was stupidity because you couldn't come to let yourself believe in that. She was waiting for an answer, watching him now, maintaining eye contact, in what he was sure she believed to be a forthright and disarming manner, no pun intended. She wanted him free to tell her anything. She wanted to know if it had been a conscious decision on his part. She was offering him an out. "Lady, I ain't stupid," he said. "It's just a truck." Judith sighed, in relief he supposed. He stepped in again, "But it was *my* decision." And that should put an end to it, but he knew it wouldn't.

The counselor seemed satisfied and redirected the next set of questions to Judith. They talked comfortably. In another circumstance, they would be friends, he thought. They were discussing present custodial arrangements—joint custody, one week with him, one with her, and alternating weekends and holidays. Judith and Em lived within blocks of each other and Brad's school, where he had started second grade just two weeks ago. Em bought a small house with the settlement from the truck manufacturer, lived on disability and studied accounting at nights.

What he lacked in natural aptitude for mathematics he believed would be overridden by determination and the physical realities. Not that he'd let his handicap rule him entirely. He'd also taken up horseback riding, which would give Judith no end of amusement if she knew about it, which was why he hadn't told her.

Before they'd married, when they were in the early days of courting and both working at the mill, Judith had been a barrel racer. Hardly what you'd call a rodeo star, but consistently good at it. She rode a dog-backed mare who didn't look like much out of saddle or under but knew how to cut an unnerving pin around the barrels and not give them so much as a breeze to tremble on. He would sit up in the stands, flick gnats out of his flat beer, and count down the events: bareback broncs, calf roping, bulldogging, team roping, saddle broncs. The afternoon would turn drowsy, Stetsons shoved back on heads, sweat stains riding down from armpits and up from crotches, elbows kinked on the bleacher backs while the announcer reeled off a half dozen bad jokes, and the rodeo clown played the crowds. Finally, the moon would wobble up over the Sapphire Range, and the fairground lights would come on overhead, moths crowding up against the glass shades sending shadows big as bats chasing over the ladies' laps, and the announcer would call out women's barrel racing as the next-to-last event, and the men would rise, half-emptying the stands to go for beer, take a stretch or a piss before the bull riding. Barrels were rolled out onto the dirt. Behind the arena he could see the women riders holding those crazy-in-the-head animals to a jitterbugging canter, warming up muscles, stretching out tendons. But he would walk down to the cyclone fence, his fingers linked to the wire, leaning close to see Judith, wearing the only fringed Western shirt she owned, smoking a cigarette and walking out her mare while the other young girls churned around her, their horses slathered with sweat from excitement. "Nothing crazier than a barrel horse," Judith once said. "Got all the usual cues ass backwards. Relax the reins they run full out, tighten up they only run half-full out."

"How do you get them to walk?" he'd asked.

"You get off their damn backs," she'd answered. They'd laughed about that over drinks on their first date, as if he'd known anything about horses at the time.

She gave it up when they married. Sold her horse to a twelve-year-old 4-H kid who was just beginning racing and needed a savvy animal beneath her. Judith packed away the trophies, ribbons, and photos and never said another word about it. None of those lawyers she worked for knew about that. He would bet on it. For all those men knew about her everyday work life, only he knew she had run barrels. He could believe it because Judith had excised that part as clean and neat as the truck had his arm. He wondered, sitting there in the failing light of the counselor's office, if at times she still felt the horse under her, the dizzy momentum of the hairpin turns around the barrels, and then stretching low, snatched tight as beggar's lice, over the horse's neck, hands push-ing the reins free, cueing the horse to run hell-bent the last fifty yards out of the arena while the crowds cheered and screamed, everybody, after all, loving a horse race, even if it's a woman. Did it come to her at odd moments that she was missing something? He felt comforted to think they might have that in common.

"You're to be married soon?" The counselor was speaking to Judith, who looked embarrassed, as if caught in a small act of van-dalism. "Yes," she answered, avoiding Em's eyes. "This spring. Ted's been offered a position in the South. Louisiana."

"Louisiana—shit," Em exhaled. He shifted in his seat. "Red dirt and water moccasins."

That was the real reason behind her bid for sole custody and his countersuit. Joint custody was no longer convenient. She was leaving. She would take Brad with her. "He can have Brad for two holidays each year and every summer," she said. "We'll take care of transportation. It'll be easier on him with his arm and all."

"That's my Jude, always thinking of me first," Em said.

"Are you being facetious, Mr. deSnoo?"

Em paused for a moment—yes, he'd been flip, but not entirely, sometimes you had to give the devil his due. He studied the counselor. He'd noticed her reverting to the form of *Mr.* as a rebuke. He wondered how he could tell this without alienating her further. "Well, let me give you an example. After the accident, it took a long time to get my balance back. I guess that's just the way it is. You feel lopsided, like you could tip at the oddest moments. Like when you're making love—"

"Oh Christ, Em."

He waved Judith back. She slumped deeper into the sofa, her left hand neatly concealing the side of her face. He might have taken some pleasure in Judith's distress, but he was watching the counselor instead. She was stolid behind the desk, her eyes flicking back and forth in interest.

"In those last months, in bed, Jude got on top of me." He paused for effect. "She used to ride horses, you know?"

The counselor leaned into her chair, tipped back like a brick wall going over, then stopped short and swayed forward again until her elbows were braced on the table, hands steepled under her chins. She smiled at Em like she'd read his mind.

He went on with it. "Jude used to half joke that once you'd had a thousand pounds of steaming horseflesh under you, it just wasn't the same with a 170-pound man." He could see a smile curling under Judith's hand. At the time he'd answered, maybe she just hadn't had the right 170-pound man under her, but once she'd straddled him with those hard-muscled thighs, buttocks clenched and fingers gripping his chest till it hurt, he knew there was little he could do to surprise her in this position. He'd flipped her over and kept her on her back most of their married life. She'd loved it, and he wasn't a slave to diversity. It had worked out well. "And she meant it. But after the accident, I was ... clumsy."

She became careful with him in the act of love, mindful of his balance without being told, as if she knew from those old days of riding when timing and movement were essential. In those last months, she took charge, laid him on the mattress beneath her. When she rode him it was with thighs still firm, a hand braced on either side of his chest, and though she never intended to make him feel so, he felt *diminished*.

"And so Judith rode you," the counselor said, her voice level and thoughtful.

"Yes," he said, and found that his throat ached. He could have given her other examples, he supposed. Judith hauling him up out of one depression or another. Judith outfitting everything in the house with Velcro, from shoes to baby diapers. Judith going back to work to support them. But wouldn't he have done the same for her? Hadn't he?

"That's to give her credit where it's due," he continued. "And more than that," he admitted. "She tried hard. We both did. But the fact is that now she's leaving and wants to take Bradley with her, and the fact also is that for these last four years I've been the one who's raised him. That should stand for something, too."

"Is that true, Judith? Has he been the primary caregiver for Brad these last four years?"

Judith spread her hands out before her, as if the counselor

should divine the past from her palms. "After the accident, I had to go back to work. Brad was still only three years old. We couldn't afford day care, hell, we could barely afford rent and groceries. So, you see, I had to go back to work." She ran a hand through her short hair, unconscious of the cowlick it raised. "And, Christ, it wasn't as if that didn't make me nervous. Em was a mess. He'd given up everything but self-pity."

Em nodded. "But that changed, didn't it, Jude?"

"Yes," she agreed. "After about six months, he seemed to be coming back to his old self, only..."

"Only what?" the counselor asked.

"Only different."

Em waited. He waited for the counselor to push. He held his breath, willing her to ask Judith as she'd asked him, "How was it different?" The counselor sat there with her stubby fingers interlocked on the desk, staring between them maybe to the door sealed behind them, or the wall clock nearing the end of their appointed hour, the first of three court-ordered appointments. Come on, he urged. Ask her.

But Judith picked it up herself. "Absorbed. Obsessed. Everything focused around Bradley. We couldn't talk anymore but about how he'd potty-trained Brad, or how Brad liked to hold the jars while Em unscrewed the lids. Christ, I might as well not have been there. It was like he lost his arm and..."

"Found his son?" the counselor asked quietly.

There was a hush in the room, as if something was about to befall them. He braced himself against hope even as his mind ran with the possibilities. Judith's head reared back. She lifted from her place on the sofa, walked over to the desk, and placed her fists on it knuckle down. "That's unfair," she said. And damn but he admired her.

"Is it?" the counselor asked evenly.

"Yes. It wasn't like that. It was like he lost his arm and Bradley had to pay the price." She turned toward Em.

Em shifted in his seat, confounded with the direction this conversation had taken. How did she mean "pay the price"? She'd become jealous. She felt excluded, and perhaps that had been partly his fault, but hadn't she excluded him those first years? And hadn't he conceded her her rights at the time? She was his birth mother. She'd given Brad her body, borne the pain. It was the natural ordering of parenthood, that first bond between mother and child, with the father moving about on the periphery, trusting that the years would close the gap. But circumstances had changed all that. The tables had turned, he'd given part of himself, borne the pain, he'd earned his fair share of the boy.

"Sex," Judith said, her face moving close to Em's. "You want to talk about sex—I'll tell you about sex. Sure he was clumsier, but it wasn't that. He was inattentive. Always listening because maybe Bradley would wake up, maybe he should go check up on Bradley. I thought it would get better, but it didn't. I couldn't hold my own son anymore because I wasn't doing it right." She was crowding Em now, leaning into the side where his arm should have been. "He knew what Brad needed. *He* needed Brad, and I didn't. Brad's his new reason for living. That's the big payoff and what the hell child needs to be saddled with that?" She was out of breath. She straightened up, smoothed down her hair, and walked calmly to her seat on the sofa.

There was a knock at the window, and Em looked up startled to see a bird slip down the glass and tumble from the sill. Where it had hit there was a spattering of color, like duff from a moth's wing, browns, rust, and a bright splurge of yellow. Was that how it really was? he wondered. Could it all be reduced to a debt made payable? Had it been?

The counselor turned her head to the window. "Ah, that happens often," she said. "I feel bad, but I'm not sure what I can do about it anymore."

Em stared out the window, over the counselor's shoulder. He could still feel Judith's breath on his cheek like a kiss. Judith called him obsessed; he preferred passionate. The morning Judith had gone out to inquire about work at her old law firm, he was left at home with Brad, stalling through the day as he had for the five months since the accident. The absent arm was still a continual ache back then, a prickling down the phantom elbow and into the hand, so that he was prone to reach for it like an arm gone dead in the middle of the night—just enough of a presence to remind him it wasn't there. Brad was restless, shy around him. By midday Em had had enough. He dressed Brad in his coat, muffler, and mittens, strapped on the new Velcro-laced shoes, and took him for a walk. They went to the mill, where he knew the first shift would be breaking for lunch. Even in the dead of winter, men would hunch outside to get a breath of air, blow sawdust out of their noses, clap their pants, and spread a cloud of yellow around their feet like pollen.

Lymon had been the first to notice Em standing at the fence with Brad tugging to run free from his remaining hand. They came over in a tidy group. They were not strangers to maiming, and so, as a group, gave him a good look, nodded, and put it into words.

"On your feet and looking good," Lymon had started out.

Tom squinted. "Lost some weight, huh?"

That was Em's cue to handle it as he would. "Mostly on the left side," he answered easily.

It was the good answer. He could tell by the way they reformed to a looser grouping.

"They going to give you one of those fake arms?" Cyril asked.

"A prosthesis, dummy," Tom said.

Cyril shrugged. "I know that."

"He better," Lymon threw in. "They just put him on the saw this week."

"If it's any consolation, Cyril," Em said, "I never missed a day because of *job-related* injuries." The men laughed, and Em leaned up against the fence, enjoying the feeling that he could still fit in. "Any work here for a one-armed bandit?" Bradley latched on to the fence, tried hauling himself up onto it. The chain links rattled under his snub-toed boots.

"Might check up at the office." Lymon looked tired. "But if I was you, I'd look at a different line of work. Less lumber, more cutbacks. Same old shit." He was fifty, old by lumber industry standards, made older with the fear they'd lay him off before his early retirement date. "That your boy?"

Em nodded.

"Quite an armful," Lymon said, as Bradley monkeyed up the fence. Em reached over and swung the boy up onto his hip. Em swayed slightly, then felt Brad latch on to his waist with his small legs. He rode there comfortably, and, for the first time in months, Em felt as though he'd found more than he'd lost. There was a quiet in the men's faces. They ducked their heads to say good-bye and went back to work. Em stood there awhile, watching the yellow haze from the smokestacks slant across the sky and settle into the hollows of the valley, homes and streets slipping into a fog. A truck rolled into the yard, logs stacked evenly, snow still packed in the bark and a few green limbs trailing over the rear wheels. He could smell the sap and the cut.

"Emmett?" the counselor was asking. "Do you want to add something to that?"

He felt tired, the act of sitting upright a matter of will. Em looked at the counselor, then over at Judith, who sat poised on the edge of the sofa. Her hands were clenched together, her nails trimmed and buffed. She'd always had beautiful hands. She used to tease him about his short square hands—a workingman's hands, then she'd slap them and say, "Get to work, man." It was a joke he'd almost forgotten. "She's right," he said. "I needed Brad. But it wasn't like that. He was learning everything; I was learning everything over again." And yet that wasn't all of it either. Unasked for, Brad had given him trust. Brad would not remember his father as Em had used to be with two arms. He had, for all means and purposes, just *become* a father. For Brad and Em this is how it was, how it is. But how did you explain something like that? How do you explain what you gain and what you lose? They'd taken it all too far, and it seemed again to Em that consequences were a tangle you could never find your way completely out of. "She says that's making Brad pay me back—the cost of my arm."

Goddamn but there were things on things unseen in every action. Even as he had been running for the truck unaware that the last things he was to feel with that hand was the sap from a tree, the drool from his child's lips, he had been full of all kinds of other awareness. He'd had the time to take measure of the situation, his own distance and speed, the incline of the road, the acceleration of the truck. He *knew* the truck would take him along. He knew he would get hurt, maybe die. But that, too, was acceptable because it was known. What he could not risk in the end was the unknown.

And now Jude had turned it on him somehow, his decision not really his to be made anymore, but bearing entitlements and debts payable like some accounting system he had yet to learn how to juggle. In what column did you put his persistent love of

Judith? Where the love for his son? And in the final tallying, what if Judith was right after all? They were both waiting for his answer, and he didn't have but one. "I do know this, I've given as good as I got. You tell me, is that bad?" And for once he hoped to God the counselor wouldn't come up with another question but would have the answer.

"I don't know," she said. It was the only honest thing she could have said, and he respected that. She kept her eyes on his until he nodded and let her go.

The room was quiet, so that Em could almost believe the sound of his heart was louder than the clock that picked at the minutes overhead. Then there was a small cough from Judith, and she spoke. "You're a good man, Em. You're a good father to Brad, just as I'm a good mother." She took a deep breath. "You would think we could be a good family." She looked to the counselor for help.

Em sat eager in the pause, his head feeling strangely light, his body turned buoyant. He would ask for a second chance. Brad would hold them together where Em had failed. And then he remembered the feel of Brad on his hip, that sweet counterbalance, but it was like the hurt of his arm, all over again. He looked over at Judith. She was waiting for him, and he found he had to do this one last thing for her. "But we aren't," he admitted, his voice soft, and she ducked her head.

After a moment, the counselor said, "Our time is nearly up. I'll see you both next week?"

Judith nodded, looking shaken.

"And if one of us doesn't come?" Em asked.

She looked at him, her eyes surprisingly soft over her stern mouth. "I am still ordered to make my recommendations to the court, Mr. deSnoo."

The window was the only light in the dark room, and the mountains grew larger as the light failed. He sat there in his chair, considering the minutes they had left, knowing they would not be enough. He could feel the lassitude in his blood, his heart winding to its own conclusions. Consider the consequences of an hour's meeting. Consider the consequences in the seasons changing, the slope of a hill and a slow-rolling truck. Or her being a woman and him a man and all the natural ordering of parenthood. Consider the consequences of love.

STIFF SOUP

L ater, that evening at the dinner table, while his parents picked at their food, the day's events, and each other, the six-year-old Billy dawdled over his first course—split-pea soup. The soup, untouched, sat in a bowl in the center of a white plate like an odious eye staring back at the child. At so young an age, Billy could hardly be expected to appreciate the delicacies of its flavor, or the resonance of blended herbs, or the savory fragrance, or the generation of cooks it took to develop the recipe, any more than he could appreciate this room with its damask wall coverings, the fretted plasterwork ceiling, doorways bracketed by teak spandrels, and the fireplace nested in Italian, slip-glazed terra-cotta tiles. This was simply the world as he knew it, this room, and this was just another cozy dinner at home, with the three of them, sitting in the unsuitable chairs, laps tarped in linen napkins, while silver chargers gleamed like polished hubcaps beneath each plate.

"Eat your soup," his mother said for the umpteenth time.

"It's good for you," his father offered, a bit of green snicked between his incisors.

The boy inserted his spoon in the soup, tipped the handle up, and let go. It stood like a silver mast in a china dinghy, like Excalibur in its stone. "It's stiff," he said, and folded his hands in his lap.

"We call it hearty. Hearty—you know, good for you." His mother was a tall, small-chested woman who wore her hair wrung like a dishcloth in a French twist. "You want to grow up, don't you? Get big and tall?"

A reasonable question, as Billy *was* small—it said so on all the charts his mother navigated through in the doctors' offices, asking each of the many physicians: "Isn't he small for his age?" and "Look at me. Do I look small? Or his father? His ancestors were Norsemen, for goodness sake."

Not that being small bothered Billy. No. Though he could see it was clearly one of the many disappointments he was to his parents. Despite their misgivings, he was, for the most part, a pliable boy. Willing to do what they wanted and genuinely wanting to please them. He eyed the turgid green with the upright spoon lodged in its center, made a halfhearted attempt to lift his hand from his lap.

His father sighed. "Well, it's cold by now. Hardly appealing, hey, Billy?" He turned to his wife. "Maybe warming it would help?"

There grew a silence between the adults then, and in that space of time Billy's mother blotted her lips with a napkin and settled it back in her lap bundled like a fist. She said, "You always have to be the kind one, don't you. You couldn't just say, 'Eat your soup,' could you? Of course not. But how like you that is."

They fell silent as the second course was served, leg of lamb, buttered lima beans. As the maid offered a dish of red-jacketed potatoes, the father speared one with his fork. "I only thought the child might prefer it warmed," he said.

"Might prefer?" she said, and then again, "*might* prefer."

The father looked up, his shoulders slumping. He chewed the potato, swallowed, and speared another. He turned it one way and another in the candlelight, then looked over at his wife. "Edith, you know I'm not good at these sorts of things. But what's the fuss, really? It's just soup after all."

She shaved a sliver of meat from the leg of lamb, and the fragrance of hibiscus, wood, and sweet pear slipped into the air. Of course, he was right. It was just soup. And contrary to the generations of parents who had universally declared otherwise over dinner tables, she knew one bowl of soup wasn't about to save starving children anywhere, anytime soon. Moreover, he was looking pained over his beans, making it clear that she'd thrown a wrench in this dinner, yet another in a long chain of circumstantial wrenches she'd thrown in his life.

It wasn't as if she meant to be a cross to her husband, though it always seemed to come out that way. Where he was perfectly happy to let the daily affairs of their home life slide, she was by nature called to task. Even now, he was leaning against the arm of his chair, his hands folded across each other in the same way they did at night when dreaming, and he lay on his side curled over his knees like a dog over a bone, while she, always the last to sleep, was compelled to revisit the waking moments of the day: the mound of bills, the endless phone messages, the butcher who denied padding the packages with fat. The cheeky pedicurist. All the tedious moments stacked for examination—each yes, no, and maybe, crowded about her in bed while he snored obliviously on through the night. The clicking of the mantel clock marched between them until she shifted in her seat. Sighed.

"You know best," he said. He leaned forward, arched a brow at her. "Clearly."

And then they were off again—and soon enough the child grew bored, kicked his legs under the table, back and forth.

That morning, sneaking away, as he was like to do of a busy Monday, he crossed their broad lawns, dodging groundskeepers absorbed in their noisy work: mowing, pruning, and hedging. In the far corner of the property, he squeezed through the bars of the large iron gate, and ran down the wide lane lined in broad-leafed sycamores. He walked past the neighboring meadow with its white fences, stopped at the farthest end where a group of horses clipped grass with long, blunt teeth. After a while, he clambered through the fence, weaving among them, the chestnuts, the bays, the dappled gray, their tails flagging flies, flanks twitching. He stepped close to their bodies, and their hides, warmed as they were by the sun, smelled of honey. The smaller of the horses, the gray, lowered its muzzle to the boy, blew its clover breath in his face, and snorted into his hair. When the horses tired of this, they browsed their way to deeper grass, or rolled in bowls of green, grunting with pleasure. Being a child, Billy ran to roll alongside them, but the horses, startled with his running, bounded to their feet, bolting away, kicking and snapping off great, loose farts. Across the long glade, he chased them, whooping and leaping, then they wheeled about as a herd and charged headlong in his direction. The child skidded to a halt, and because he stood with knees locked and arms flung over his eyes, he never knew how they had parted as the sea before him.

· · ·

His mother tapped her spoon on the side of her plate, rapping for his attention. Billy roused. She was pointing at his arm with the fork as if she meant to skewer him. He lifted his chin from his palm, removed his elbow from the table. He looked down at his plate, where the complacent soup waited. He believed it had gotten bigger. He blew a breath out through his teeth, and the cropped bangs flopped over his eyes.

"Let's try something different," she said, and leaned forward, waiting.

"Different? From what?" the father asked.

"Different from the usual. You know. Where I give in and take care of it."

"How did I know it wasn't over?" the father asked.

She tipped her nose upward.

There was the bonging of a pot from the kitchen and a muffed voice, then the door winked open on the cook's moony face and, closing, was as quickly eclipsed. The parents studied each other while the chilled water glasses grew translucent, moisture slipping down the long stems.

"Well," the father said, looking about the room, his gaze glossing over the furniture, the pictures on the walls, and coming full circle on his son, taking in the chunky arms, plump hands, and ruddy cheeks. Wondering what it felt like to be that…meaty. As a child, he'd always cut a slight figure. Easily overlooked, most often by his father, whose gaze always passed over him as if he were more afterthought than substance. He looked at his son again. Thought there was something to be said for being so substantial, at even this early age. In a perfect world, the boy would have been born a logger's son, or a long-haul truck driver. Those parents would have named him Olie, or Augustus—a roomy name, with space to fill. He had a sudden misgiving, that perhaps they'd slighted the boy with the slip of a name like Bill, and he found a tenderness for the boy that he hadn't known in a long while. He felt simultaneously gratified by its presence, and stung by its infrequency. He inclined his head toward the boy, said, "You must be hungry?"

The boy shrugged.

"How about we make a deal?" the father asked. "You eat your soup, and after dinner we'll do something special."

"Oh," the mother said, "that's different."

It was the father's turn to sigh. He looked up at her. "I guess, then, I don't know what you want from me."

"Bribery," she said. "Bribery's not it."

He sat back in the seat, at a loss, confounded as he was so often by her vagaries, her inexplicable expectations. And truthfully, what did he know about being a father? If he was a success at all in this world, and he liked to think himself moderately so, it was because he had kept to one hard-and-fast rule—do what you do best and leave the rest to the experts, and in this less-than-perfect world, what he did best was choosing the *right* experts. Most of the time. Nine out of ten.

The father set the iced dish aside. "We're really making much more of this than we need to. Listen, he does something well, I reward him. That's how the world works. You do something right, you get a reward. Do something wrong, you get punished."

The boy watched his mother. She slipped a spoonful of ice into her mouth, held it on her tongue until it melted; he could tell by the way her focus went distant a long moment and only reluctantly returned. She looked down at her dish, settled the spoon alongside it.

"By that measure, what did I do to deserve this?" she asked.

The father frowned down at his plate. He hated being pushed. More and more, with her, it seemed he just couldn't cut a wide enough berth. "Damned little," he said.

Across the room, a log popped in the fireplace, and a spark zizzed against the screen. The boy watched the ember lodge in the mesh, glow and dim.

Having had enough of horses, Billy found his way into the woods beyond. It was a stickly wood—all hawthorn and bramble—with a narrow game trail. Deeper in, oaks shouldered aside the upstart saplings of maple and aspen. May apples bloomed in bunches, like small parasols about the trunks of trees, and the solitary jack-in-the-pulpits bloomed among the maidenhair fern.

He found his way through the wood with a skill that would have startled his parents. Believing, as they did, that he was in general mostly unaccomplished. Believing, for the most part, that what you saw was what you got. And so he knew that soon now his mother would be worrying, having exhausted all his usual hiding places, and would turn her anger once again on the dim nanny, who would be wringing her hands on the outside while being covertly bored on the inside with the whole, routine ordeal.

It wasn't that he meant to be bad. And truth to tell, how was a boy to be clear on what constituted being bad when there was nothing clear-cut about it. All of it being this haphazard business of trial and error. You ate what tasted bad because it was good. Lessons were good, but felt bad. Farts felt good, but smelled bad.

He wound his way through the wood, stepping through the bright coins of sunlight that dappled the forest floor. No, it wasn't that he *meant* to be bad, or good for that matter; rather, for him it was all just a means of getting from one end of the day to the other.

. . .

The cheese platter came next. And sliced apples, pears. Still the soup on his plate. His mother had been silent, hands in her lap for the last several minutes while his father turned his napkin over and over.

"This isn't easy for me," the father said. He leaned forward, his shirt pressing the edge of his plate. "I know that sometimes, I'm"—he laid his hands palms down on either side of his place setting—"let's say, inattentive." He smiled.

She'd always been attracted to his smile, most especially in candlelight, and felt it, even now, even after all these years and the revelations of broad daylight, the spontaneous quarrels and staged regrets. Then there was a shifting around his eyes, a sudden softening like a long-forgotten tenderness revisited, and she thought about their early days, at the poolside, how he swam with broad swift strokes, sat on the concrete ledge, the water puddling between his thighs, and then she remembered where she was, and blushed, as if caught in a rude act.

"Would you agree with that?" he asked. "That I stray into inattention?"

She sat forward, pressed a new edge to the set of her shoulders. "Are we being honest?" she asked, spearing a slice of pear.

On the sideboard a silver coffeepot shone, and the maid rolled up the linen runner where a guttering candle had pooled its wax. When she left the room, the service door swung like a slowing metronome.

The mother looked up. "Now you're angry."

The father took a deep breath, then another. "No. No." He sat back. "But let's be reasonable. Why can't we just let him get on with the rest of his meal? After all, he can't go hungry." He lifted a circle of cheese from the platter, sliced it into small and smaller pieces.

"But it's perfectly good soup," she said.

"But he *obviously* doesn't like it."

"He *obviously* hasn't even tried it." She drew in a deep breath. "Today, he ran off for four hours, and this is where it starts. Right here. If I tell him to stand up, you offer him a chair. And then you ask him if it's comfortable." She shook her head. "Headstrong and willful."

"Him or me?" the father asked.

She tapped the tabletop with a fingernail. "With the soup. It begins with the soup. Are we together on this?"

The child would not look at either of them anymore. Nor at the cheeses, the gutted rolls and softening butter pats. Not even at the soup squatting cold on his plate. Instead, as he so often did during these dreary family dinners, he looked at the wall, at the tapestry, a late-seventeenth-century Beauvais of a wood—dark and deep—that had at its heart a pond. He stared at the needled bits of color: the undersides of leaves, tree trunks, grass, the great white bird at the bank of a too-blue pool.

"Eat your soup," the father said.

The wood opened into a glade, and in the low corner was a pond thatched round with rush and willow, an abandoned wicket on the creek side. The air was hazy with insect hatches: lacewings, damselflies, ladybugs. Dragonflies fed on the mosquitoes that humped up off the pond's surface, and thickest in the under-brush was the hum of bluebottle flies and bees. Billy swept aside the skin of duckweed, pressed his nose to the water. Scooped out a clump of mud, spent snail shells and the homely accretions of caddis fly. He mucked about until, tiring of that, he lay on his back in the reeds, contemplating the course of clouds. He didn't measure time, except in terms of his mother's worry, and then, only occasionally, felt a twinge of guilt and as quickly set it adrift. Hurt for him was still more a matter of surprise than consequence. He never feared getting lost, trusting that having found his way in, he would always find his way out. It was a small world after all: the woods, the meadow, the thickly tarred lanes. When he saw the first frog lap past him, he was sitting on the bank, his toes wrinkling in the water. It was a long wait before he saw the next, and even longer before he caught one, swimming in the bloom of weeds, snatched it into the air by its rubber-band legs to dangle in front of his face. Its throat worked like a tiny bellows. He raised it to his eye, its webbed toes splayed to swim the air. The skin dappled and slick between his finger and thumb.

He put it in his mouth.

It seemed a good thing to do, at the time. Or perhaps it wasn't nearly that well conceived, but just another one of those inexplicable things he found himself doing, like packing grape seeds up his nose, or putting a spoon down the garbage disposal, or sitting in his underwear, in the birdbath, in the arboretum. Of a sudden, there was a frog in his mouth, sitting on his tongue, the small creature shifting about, one leg and then another, snugging itself into a comfortable package. The boy kept very still, held his breath. He believed he felt it blink. It tasted of mud and fish, of green and bitters. It croaked, two stuttering syllables that caught Billy so by surprise that he opened his mouth, shouted, "hah."

Perhaps it was the sudden light, or the startling sight of enameled molars, or even the shifting tongue, but just as unexpectedly there was a small quake in the child's mouth, as the frog flexed, snapped its limber legs behind him, and, bracing against the child's bottom teeth, pushed off like a boat from shore, bob-bled a moment against the safe berth of tongue, then leapt into the dark. The deep.

It swam down his throat.

Because the frog was small, it slipped down whole. Still, a gag reflex kicked in and a swampy smell swilled up through Billy's si-nuses, filled his mouth with a warm brown taste, rather like the teas his mother favored. And then he felt it go still, lumped in his gullet, the inert mass of it lodged frighteningly behind his breast-bone for a full count of three before there was another curious stretching, and plunging, and kicking downward. The boy, still locked in surprise, felt, for a flickering moment, what it must be like to be the water, say, or even the atmosphere he himself moved in—to have this blunt-headed creature fumbling a path through him, setting off the rippling wakes of stomach and throat. The boy stood very still, breathing through his nose, and then he felt the quickening, a bounding—once, twice—a thumping at his center.

"I just want to get through this damnable dinner," the father said. The boy could hear the edge to his voice. And then they were quiet as the maid brought out dessert: flan with its caramelized coat, a side of fresh raspberries, coconut macaroons. She poured coffee, centered a bottle of port on the table before leaving the room, spent dishes in hands.

"Eat your soup," the father said again. "No more dallying." He looked over at his wife, and her face closed like a screw being tight-ened down, but then she nodded and served herself a cut of custard.

"Do as your father says. Do you hear? Do you want to stay small all your life?" she asked.

The boy shook his head, shifted in his seat. He looked at the soup congealed about the spoon.

The father bit into a macaroon topped with dripping berries, chewed, swallowed. "Eat your soup, son." He took another gory bite.

The boy wanted to answer. He meant to say, *yes Sir* and *no Mother*, but he felt a rising in his throat, like a shout, and a belch erupted instead, filled the space about the table with a stewed smell: leeches, bluebottle flies, and duckweed. It was milfoil and rush, squirrels tail, a marl of old leaves, and bark. The smell moved across the table, had legs like a fine wine: molds and musts, blight, puffball, bladderwort, and worm. The room narrowed. Owl pellets, rodent hair, night crawlers, and stinkbug. Skunk cabbage, sawgrass, beebalm, catnip, and newt. And above it all was the smell of frog: green on green, sun and mud.

Long years after this time, when the boy has grown tall, comfortable with success and little else, while of an evening, alone at his meal, he will find himself reconsidering his childhood, in a manner not unlike tonguing the hole where a tooth once was, and he will dimly remember, though the eloquence of it will be lost, how in that moment the character of his world had changed—the green walls with its the tangle of wood beams, the light breaking in ripples across the table, and his parents watching him, their unblinking stares, their pikeish teeth. He will recall how the boy he was pushed off from the table and, stepping one foot and another onto his chair, struggled up for air. How from the back of his throat there was a fidgeting, a rushing, a sound like a glottal knocking.

"What in heaven..." the mother said.

The father stopped chewing.

And when next the child opened his mouth to speak, it put an end, at last, to dinner.

GROUNDED

Only an hour ago Wava Haney had grounded her son Kyle forever, but there he was, kicking down the gravel driveway as though he had every right. She knelt on the shop floor, the chair braced against her thigh, one hand supporting the dowel while she cranked on the wood clamp with the other. Her fingers were glossed with glue, and the chair, her best work yet, teetered on the edge of completion. Lifting her fingers from the clamp, she eyed the configuration for balance. She knew what it *should* look like, this Shaker-style, ladder-back chair, bird's-eye maple, with a plank seat chiseled and sanded by her own hands, those hand callused until she'd lost the tactile details of every day—the embossed flowers on her favorite teacups, the hairs blushing her arms. The chair lingered in a suspension of glue and faith, eminently perishable. On her haunches, she looked out the door. Two precious days off from waitressing at the cafe. Two days in which she'd planned to finish this chair. Start another. She'd as soon pretend she hadn't seen Kyle, wipe her hands and wait in the shade of a tree for his sorry return, then give him a righteous piece of her mind. She rose to her feet, studied the chair. This was a critical stage; it could all go so badly.

She slapped her hands across the butt of her jeans, thinking too late, as she always did, that she should have used a towel. He was on the turn in the drive, and if she didn't hurry, he would be gone. She hiked her arms and tried running, but her ankles wobbled. Should it feel this way at thirty-six? Her upper arms jiggled, and she felt absurd. She slowed to a jog.

The driveway was a piece of work—a half mile of pitching turns, hills, and dips that in winter meant night shifts burrowing through drifts behind the plow in her four-wheel-drive Custom Ford pickup. You wouldn't think it, to see it now, in the dog days of summer, trees wilted, waiting for the final crisp of autumn. Roadside weeds were varnished with dust. The green grasshoppers of June had turned brown and percolated in the shrubs.

She caught up as he turned onto the highway—two lanes and no shoulders, common to Montana. "Where do you *think* you're going?" she asked.

He slowed. She could see her effect in the set of his chin. She touched his arm, and he didn't snatch it from her, and even in her anger, she was grateful for that.

"Did you hear me?"

"Yes, ma'am," he said, as he always did when angry, as though he needed that distance of courtesy.

"You're grounded."

"Yes, ma'am."

"Then where are you going?"

"Away from you."

He'd stopped and was watching her with all the astuteness of a fifteen-year-old already gathering his defenses. She stepped to the high side of the road, trying to appear taller. She was no more used to looking up than he was looking down. All that bone didn't fit him yet. He used it like a borrowed body. She supposed he'd gotten his height from his father, though she preferred to think it was some wild-card gene from her own short side of the family. He was dressed in Levi's, T-shirt, and high-top sneakers, a jacket tied around his waist. No water, no food, no spare clothes. "You won't last a day," she said.

"You going to give me the chance to find out?"

"Probably not."

She could see them as others might—a logger, or better yet, a couple on a leisurely drive, startled by the scenery, heads ducked to better see the mountains packed in the frame of car windows. They would welcome the sight of a mother and son on the side of the road. *Isn't that nice*, they would say.

"Get home," she said. "We'll forget it happened."

He walked ahead. She stood a moment in disbelief. "You're too young to run away," she called, though the fact was, he was too old. At five, ten, even thirteen she could have bullied him back up the drive, hauled him by the arm into the house and sat him on the couch for a dressing-down. But at fifteen he was becoming a man, too strong to tackle.

He lengthened his stride, one to every two of hers.

"Eighteen is old enough. When you're eighteen, I'll lock the door after you." She tried not to breathe heavily. She was past showing weakness to anyone. It had been her first lesson as a single mother in rural Montana, where a woman alone didn't so much gather disapproval as disinterest. "This is ridiculous," she said.

He cut into a fallow field, sour with leafy spurge. Knapweed broke flower heads down their jeans and bunched in the cuffs. She chugged behind, convinced he would tire even as she did, that he would grow hot and thirsty and bored with his own dogged rebellion. Wava settled into walking, and jogging in short bursts when she got too far behind. He was having an easy time of it, while she struggled: weeds, hummocks, and prairie-dog holes. Three-foot conical hills topped the wild oats, the industry of ants shivering on the surface. She believed he could be worn down. There was nothing beyond this valley but the Swan Mountains to the left and the Missions hard on the right. When Kyle hit the bog edging the Clearwater River, his high-tops swilled with water. He looked for a shallow wade, or a felled tree to cross. He must have known he'd be stopped by the river, she thought, and beyond that by the mountains, all that implacable rock. An innocent in the pitting of wills, he must have thought she would give up. She felt disillusioned. He simply did not believe in her.

He appeared disinterested, turning away, his neck craning back to study the side of the mountains where a red-tailed hawk circled on the thermals. "Sharp-shinned hawk," she said, giving him an excuse to talk, an argument to cover his embarrassment. She had a keen sense of what it felt to be fifteen and daring and foolish. She was less certain as to how it felt to be thirty-six and a mother whose son was running away. He started back toward the highway, his sneaker squeezing water with each step. Good: easier to keep up on blacktop.

Given other circumstances, taken at her own accustomed pace, she'd have enjoyed this walk. In the fourteen years she had lived in Montana, much of it had been spent doing just this, striking off across fields, bullying her way through cheat grass, or forests with the pine-pitch smell she'd come to love better than her own baking. It was something perverse in her that preferred this above everything—putting herself in a place where everything most precious could be lost. Time. Direction.

She suspected Kyle had been incubating this idea for some time now. In this he was her son, predicating each move, imperfectly planned perhaps, but planned. It went beyond their fight. It was a product, she thought, of the hours he spent sitting on the back stoop studying the commotion of wind in grass, or the flight of birds. It came of example.

When her husband Joe had first brought them to Montana, enacting the whim and transporting her and one-year-old Kyle out of the Midwest and into the West, she was still young and able to be swayed. Joe was a woodworker, neither adept nor inspired, but he tried. "All that lumber," he'd said. "We'll buy a small place with lots of trees." He chucked her under the chin with a finger. "Don't you see it's like free wood then. We're dying here. All the costs—you, the baby, the wood." She wondered how she could have been so witless as to believe that. Five years later he ran off with Katie Hitchet, who'd commissioned a set of bookcases. The only redeeming grace was that he'd left his tools. The bookcases Wava burned. She regretted that, in a way—those beautiful birch planks. But it made a hell of a bonfire.

On the highway, Wava kept her pace and temper at twenty feet behind. To the right, a pileated woodpecker knocked its head against a tree, rapping like a determined visitor. They passed the Riding High Ranch, the signpost listing over an assemblage of derelict Studebakers. A flock of peacocks roosted on roofs, shat on windshields and dismembered fenders. They screamed in a frenzied chorus, their fanned tails trembling in the sunlight. Wava and Kyle passed a lumberyard, then a small herd of cattle stupefied with the first heat of the day. When she looked at Kyle again, he'd struck his thumb up for a ride. What next, she wondered.

"Have you ever heard a thing I've told you?" she asked. "Hitchhiking is *stupid*. You don't know what's out there."

He was jogging backwards, joyfully wagging his thumb in the air. Wava's heart thickened as she looked over her shoulder and in the distance saw a car, a glint off the windshield like the proverbial light at the end of a tunnel, like the oncoming train. Kyle was running to leave her behind, and the car was coming on, nearing, then passing and slowing to a stop fifty yards ahead. The passenger door swung open. Kyle loped up to the car, leaned down to see who was driving, then glanced back at her, and got in. The door slammed. Wava ran. She ran, wishing for better shoes. She thought to get the license number, but all she could see was sunlight, a frieze on the bumper, two blurs in the front seat. She wanted, more than anything, to see Kyle's face while he was still here, still hers to look at. She was within twenty feet when the gears engaged and the car started pulling away. She could see the driver checking for traffic. "Wait," she yelled. And the taillights flickered. "I'm coming," she called. The exhaust fumed, but the car waited on the side of the road.

The Mission Mountains veered off as they drove down the highway, she in the back, swathed in dog hair—golden retriever, she thought—Kyle up front, his head rigidly forward, and Jessup Taylor driving. Sup he called himself, with liver-spotted hands and a face of indeterminate age. Sup hummed, his bass voice lush and resonant, out of place in the small car with upholstery tufts seeping out of torn seams and dog hair pooling on the floor. Glancing in the rearview mirror, he smiled. "Where you two going?"

"We're not together," Kyle answered. "As far as you'll take me," he added.

"Seeley Lake," Sup said. "Once a week, need it or not, I go to Seeley Lake for a little excitement. Course, given my age and the nature of the place, it's an exercise in futility, but I try. And you, ma'am?"

"Wherever you take my son."

Sup flicked a look into the rearview mirror, then over at Kyle. "Thought you weren't together."

Kyle flinched. His neck looked delicate from behind, white beneath the short-cropped black hair. She'd never seen anything so vulnerable. "He's running away. From me," she said.

"He's not doing a very good job of it," Sup said, downshifting into a turn, five feet from where the bank dipped down into trees brazed with the noon light—ponderosas, fir, scrub larch, and lanky aspen whose leaves had already gone gold above the red dog-wood and bunchgrass.

Sup's head bobbed into each turn, his passengers ignored, as if it were normal to find himself transporting both a runaway and the runned-from in his car, as though there were a world of mothers tethered to runaway sons, and perhaps for him this was true because he was old, had seen enough to believe anything possible, and life with all its attendant quirks was no longer a dilemma. Wava envied him.

"Everyone runs away least once in his life, or contemplates the idea," Sup said. "I thought about it, once, maybe two, three times. But it always seemed a coin better saved." They drove in quiet, the road paralleling the forest and link of lakes—Summit,

Alva, Inez, bright glimpses in the foliage—unfolding like a drunken stagger, one mile forward, two back on itself in a series of horseshoe curves. They passed a stand of tamarack and a falling magpie. Wava cranked her window open, and the dog hair drifted and fell.

"Your dog still got any hair?" Wava asked.

"Sorry," Sup said. "He's lost more than I ever owned." He rolled his window down, and the hair wheeled in the air and drafted out. Sup hummed a few notes. "But he's a good dog." He looked over at Kyle. "Stays put where I tell him. Where's it you plan to run to? You got somewhere to go?"

"You can let me out anywhere, sir."

"You trying to get rid of me, too? This is not your lucky day, boy." He drove on.

Minnesota, Wava thought. That's where they all go eventually, Minnesota or California.

Kyle leaned forward, his hands fidgeting with the seat belt. "Idaho," he said.

"Idaho?" Sup slapped the steering wheel. "Now *that's* a change for the better." He grinned. "How you going to live?"

"I'll get a job."

"You don't look a day over sixteen—minimum wage and a handful of hours." And from the backseat, Wava could see how Kyle blushed with pleasure to be thought older than he was, even if only a year. "You got money?" Sup asked.

"Yes, sir, seventy-three dollars," Kyle said, as if it were all the money in the world—one year's savings, chopping and stacking wood for the elderly Geneva Norwitch, who lived alone with her dogs and spavined horses down the valley.

"Well, you're an accommodating boy. Seventy-three dollars, sir, he says. Why don't you just hand it over and get it done with—

save yourself a knock on the head?" He shook his finger at Kyle. "You got to consider who you're going to meet on the road. But you're thrifty. I'll say that for you, if not real smart."

"He's an *honors* student," Wava said, intending irony but sounding defensive. And why not? How could she not be proud? Kyle was gazing out the side window.

"No offense, ma'am," Sup said. "We'll be coming into Seeley Lake soon, and all the better that I'm out of it." On the outskirts of town, Sup asked, "Can you tell me why you're leaving?"

"She thinks she owns me." The answer was practiced. Believed.

"She does. Heart and soul, boy," Sup said.

As if that didn't work both ways.

They walked Highway 83 eastbound out of Seeley Lake. As earlier, Wava kept a few steps behind. The road—two lanes of long, slow ascents. She thought about the chair in her wood shop, about the glue that might shirk its grip, the laddered rungs slipping, then she looked up and saw her son moving farther from their home with more determination than she could ever account for. He was furious. Embarrassed. His shoulders were slumped under the new backpack he'd bought in the hardware store. He hadn't spoken a word to her since Seeley Lake. And didn't he have every right to feel angry with her? Wava punched her hands into her jeans. No. How was she supposed to know what that old man was going to do?

Sup had dropped them off at the True Value Hardware store, an oversized log cabin like all the other Seeley Lake buildings—a tidy collection of logs gummed with oil, antlers and skulls lofted into every available cornice. In the store, Wava veered off into the wood-finishing aisles. She loved the color cards—pecan, cherrywood, mahogany, teak—the stacked cans of stains and oils, lacquers and waxes. She loved the hiss of a newly opened can, the look of grain revealed with stain, how cheesecloth glided over well-sanded wood. She could use some tung oil. She pulled herself away and followed Kyle. He was looking at hatchets. He eyed the top of the line then pulled a midpriced one from the shelf.

He ran his thumb lightly down the steel while Wava winced. "Good edge," he said.

She took the hatchet from him. The balance was wrong: wrists would pop and ache. It would not cleave cleanly. That's what novices didn't understand. For them the edge was all. She pulled a better one from the rack, placed them both in his hands. "Feel the difference?"

He held them awkwardly. "No," he said.

She moved his hands down the handle. "Yeah," he said. "Oh, yeah." And he handed the new hatchet to her to hold as he moved down the aisle. She swung it as she walked. They could use it at home. A person could always use a good hatchet. It had become an excursion, she thought. There was really nothing desperate about it.

She loved tools—oiling wood handles, cleaning and sizing router bits in the proper felt pockets, alert to the dings, flakes, and splinters that could undo months of work. Joe had respected the function of tools but not the tools themselves. The labor and the means always secondary to the product. And wasn't that indicative of something larger in him? "You're too damn critical," he'd say, one foot raised on the table or chair he'd just finished. "I'm just trying to help," she'd offer, and he'd look her over while picking his teeth. *"Yeah,"* he'd say. *"I can tell,"* or *"Who asked for it?"* And so, wasn't it a relief when it all came apart? Yes.

At the counter, Kyle bought the hatchet, a pocket knife, and backpack. He was down to a twenty, some singles and odd change. He slipped the items into the pack while she looked at postcards. "We could send this one to ourselves," she teased him. "Having a good time, glad you're here." He broke into a smile. Yes, she thought, this could be turned around.

"Anyone here got a runaway?"

A sheriff stood in the door. Kyle ducked his head and started to move. Wava reached out and snatched at his sleeve, hauling herself back to his side.

"Who's got the runaway?" the sheriff repeated, then spotted them. He was a squat man, a lightweight, bearing down with all the authority of Swan County winking from the badge on his front pocket. "You the runaway?"

Wava nodded while Kyle shook his head.

"How old are you?" he asked Kyle.

They spoke at the same time.

"Eighteen."

"Fifteen."

Kyle pulled away, and the sheriff's strangely delicate hand circled Kyle's wrist. There were handcuffs prominent in the sheriff's back trouser pocket. She could see Kyle and herself in the back of the sheriff's car, the siren silent, no blue lights, but cruising at sixty with intent down the highway, back to their home and abandoned on the front stoop. Then what? Wait for Kyle to run again. She blamed herself—what, after all, did she know about raising boys? She was an only child, from the Midwest, where all the boys, she knew in childhood were corn-fed at proper tables, wore tight jeans, and carried themselves with the arrogance of their fathers.

"You got some ID?"

Kyle shook his head.

"He's got his mother," Wava said. "Is that ID enough?"

"It is *if you are*."

"I am."

"Is she?" He turned to Kyle and the boy kept silent. People were gathering in a clutter, slowing down to see better, leaning in as they walked by.

Wava jabbed Kyle with an elbow, and whispered, "This is no time to fool around."

"Maybe we should just go down to the office—"

"She is. She's my mother."

Wava smiled. "Told you so."

The sheriff was breathing through his nose. "This is not a game. I got some old man at the office worrying about a runaway. Now I *got* to investigate."

"I can handle it," Wava said. "I know you're trying to help." She saw herself as he saw her, shirt slipping out of her jeans, sweat stains under her arms and breasts, her hair coarse from the sun. She looked small, foolish, and fierce. The sheriff's eyebrow hitched, and she knew he did not believe her. If she could handle it they wouldn't be here. "You're just interfering—"

"Where's your father?" he asked Kyle.

Wava settled on her heels. "I'm divorced," she said, not that it was any of his business.

A woman standing at Wava's elbow, nodded, and whispered, "It's a hard road."

Wava singled out the woman. "You got something to do?" The woman backed away. And then Wava rounded on the sheriff, because he was the cause of it all—her snapping at the woman who meant only sympathy—because he assumed any father was better than none. She lifted her chin level with the badge on his chest. "Are you done with us? I'm his mother. We're out for a walk." She leaned up into his face. *"This is not your business."*

The sheriff released Kyle's wrist. He was steadying his temper with deep breaths. "Then take your walk somewhere else. Ravalli County maybe." He stepped off, and said, under his breath, "Goddamned ungrateful. I'd probably run, too."

After that, nothing remained in Seeley but to stand by as Kyle made his purchases at the IGA: a loaf of bread, peanut butter, a six-pack of Coke, and two apples.

They were heading up yet another incline, and it stretched onward for a half a mile. They were entering the real heat of the day. Her underwear, damp with sweat, bunched and crept where it had no business. She twisted her hair up and wiped her neck with her shirt collar. She was stewing in her own skin. She considered the sheriff's parting comment. What had she done to merit it? Lose a husband, take on a job while trying to learn a skill to keep the clothes on their backs, the food in their bellies, the sky from falling. *I'd probably run, too.* Well Goddamn it, when was the last time she'd had that luxury?

"Slow down," she yelled. The highway edged a lake sheltered in a hollow of hills, the reflected trees more significant than the real. They passed the island where the millionaire built his log-cabin mansion, six kitchens, fifteen fireplaces. A FOR SALE sign hung roadside. He had one year on the lake before burning his yacht for insurance and blowing off his own head. She could not conceive a proper reason for suicide. She could not imagine the necessity of it. The whole prospect of death and dying was deterrent enough. But how much did a person have to lose before the end was worth more than the means? Her mouth went dry. The water looked clean, the hills unmoved. "I'm thirsty," she called.

"You should have bought something to drink," he yelled back.

She jogged to where he waited, pulled her pockets inside out. "No money."

"You should have thought of that before," he said, and started walking.

"What? I should have read your mind, grabbed my purse, packed a dinner—"

He stopped.

"I'm thirsty," she repeated. "Pretend I'm a stranger. Pretend I'm some bum on the road who needs a drink and not the mother who gave birth to you, who watched your head crown between her knees."

He opened his pack. "That's gross."

"You don't know the half of it," Wava said as she pulled out two Cokes, handed one to him. "Thanks." She took a long pull. He shrugged the backpack, seated it in the duff of pine needles, then walked down to the lake. Wava folded herself to the ground. Mushrooms whoofed under her, and a cloud of brown spoor patinaed her arms. She wiped the sweat under her breasts with the tail of her shirt and leaned back against the tree. Kyle was bending over, picking at the knots in the laces, taking off his shoes. When he was five, she'd bought him a pair with Velcro fasteners. When she showed him how they worked, all he'd said was, *I can tie my shoes.* He put them on, but there was no delight. It was clear he believed she hadn't enough faith in him.

Kyle dove into the water. The afternoon light sliced through the trees. She counted the limbs overhead like a blessing. Pine was good for primitives—plank tables, benches, bookcases. The soft imprint of hammers gave them character, the respect of use and age. After three years of working with the more expensive hardwoods, she retained a fondness for pine. She loved the open-hearted wood with all its knotholes and failings that relentlessly taught forgiveness. If she had a single great attribute, it would be her belief in the character of wood, that each wood had its own best use, each plank its order in design ordained by the symmetry of grain, and that grain preordained by the clemency of weather, by soil or rock face, by the event of seasons.

Belly-up to the sun, Kyle floated in the water. Wava's kidneys felt battered from the long walk and the sudden intake of fluids. She relieved herself in private then walked down to the lake. She set her shoes next to her son's and stepped into the lake fully clothed. The cold water wicked up her thigh, her buttocks. She slipped deeper until her breasts floated and the sweat washed away. Dog paddling awhile, she kept her head dry above the water. She had always been a coward about full immersion, each time a battle of will between herself and the unknown. And yet she persisted. She held her breath, squeezed her eyes shut, and ducked under. She floated beneath the surface, and when the ringing in her ears faded and her heart calmed, she heard the hum and kick of her son swimming.

Her shoes squeaked when she walked, the lake water trickling from her jeans into her shoes. But she felt refreshed, ready to do battle. She tried to vary the pitch. "Hey, listen to this," she said, and pumped her foot in her shoe. When she finished he stood there, uncomprehending. "It's 'Stars and Stripes Forever,' you know, John Philip Sousa."

He rolled his eyes. "Don't you ever get tired?" he asked.

"You should try an eight-hour shift with the meat-loaf special," and she balanced her arms out in front of her. "How about you?" she asked, trying to keep the hope out of her voice.

He turned away and started walking.

"That's my boy," she said. "Never say die." And that was probably her own damn fault, too. His stamina—built on long nights at the cafe as a little boy when she couldn't afford a babysitter, and he'd play quietly at one of the tables, sneaking sips of cold coffee left by customers. When he faded, she carried him out to the parking lot and laid him in the back of the truck bed—the cap windows cranked open or shut depending on the weather. She'd check on him in the spare moments, between late-night customers—drunks trying to revive with food, or the truckers hunched over tables talking into the tableside phones, hands cupped around the mouthpieces. Hamburgers hissed, fried chicken crackled, and she'd bolt through the back door to lean against the pickup and listen to her son, still safe, still asleep while coyotes choraled in the distance. Hardly an ideal childhood. Not even a reasonable one.

All totaled, including the ride from Sup, they had covered nearly twenty miles. They were still on 83, alongside the Blackfoot-Clearwater Wildlife Management Range, an elk and wildlife preserve. A long flat pasture, with hills bucked up against its western border. They passed signs with binoculars stenciled on—wildlife-viewing areas—though in summer when tourists arrived, the elk ranged miles up and away in the high country of the Bob Marshall Wilderness. Preserve. A curious idea, given that in-season hunting was allowed, the hunters advised to return the radio collars to the department of fish and game. Didn't that make it uncomfortably like shooting a pet? Removing the collar after the dog is hit on the road?

"Could you kill something?" she asked Kyle.

He stopped, shifted the pack on his shoulder. "Why, is there something you want dead?"

"I could carry that pack for a while," she said.

He shook his head. "I can do it. You *never* think I can do it."

"No." She shook her finger at him. "I *know* you can. Why the hell do you think I'm here?"

He stepped back, turning his head so she wouldn't see how pleased he was. Maybe she had done too much. Maybe all the years she worked the extra hours, did the extra chore herself, she hadn't so much given as taken from the boy?

"You never said—could you kill something? Elk? Deer?"

He led off again. "I won't make the county line by dark."

"I could—kill something—but I'd have to be damned hungry first," she said, and thought it couldn't be wearing a collar. He slowed down, and she trotted up alongside him. Her son hadn't answered, and that seemed significant. There were things mothers should have of their sons before handing them over—a sense of their experience. "Did you ever see anything die? Something sizeable." Her hands spread apart. "Something that counts?"

"Sure." Then he reconsidered. "Do roadkills count?" he asked.

She nodded and thought about her parents, but that was unfair. They had been *in* the car. She had been fifteen hundred miles away with the excuse of raising her own son. She would spare Kyle that, if she could—leaving too soon, too angry and too proud to go back. But she couldn't think about that now—the wages of being someone's child. She had her hands full being a parent. "My father used to slaughter hogs—a sledge to the head." Her arm swung down, and she stopped, fixing the spot at her feet as if there were a pig at the end of her reach. "Jesus, he had *arms* on him." She looked at her own. "Then he'd hoist it up by the hind feet to a crossbar and slit its throat." Kyle was staring at the road, his nose wrinkled. "They were big hogs, hung their length from a crossbar, their heads swinging just about the height of my head. I could look in their eyes if I wanted to." She stepped off. The sun was over the western hills. Meadowlarks sang, perched on the tips of lamb's ears, and the shadows of clouds rolled over the fescue like animals grazing. They stood side by side, watching the shadows, the mountains, the sky around them, everywhere but at each other.

"Did you? Look in their eyes?" he asked.

She nodded. "Always."

"Cripes." He walked away. "Why?" he asked over his shoulder.

"Because I was ten years old. Because nothing frightened me then." What kind of child does that? Touches the dead, looks it in the eye? She had been a strange child. So who was she to question Kyle's behavior? Though the only time her father had been upset was when he'd found her, knees crooked over the crossbar and swinging like one of the hogs. She'd wanted to know how they saw the world, inverted, the sky become ground, the grass heaven. Her parents had been horrified. But then what, after all, frightens parents more than their own children's curiosity?

They laid her parents out in oak coffins. Closed caskets. Their neighbor sent her pictures, printed on the back of one, "your father," and on the other, "your mother." A car passed, and another, none slowing down for a better look at the odd pair in the road. Wava slipped a hand into her blouse to ease the stitch in her side.

"I killed a rabbit once," he said.

Wava nodded, as if that were reasonable.

"I lobbed a rock at it, hit it square on the head. It didn't have time to be surprised." His eyebrow lifted, as though he still found that surprising himself. "Never thought I'd hit it. That it would die."

She studied him from the corner of her eye, the sweat bead-ing on his lip, the chin still hairless—skin like the bottom of a baby's foot. He seemed impossibly young, still bewildered by his own actions, a rock and a rabbit, cause and effect. "Why?" she asked.

He blushed, swiped at the hair over his forehead. "I wanted a lucky rabbit's foot."

The day's sun had wilted the weeds. Wava's arms were lacquered with sweat. In the grasses, beetles drowsed on the undersides of the blades, and dragonflies fumbled through the air. She was thirsty but reluctant to ask him for another drink. The meadow was spent with the day's heat, and the first early-evening breezes were still moments away, the land pendent with expectation.

"Did you take it?" she asked. "The rabbit's foot?"

"No," he said. "The rabbit was dead. How lucky could it be?"

It was dark by the time they stopped. Their clothes had dried, though the inseams in Wava's jeans remained damp and chafed her thighs. She took off her shoes, rubbed the weals on her feet. Her hair had hardened in snarls. They camped in an abandoned shed, one of many sagging houses and barns along 200 heading south to Missoula. They were in the Garnet Range, which had drifted from Idaho almost 90 million years prior, along with the Sapphire and Bitteroot mountains, escaping to Montana. All this traffic, coming and going, Wava thought.

Her skin itched—no-see-ums, whose bite didn't bother until after they'd fled, and what kind of defense could you have against that? Still, she slapped at her arms, disinclined to let them get away with it. It was chilly. They had a hatchet and wood but no matches. She sat on the dirt floor, under a star-pierced roof. The wall across from her buckled outward, and through the yawning pitch between wall and foundation, sage and knapweed grew rampant.

Coyotes yapped from the fields outside. "There are big cats around here—mountain lions. Wolves. Rats," Wava said.

"Elk, mule deer, skunk," Kyle said.

"The occasional psychopath," Wava added. "He can use your new hatchet on us."

"You're not going to scare me back home."

Wava stretched her feet in front of her, locked her arms over her chest. "Steaks would taste good."

"We don't have a fire to cook them, anyway."

"I'd eat them raw. Damn I'm tired." She took a bite of the peanut butter sandwich he offered her. "So, remind me. Why are we running away?"

"You grounded me. *Forever.*"

She shrugged. "And you can see how long that lasted. If you'd just done what I told you in the first place—"

"I can't do a *damn* thing without you ordering me around."

"Watch your language. I do not."

He pointed a finger at her. "You don't even know when you're doing it."

"I'm a parent. Your only parent. I'm *supposed* to give you order in your life." She wished she still smoked. She'd have matches then and could light a fire. Maybe the whole goddamned shed. "I take orders every day of my life." Bucking hot plates to customers until her arms were pinked with the heat, Rod, the owner and cook, shuffling kettles countertop, waiting for the next spurt of customers. He had six daughters, none of whom he thought lev-elheaded enough to work for him. And Wava figured that was his own damned fault.

Kyle had moved off to the far side of the shed, kicking at the sagebrush. She was tempted to list her acts of benevolence like a catalogue of his sins. "Checking for snakes?" she asked, and he returned to sit ten feet from her. "You want to be an adult? Then act like it. Adults don't run away." And that was nonsense, of course. They ran with regularity, off to work, to lovers. Put holes in their heads. They had better timing was all, a greater ingenuity for excuses—financial ruin, change of life, you don't understand me. I never meant to fall in love with her, meaning I never meant to fall out of love with you. But there it is. Take care of the boy.

"Well, you're the adult all right," Kyle said. "*You* don't run from nobody."

"You talking about your dad? Christ. Don't bother. He invented his own excuses when he left. No. This is not his doing. This is yours. You take care of your own reasons." She walked over and squatted in front of him. "But you tell me of one time, just one, when I wasn't there."

She stood, dusted her knees, and walked to where her shoes slumped in the dirt.

"Maybe I just want to be alone," Kyle said.

"Funny you should say that. I don't." Wava slipped her shoes on and limped to the door. She leaned on the remnants of the jamb. People were selfish. They learned it as children. They were generous only in blame. The moon hung low and huge in the sky. It would ascend and shrink, but still it would be there, night after night after night. As a child, how many times did it have to rise before she'd believed it would always rise to fall? Such things must have come easier back then.

She could have left. Fifteen years ago. Ten years ago. It was done all the time. She had simply chosen not to. It was all so absurd, her son running from the only one who had stayed, her standing there, tired in the doorway, the moon rising yet another time. She could sleep, and Kyle would run. She could stay awake, and Kyle would run.

"You go on," she said. "You meet other people. Someday, you'll find yourself a woman who knows that you save your peas for the last and assumes it's because you like them least. You'll have to tell her otherwise. Then some morning, you'll slip out of your wife's bed, maybe step on your children's toys, and you'll wonder if it's worth it all. You'll think about leaving. I suspect it comes easier with practice."

She shuffled back into the room. She could barely make out his shape against the wall.

"You going somewhere?" he asked.

She shrugged. "Maybe."

"You can hardly walk."

"I'll hitch," she said.

"That's stupid."

She walked out the door. The wind ruffled the grasses, and she stepped off into the gratifying silence. She was cut loose, and it was terrifying. Wonderful. Wasn't this what she'd been preparing for all along? Marriage and friendship, sons and daughters, were just a respite between you and the knowledge that every choice you make is yours alone. The moon was nearing its zenith, and trust seemed a damned thin thing to rely on. She crossed a small hummock, stumbled on the downside, and caught herself short of falling, or turning back to look at the shed a last time. She could not afford to consider what she left behind. The field seemed deeper in the night and the hills kinder—the edges planed clean in silhouette. It was seductive, she thought, this running away. She could just keep going. She watched her feet carefully, stepping clear of the prairie-dog holes, through the chewed turf and buckled grasses where elk had rolled out of sleep. Her arms swung at her side and she waded through the knee-high grass. She heard the clatter of Kyle's possessions banging in his backpack as he raced up from behind.

"You act like it's my fault," he said.

"It is. Surprised?" She struck off toward the road.

He caught up to her, his feet catching in the grass. "How do *you* like it?" he asked.

"I don't know. I haven't been on this end long. Does it scare you? Now that it's me leaving?"

"You going home?"

She stopped. She could see his face in the moonlight, his eyes bright and frightened. She turned away and kept walking. Kyle hesitated and then there was the sound of his feet treading behind her own.

She struck off without direction. They would argue and talk. Perhaps they would walk east, or south to discover what came of the moon's progress. She wondered what they would see, what would become available to them because they'd placed themselves here and now. They'd flush deer whose antlers oriented like a compass against the stars and range behind them to the edges of cities. They'd walk the concrete sidewalks and loiter to hear the streetlamps buzzing. Avenues lined in maples, oaks, and weeping birch. There would be homes with dogs yawning on the stoop, doors clamped tight and hallways they didn't know by feel. Where men and women clung to each other, their children spent in fretless sleep under the benediction of gabled roofs. They'd pass like shadows, the city falling behind. Past cemeteries, a march of crosses and stone angels anchored in decline. They'd traverse water and mountains, hillocks of cedar—old-growth groves with hoary skin. And on the downslope where wind shears toppled trees and lightning forged revelations, they would trace the wood beneath the skin. She would instruct her son—the cambium, the heartwood, the pith, the soul—she would speak as mothers never can, and he would understand as sons never have. And in this world, where all things *are* possible, they will turn the corner to find their house, tied to the land, open as they'd left it with the wood shop still redolent of glue and all the clever tools in their ordered place, safe beneath the crown of cottonwoods, beneath the sky, the night suspended.

LABORS *of* THE HEART

The remarkable thing in dreams: People say what he never hears in waking. Fat. They say it to his face, not behind his back, or clear of earshot. The word is succulent in their mouths—Faaat—stretching out like the waist on his Sansabelt pants. Nothing derogatory about it, only an unabashed honesty. On these mornings, for a few moments, he wakes feeling curiously relieved.

Clarence John Softitch, Pinky to his friends, at five-foot-eight and 482 pounds on a good day, *is* fat, not large, big, or big-boned. Not hefty, husky, generous, or oversized. Nor robust, portly, or pleasingly plump. He is fat. Enormous. Corpulent. And no delicate euphemisms or polite evasions can relieve him of this knowledge when every movement, whether tying a shoe or climbing a short flight of stairs, becomes a labor of the heart.

Not that he has much to do with people in general. He lives in Clarkston, Washington, a scrappy town of twenty-odd-thousand on the eastern edge of the state, where the paltry rainfall encourages prickly pear in lawns and 12 percent of the population is on welfare. He works as night janitor at Loyola High School, and when most the town's folk are gathered in families for dinner, or socially at Hogan's bar, Pinky's company is the clatter of scrub bucket, mop, and brush. For solace he has his voice—a fine, clear tenor to fill the empty rooms. He sings, "When the moon hits your eye like a big-a pizza pie, that's *amore*."

Not that he knows anything about that. *Amore* that is.

For he is virginal, a moderate embarrassment at his age, having come to terms, he believes, with the reality that no one loves a fat man. And so he has given up on love, the daydreams, the hope, the mooning about, the unsightly chase and precipitous rejections. Until this Monday, that is, on one of his twice-weekly food-shopping trips, when he sees *her* in the produce aisle of the north side A & B grocery, a rutabaga under her nose, a peckish look about her mouth. She's little. A narrow, neatly planed body. There is about her the solidity, the starkness of a lightning rod.

He finds this fascinating; more than that it stirs him in a way he's never imagined, his feet locked like a stammer, his breast tightening unlike the usual angina. But what is it about this woman? Her shoulders pinned at attention, the fierce way she sniffs out the proper rutabaga, so that he feels intimidated. Dwarfed, really. For although Pinky *knows* himself to be large—talcums each pant leg to keep his thighs from chafing, avoids chairs with arms—he's always *believed* himself small, just a tiny voice chirping on the horizon, flotsam in an ocean of flesh. He's amazed at how his vessel sloshes and wags, jiggles and rolls. The *real him* adrift inside like a buoy at high tide. He cannot imagine being of consequence in the larger world beyond bumped tables and broken chairs, the numerous bruises and insulted flesh so common that he has ceased to wonder at the many ways the world is rigged against the fat.

But standing in the grocery aisle, he knows for the first time in his forty-odd years what it means to be *struck* by love.

She passes on the rutabagas, and even as she's whisking out of produce, he's slipping the vegetable under his nose, then into his cart, perhaps as a keepsake, as he's never actually eaten one, doesn't know what to do with the thing bowling down the cart's length, toppling stacked, frozen dinners—breaded fish sticks; Hungry-Man slabs of salisbury steak, mashed potatoes, and gravy; lasagna; chicken Kiev—and the comfort foods: donut holes, potato chips, a baker's dozen Hostess Ho-Hos, chocolate cheese-cake as a chaser. A front wheel turned sideways thumps, ba bump, ba bump, ba bump, calling everyone's attention, he thinks, as he trails her to the checkout lane before he's actually ready.

He tries not to stare but admires the efficiency of her moves. She retrieves each item with a lean elegance, and he hangs on to the cart handle, dizzy with love, half hopes she notices the rutabaga. When she leaves the store, she's burdened by six plastic sacks hanging plumb from her fists. She staggers out and pauses in the sunlight, the door frozen open at her back so that the heat wafts in, and he imagines her body, that small dark column, immune to the glare of sun on concrete, her clothes dry, armpits forever fresh.

By the time he's checked out, she's gone, and as he pulls onto the street he sees her struggling down the block. He closes his teeth against the knocking of his heart and idles behind her, the wide-body Chevy wallowing like a whale in the shallows as he leans across the seat to roll down the window.

"Can I give you a lift?" he asks.

She angles a suspicious look at him—the friendly stranger— but then she stiffens her back along with her upper lip and marches on.

"Just a ride. I'm safe," he says, and has to steer around a parked car.

She glances over her shoulder. "Do I look like I need help?" she says. She crooks her elbows and flexes tidy biceps, causing the plastic bags to twist in slow revolutions, and from the cotton- woods white duff spindles down into curbside drifts, a goldfinch flits overhead—a stab of yellow and gone—and still she holds the bags high, until Pinky begins to feel *he* is that assortment of odd bulges and bumps bundled in an unsightly sack turning this way, then that.

Of course she doesn't need help, certainly not from him, and he ducks his head in apology, cheeks flushing with an old but fa- miliar heat. What is left him is this small dignity—he touches a fin- ger to his forehead, as if to tip a cap, and accelerates down the street as though his heart were still intact.

It's a full week before he sees her again, which is odd, because it turns out she's his new neighbor, rents the old Grieger house kitty-corner. Though given his daytime schedule of sleep and hermitage he hasn't noticed the lights on, the mail delivery, the mowed lawn, before this moment. Curious also is how he recognizes her, half-concealed as she is beneath the draped branches of a weeping birch, her back to him, head tilted so that the short nap of hair twists into something like a question mark against her neck. No more clue than the spine's rigidity, the belligerence in her stance, and still Pinky's heart begins to toll. He wishes he were driving, but these last three nights he's begun an exercise program—walking the three blocks to work and back. *Morbidly obese*, he's been categorized. Morbidly. As in deadly, not sadly, which is the way he's preferred to construe it. Midway second block, he'll be winded, and by the time he reaches the school door, the back of his shirt will be sweated through in the early-evening cool. He'd walk by her house without stopping, but she's noticed him, turns, and by the look on her face he can tell she can't place him. He tries not to waddle, wishes he were wearing something other than Carhart coveralls. He tips his finger to his forehead and gives it away.

"The man in the car," she says.

He nods, pleased in spite of himself. He toes up to the lawn to extend a hand. Her own hand disappears in his, but her grip shakes him. "I live in the yellow house." He points over his shoulder. He tells her his name, says, "Call me Pinky," and he wants to say *All my friends do,* but thinks *What friends?* and feels a surge of despair. What folly. What gall. What enormous odds. It's overwhelming, this business of love.

"Pinky," her voice rises. "Rose. I'm Rose Spencer." She doesn't release his fingertips, instead stalks up the lawn with Pinky in tow. "Tell me what this is." Rose disengages her hand to point at a branch. In the upper reaches there is a cocoon, a tented web, with freckled bits splotted here and there. In yet another branch, he sees the start of another, and how is it that he hasn't noticed them before? He sights down the row of cottonwoods streetside, the upper reaches. He sighs.

"Tent caterpillars," he says. He hopes she doesn't register the way his flesh quivers as he thinks of the frantic shivering of worms overhead. A phobia, like some folks have for snakes, spiders.

"Are they bad? For the tree?" she asks.

He knows they'll eat their way down a branch, mature, and drop like fruit. He backs up a pace. No more than a couple tents. Not so bad. "We'll keep an eye on them." And suddenly he's using "we," and such audacity stuns him. But she lets him get away with it, nodding her head and escorting him off her lawn.

"If you need anything," he says. "I have a car," he says, "for groceries, anything." She's watching, and he has the sense she's backing away though her feet are still rooted to the edge of the lawn. "I'm safe," he says, ducks his head.

"How's that?" she asks.

He flushes. Can't believe he's saying this. "Well, you can probably run faster than I can." He laughs as he's always had to.

Rose arches an eyebrow at him. "I don't know what you expect from me." She crosses her arms, cups an elbow in each palm. "But I'm tapped out when it comes to men. Pity, love, anger, compassion—you name it, and I've exhausted it."

"I'm sorry," Pinky says, and he means it. He wonders what could have hurt her so deeply, briefly envies her pain, the experience of being close enough to wound or be wounded. And then, of course, he realizes that's nonsense. Believes he has the perfect vantage for sympathy, from behind this great bulwark of flesh. He's thinking of himself now—the lifetime alone, avoiding pain. He runs a hand down his chest, down the globe of his belly, a gesture he's developed over the years familiarizing himself with the expanding boundaries of his body. "We're neighbors," he says, and she seems puzzled, but there's something in his face, or his tone that puts her at ease.

She relaxes the grip on her arms, and says, "Neighbors. I can handle that."

It's his turn to be confused now. He checks his watch, then looks west, to the sunset, as though that might be more accurate. "I have to get on to work—over at the school? I'm the maintenance technician." A smile sweeps across his face. "Night janitor." He avoids her eyes, looks over her shoulder, and the hills rising above the town turn amber, then the color of autumn rushes, and where the light catches the grasses, the bunched sage, it is a luminous fire. It occurs to him just how long it's been since he's *seen* the hills, wonders how it is that he could have moved through these days, these months without noticing how the crowns levitate with light above the rim rock, the dimming crevasses. He backs up a step, and as she turns her attention once again on the yard, he starts away, first one foot, then the other, until he finds himself three blocks gone and on the steps of school. He unlocks the door with a jangle of keys, lets them loose to the satisfying snatch and click of the take-up reel, then enters the building. He clamps the door shut, and flipping on hall lights, he breaks into his best Johnny Mathis voice, *"Chances are..."*

They shop together now. One day a week. Separate carts. He's taken it upon himself to keep Rose advised on lawn maintenance. "It's the first yard I've ever taken care of," she confides, and so he understands she's always had a man, and no he won't infringe because it's obvious she takes delight in adding oil to the lawnmower gasoline, or pruning the boxwood hedges, regards each task as an indication of competence in the larger world. "I believe a person could fix anything," she says in the house utensils aisle, "given proper instruction and duct tape." Then she adds, "Except trust." And this is the first hint she's given of what keeps her so clearly focused on staying "neighborly."

Not that he's done much more than buddy his grocery cart up to hers, and although it's true, the contents have more and more begun to resemble hers, still he keeps a cautious distance. He's at a standstill, and all the month of long hours mulling over the mop handle at work, dreaming up ways to woo and win her, have yielded nothing more than any neighbor could claim.

Until today, when she lets slip the tidbit about trust. And then the store manager, Ray Tipp, an old classmate—a starved-looking man who keeps himself anxious with coffee—checks out Pinky's groceries, says, "Got a sale on Hostess Ho Ho's." He lifts a head of broccoli and Roman Meal bread. "You on a diet?"

Pinky can't even run. He feels Rose, next in line, caught up in his embarrassment. He shuffles between the checkout stands, the backside of his trousers snag on a magazine rack, and he endures Ray's curiosity while he frees himself without spilling *Vogue* and *Look* into the aisle. He pays Ray, lifts his bagged groceries from the grinning stock boy. He knows that this too Rose must see, how the young boy's eyes widen and the whites shine like twin moons, roll in their sockets.

Stupid. Stupid to have invited her along. To see this. Still stupid—after all these years—to aim yourself at inevitable hurt. But the damage is done. Rose, after all, is guilty by association and so he pivots on his heel, the great slowing mass of him, to face this small woman and take her disgust in stride.

She's handing money to Ray. Two twenties, a ten. She fishes out a single and another. Some change. She takes her bags from the boy and waits for Pinky to lead the way, which he does with all the grace he can muster. When he breaks out into the sunshine, his heart is cluttering his chest, so huge, so full it's become. He puffs crossing the parking lot, the bags swinging at his sides, and he sets them on the ground to open the car door for her.

Two blocks from the store, she says, "Why don't you pull into the park? I've bought a melon. We can have a bite."

Just like that.

And why not? he thinks. A picnic, something he hasn't done since his mother passed on, and for a brief moment he can almost hear her, see the woman she was, all comfort—bosomy and dimpled elbows—pressing food onto him, the sound of other children chasing and laughing. He is hiccuping tears. "Eat," she says. "Like a good boy. Never mind those others. They're jealous you gotta momma can cook." She chucks a finger under his chin. "Your daddy was a *big* man." By this he understands that he, too, would be...large...and in her eyes that was good.

Rose directs him onto River Street and down to the small riverside park. He used to come here as a younger man, walked the levee at night to imagine himself with a woman, strolling the paths or swooning on a bench in the grip of passion and the moony night, like any one of a number of couples whispering from behind the willows' curtains, or lolling in the tall blue grasses riverside.

He follows Rose's lead, carrying the plastic-sacked melon in both hands like a gift, an offering of the magi, and she brings them to the base of a cottonwood. He is breaking a sweat, and the air is brilliant with light on water so that he squints the moisture from his eyes, releases a great round sigh, "Aaah," and he's just so damned grateful for these simple pleasures—river, melon, woman—that he's unlikely to recover his voice anytime soon, so he sighs again.

Rose has seated herself in the grass. He wishes she were

wearing a flowing skirt, frilly blouse, a wide-brimmed straw hat, instead of the baggy jeans and T-shirt that slouch on her tiny frame. And then he feels an ingrate. Clothes. What do they signify? Certainly not the moment. She takes the melon from him, plops it in her lap like a placid child, then pats the grass beside her, and he faces the task of lowering himself. Pinky thinks to remain standing, strike a noble pose, but she's already gazing off across the wide, blue river to the hills opposite. He braces one hand against the tree, crooks a knee, stretches the other leg behind and bends cautiously forward and down and down some more. It's a struggle against mass, gravity. His joints pop in series. He tries not to gasp or puff, and that's nearly as much effort as kneeling. His crotch feels like a wishbone, ready to snap, and then he's down without having fallen. His face is red; he can tell. He filches a handkerchief out of his rear pocket and towels off his forehead, neck, the skinny V of flesh between the unbuttoned top of his button-up shirt.

"Do you have a knife?" she asks.

And he does, though he must lean back, lift his stomach and squeeze his hand in the narrow flap of cloth, cutting the blood to his fingers as he feels for the knife. Finally, he frees it, a pocket Buck knife with all the appointments—even a corkscrew. But she lifts the knife away, slaps the screw back into its steel nest, and locks open the large blade. She stabs into the melon's meat, saws a chunk free and scrapes the seeds back into the exposed heart of the fruit. She hands the wedge to him, and he waits for her to join him.

"People on the whole are an unlikable bunch," she says, sinks the knife to the hilt into the melon's rind. "Take my advice. Never fall in love with them."

Pinky laughs, but it's a squeezed little thing, his chest constricting.

"You think you know cruelty, I know you do." She saws into the melon. "But the cruelty of strangers, or friends, is nothing"— she wags a finger in his face—"compared to what love can do." She is tight-lipped. Her brows beetle, and the air about her seems charged with a static energy. She bites into the melon, tells him about her first husband, his one-night stands, moves on to her second husband and his affairs. Tells it all in four short sentences, as if she can't bite off the ends of words hard enough, spit it out fast enough.

"What did I learn from it, you want to know…"

She dabbles at the corner of her mouth with a fingertip where some melon juice drips down, and Pinky thinks he has never seen anything more delectable. He'd like to take her finger into his mouth and suck it dry.

She stretches her legs out, leans against the tree, and tells him of her third and last husband's affairs. How she then called the woman, wanted to see her. "Couldn't help myself. Called a complete stranger— though it seemed I had the right, we'd shared so much. I don't know what I expected. She came to my house. Not the first time, I could tell that right off—the way she found her way to his chair."

Rose rubbed the back of her head against the tree's bark, a leisurely scratching. "She was a short, stumpy-legged little thing, not cute, no, not even handsome. But interesting. Perky. She says, 'I didn't mean to ruin your life.' She was being sincere, but of course, she was flattering herself. After all, my life wasn't ruined. Merely changed. I told her that."

She looked over at Pinky. "Don't you wonder at how I could be so collected? So smug?"

"I can't imagine," Pinky says.

"No." She leans over, pats his hand. "Of course you can't. And, of course, I was full of crap." She sighed. "If my life wasn't ruined, it was the next thing to it. Rubble. That's what I was left with. Rubble."

She squeezes her left breast and Pinky knows it is her heart she means, but all he can picture is the tender flesh crumpled in her fist, and he wants to loosen her fingers, cradle her breast and heart in the palm of his hand, which he discovers is sweating so he swipes it down his pant leg. And then, wonder of all wonders, he reaches over with his newly dried hand and takes the melon from her, lifts the knife away, slices another piece, skins and offers it to her.

Which she declines.

"Three strikes, you're out. Isn't that right?" she asks.

"In baseball," Pinky says, and he wants to sound decisive, but hears how his voice trails off. He's stuck with the melon wedge, dripping through his fingers onto his pant leg.

"Yes," she agrees. "In baseball *and in men*."

And what can Pinky say? He eats the melon slice, wipes his hand on the grass. On the river, a pair of Canada geese paddle upstream, six goslings drafting in their wake. Sunlight crooks across the water's surface, and shadows swim the face of the hills opposite. Pinky blinks, feels moisture budding behind his eyes, and blinks again. He begins to comprehend the scale of his task—wooing this woman—even if he weren't hobbled by his own body. He's still holding the knife, and he looks down at his belly, wishes he could slice away the flesh, pare down to some more supple version of himself that would be capable of the acrobatics—walking, sitting, bending over—that normal, everyday people perform in everyday courtship. He wants to be handsome for her.

A pair of young girls roller blade down the sidewalk, the wheels buzzing with the sound of enormous hummingbirds. They wind down the path, skinny legs and arms knotted in protective pads. Their laughter is a shouting, and Pinky admires the honesty of it. He wonders what Rose sounds like when she laughs. He wonders if she laughs.

Rubble, she'd said, and he questions the state her heart's in now. "I'm not like those men," he says.

"Why?" she asks. "Because you're fat?" And it's just a statement. "Because you think other women wouldn't find you attractive?"

Truth is he hadn't thought of it that way, but he begins to see this could work for him. He nods.

"Another way that you're safe?" she asks.

He nods again, though he feels like he's stepping into something unseen, something with teeth.

She stares across the river. "Do you think that little of yourself, or me?"

It's worse than he'd feared, certain now that she despises him for his clumsiness, his transparent eagerness. He blames himself and his lack of experience; he blames the hour of the day and the bristling grass that torments his ankles. He tells her he's a fool and that he respects her and her friendship. Those are the words he uses, *respect* and *friendship*, and she continues to stare out across the river. He asks her to understand, he's not used to … to … picnics.

Her brows furrow and she says, as if she hasn't heard him, "My last husband was different. Where the others'd been tall, he was short. A bookish man with a sense of humor. He couldn't change the oil in the car, but he was mad for opera. I believed he was different, as day is to night." She wags her head. "But this is much too lovely a day"—she leans back on her elbows—"to quibble. I'm done with men." Rose rolls onto her side facing Pinky. "Except as friends. Take it or leave it."

Pinky nods and heaves a sigh, but even as she pats his hand and closes her eyes to rest, he is studying the logistics of getting back on his feet.

Late at night, in the gym, Pinky plots strategy. He turns on the overheads and the constellation of bulbs shine from the floor's mirror finish. He has cleaning down to an art, dry-mopping the area in under an hour, starting at the foot of the bleachers, left to right, and threading his way in overlapping lanes down and back until he's dusted his way into the boys' locker room, where the real work begins. Though, as it is summer, this chore is reduced to a twice-weekly touch-up instead of the nightly tour during the school year. He switches to a wet mop, fills the big steel bucket on casters with hot water, a splash of disinfectant Sparkle, and bleach. He works backwards, kicking the bucket ahead of him like a troublesome dog. The mop bangs against lockers and Pinky loves the rat-a-tat-tat off the empty doors. Sings "Frankie and Johnnie" to their machine-gun accompaniment. Sees himself as Johnnie, but can't imagine doing her wrong, can't conceive of such discontent. He rolls the bucket into the boys' bathroom. He buffs the floor, glances in the mirror.

His face seems different, and maybe it's just love has transformed him. Or has he lost weight? He lifts the putty knife from the cart, scrapes at a wad of paper toweling glommed to the underside of a sink. When he straightens up, he fidgets a finger into his waistband, snugs in two. Yes. Oh yes. He's lost weight.

And this is the tough part. He enters a stall. How can he

convince Rose of his own true heart? And damn it. He slaps the brush in the toilet bowl, squirts in blue disinfectant, swabs, and flushes. He deserves one good shot at it, doesn't he? He slaps the seat up—scrubs—seat down—scrubs—backs out of the stall, then moves on to the next and the next. Patience, he tells himself, and though he's only known Rose as a friend and neighbor a little over two months, he's got a forty-year backlog of empty nights, and Pinky stops, envisions the calamity of another forty empty years, and finds himself doubled over one of the toilets. When his heart calms in his chest, and the angina eases under his left wing-bone, he backs out of the stall. The room is bright, as only locker-room bathrooms can be with the high banks of fluorescent lights buzzing and reflecting off the mirrors and stainless-steel doors, the white, porcelain sinks and urinals all ablaze so that when he looks in the mirror this time what he sees is his forehead shining with sweat and the enormous bell of his body overexposed in white overalls, and for a moment he loses himself against the white wall tiles.

He leaves the bucket and mop, the toilet brush and disinfectant, and crosses back through the locker room, turning off lights as he goes, through the gym, and out the side door. He stands on the asphalt stoop. In the school parking lot, the arc lamp's cone of light seethes with winged insects—swirling, bumping, a luminous feast that the nighthawks scoop through. Pinky breathes deeply, feels the moist back of his shirt cooling. Crickets pick up where they'd left off. He steps away from the building and walks until the locked school folds into the night. He walks slow and steady, his heart easing, chest lightening. He knows he will have to return to work, but for now he turns up a side street, where lamplight streams out onto porches and grass.

He stays to the sidewalk, but glances in each house. Where

drapes are open, it's the furniture he notices—which place has a
piano, or a lamp centered in the window like a beacon. Then there
are all the dining rooms, with tables bunkered by chairs. So many
chairs. Seascapes over the sofa, mounted deer, or the grouping of
family pictures like a lineup in the post office. Once in a while he
glimpses the people. Sometimes he believes he can smell their
dinner: chicken, hamburger, barbecued ribs. Or more vaguely Italian cuisine, Oriental, Middle-Eastern. He feels a stirring of
hunger, but he tucks his two fingers into his waistband again and
thinks apple instead of apple pie. He journeys down another side
street and exchanges greetings with a man smoking a pipe on his
front porch. He passes a young couple, and the woman titters,
but they don't notice Pinky, so wrapped up are they, and he finds
that utterly disarming. He meets more people strolling under the
streetlamps. Why, it seems to him, the whole town must be
spilling out into the warm night. Or maybe this is the way the
world congregates when he's alone, in his school, his home. And
there it is. His house. Locked tight and shuttered close. He opens
the front door, the drapes, turns on all the lights. Then he steps
back out on the sidewalk to see what he can of himself. He's reluctant to look, but discovers he doesn't fare so badly. Tomorrow,
first thing, he will dig out the old photos, frame the one of his
mother and father's wedding, the portrait of his grandfather—big
chested, with thighs like a Percheron. It will take so little, he
thinks, and pivots on his heel to look across the street, to the
house of his beloved. The lights behind the drapes are a wan
glow, and he's stricken with how tidy the place is, how self-
contained. He feels…what is it? not exactly love, but a stirring
that is equally unfamiliar from his end of things, and…discon-
certing—call it pity. He wishes he could step into her life as easily

as his home, open it wide to this sweet night. He heaves a sigh, and looks up, over the trees and over the tops of houses to where the distant hills shoulder the dark beneath the quickening stars.

He means to take her on a date, but he doesn't call it that. He doesn't dare. He mentions the movie, casually, over groceries. He tells Rose, "Dutch treat," to allay her suspicion. It's a love story, but he doesn't mention that either. She offers to buy the popcorn. "Only fair," she says. "All the gas you've used on grocery trips."

Pinky accepts. He feels pretty smart. Of course he hasn't thought about the theater seats, and though his pants are looser now and sitting upright no longer cuts off his wind, still it's a tight, tight squeeze, but he manages. He's appreciative for her small kindness of unbuttered popcorn. She'd noticed his weight loss a couple days ago, "Hope you're not doing this for me," she'd said, and when he replied, "No," he could see she was unprepared for the truth, some small part of her stung by his admission. He felt encouraged.

It *was* a sappy film. Any other time he would have been the first to ridicule the sentimentality. Except, now it is Rose scoffing, and that provokes in him a desire to defend it. She curls her lip, and Pinky lets his heart go soft. Walking back to the car, she recaps some of the *lowlights*. When she snorts at the dialogue, Pinky taps her arm with a finger, says, "You could give it a chance."

"You can't mean it."

"It had heart," he says.

She pinches his arm. "It had a lobotomy. Not the same thing."

"Ouch," he says.

She goes on, "What you don't know"—she shakes a finger at

him—"is this kind of willful ignorance about the *realities* of love wearies me sometimes."

They drive away from the theater in silence. He wants to talk, but is embarrassed to admit that there's little willful about his ignorance. Inexperience, certainly.

He suggests the 410 Drive In for a bite, and she agrees. Rose's hamburger fills her hands, drapes over fingers, lobs chunks of lettuce and pickle into the napkin covering her lap, while Pinky's grilled chicken breast sandwich is a pale, insignificant thing in comparison. It hardly seems worth the effort. He takes baby bites to stretch it out. She offers him a sip of her malt, and it's so intimate a gesture he's dumbfounded. He accepts the plastic cup from her hands and takes the straw—squeezed between her lips just moments earlier—into his mouth, tongues the tip tenderly. It is a jolt of pure chocolate, cold and clean and sweet. His eyes close.

So this is what it's like—the taste of a woman, and there's a curious quivering at the base of his spine. And of course he *knows* that's not the case, but he enjoys the *idea* of it and has to stop himself from draining her malt.

"You think I'm harsh," she says, "about the movie. But the point is"—she crumples the emptied hamburger wrapping—"romantic love suggests we are incomplete without another, in need of salvation. You're led to believe that you'll be a better person if there's someone around to expect it. But somewhere down the line, you find the cost of these expectations too dear. What? you say, Eat the same cooking? Sleep on the same side of the bed? Give up variety? Implausible if not impossible. All you will *ask* for is a little kindness, but what you will *want* is more than anybody can give—their undivided attention for the rest of their life—and so you struggle and struggle and hurt each other endlessly.

"Three marriages, over twenty-five years' worth. Imagine—twenty-five years attempting love. Trust me. It's a complication you're better off without."

Rose sighs, pats her lips dry, then sets the soiled napkin and empty malt cup back on the serving tray. "Take me home," she says. She sounds utterly weary.

Pinky takes a deep breath, resettles in the seat. His stomach bumps the steering wheel. He drives the long way, down Bridge Street, over to Riverside, up to Highland, slowly. How painful she makes it sound, *twenty-five years*, but all he can think of is turning over in bed to find someone there, of eating someone else's cooking, and it sounds grand to Pinky, worth the risk, the heartache. He *knows* what it's like to be alone—the long haul of it, not just the early phase, when the day winds down because *you've* nothing better to do and stretching across an empty bed still seems a luxury.

It's coming on to seven in the evening and the sky is yet bright with daylight. He stops at the school, invites her in. He shows her the broom closet, the mops. He shows her classrooms, the new computer lab—shakes his head, feather dusting, he explains. He takes her into the gym, throws on the lights just to show her how the floor shines. He stands center court and lobs a high A at her. He could almost swear she blushes. He proceeds to sing the only song he can think of with her name in the title, "The Yellow Rose of Texas."

On the way out of the building, she says, "A most unlikely, but lovely serenade. Thank you." They leave the car there to walk the three blocks home. He knows she slows her pace to match his. It is early evening, and the shortening daylight lapses into a dim gloaming. Dusky-winged ash aphids are swarming, bumbling clouds of blue-bodied mites that rise like yeast from the grass. Late summer, they come down from the Camas and Palouse

Prairies to swim in the warmer valley air. By full evening, they will web together in gray winding sheets around the south side of the ash tree trunks, where they will shiver into their final, short-lived ecstasy. But now they are a squall, riding the turmoil of heat convections and cooling drafts. They speckle the couple's clothes, dust their hair. Pinky is enthralled with the tiny creatures, the enormous bulb of their bodies and improbable flight. They bobble and fall, rise and fumble. This is not a matter of grace.

Rose waves a hand through the air in front of her. They stop on the far edge of the cloud, and Rose ducks her head, swipes at an eye. Pinky can see a bead of aphids riding her eyelashes.

"Ow," she says, her eye tearing.

"Here," he comforts, nips her chin between thumb and forefinger, lifts her face to what is left of the light. Rose is a woman who has little truck with makeup. There's no attempt to disguise the lines, the thinning skin. He is captivated, as he was the first time he saw her, by the static energy of this woman, her relentless honesty, all her life available in her face, her eyes. And this is the thing he both fears and admires, how she has been pared down to the bone, tried and fired as he never has been. Though his fingers barely grace her chin, he feels her energy, some galvanic current of old doubts running through her, and she sidesteps under his hand. He takes a steadying breath, says, "Hold still." He spits on his free thumb, touches that small drop of moisture to the corner of her eye. The speck of blue floats off the white, onto Pinky's thumb, and he neatly lifts it away.

Up and down the block, house lights come on, and children shoo cats out of front doors. The hills over the town flatten, grow larger with the dark. There's no help for it but Pinky feels a melancholy he's hard put to explain, and it has to do with the onset of dark and the sudden still. It has to do with the small woman at his side, her mistrust, and his own lifetime of hiding, in his house, his work, and foremost his own flesh. And, he sees it has to do with fear—the way we run through our lives in terror of it—and everything to do with despair, and perhaps, he thinks, that is what despair is, finally, a lack of daring. He feels savvy. Overhead, a crow lifts from the treetop, banks toward the river with a hard laugh—ha-ha-ha.

In another block they stop again so that Pinky can catch his breath. He pants in the quiet, shakes his head. He will lose weight—he will because he cannot go on as he always has, he understands this now—but he also knows he will always be big. Not small, or even trim, and he is struck by this. It has been with him so long, this ocean of flesh. Pinky feels he must tell Rose. Warn her. "I will always be fat," he says.

"Yes," she agrees. She lays a hand on his forearm. "As I will always be bitter," she says.

They stand that way in the new dark, and he thinks, should a young husband look out from his living-room window, or should the young wife hurrying home from errands come across them standing so, they would think Rose and Pinky some middle-aged couple of long years—the way Rose's hand is anchored on his arm. And he wonders about the couples he has so long envied, how much is illusion, a public face for the private griefs and hurts they harbor? He thinks of the depth of Rose's bitterness, the earnest way in which she confirms it, and he understands it's as deep and abiding as the bones seated in the continent of his flesh. It humbles him, how fiercely she is grounded in her resolve.

And he does not feel up to the task. Sees himself as the lightweight in this struggle. His stomach gripes, and will not be consoled by the pat of his hand. How he already misses the easy comfort of food, the anonymity. He feels a nervousness, an anxiousness like a missed meal, or the temptation of chocolate before sleep. He sways from foot to foot, rocking in place. A terror steals upon him that he cannot fathom, so that his feet are seized in place, and his fat plumbs him to the earth while she stands stark and quiet at his side as if forged of consequences larger than his imagining. He sees she is not the rod, but the lightning itself, flinty bits striking off—old loves, grudges, misfortunes, a hundred errors in judgment and more—quizzing his friable heart. He should run. He should bolt, for he senses this is a struggle deeper than the naive courtship he'd embarked on. Not the territory of novices. Not for the uninitiated. It is a journey of days, years, a chronic case of heartache, the relentless wooing to win and lose, again and again. He almost laughs, for all his assurances to Rose of how safe he is—he sees now that it is *she* who is the danger... always has been.

Overhead, the clouds quail beneath the rising moon. He turns his face away. He slows his panic by imagining the imaginable: the march of days, the orderliness of work—nights, cleaning, trips to the grocery store, lawn care, and diets. Conversation that spills over from day to day, and running jokes. He wonders how they will look in a year, two, five. Will she grow generous as he grows slight? He steadies, takes a deep breath. What he wants, he realizes, more than anything, is to imagine a time when fear will carry no weight in his heart. When love will need no proof. He squints into the dark, as if to make out the features of that distant time—the heel of a foot striking the floor as she steps down from her side of his bed, the shape of her face, is it Rose? But he cannot know this. Not now. Not yet. And, perhaps, for now, the question is enough. He quashes the impulse to push back his sleeves. Instead, he leads them arm in arm, their bodies swaying each its own way, beneath the steepled canopy of sycamore where the first flush of moonrise swims the wavering shadows in a school of light.

MOUSE RAMPANT

It had been a deeply unsatisfying spring. In the five years Phil had lived in Clinton, Montana, there had never been one like it: unseasonably cold, relieved by rain and sleet. The old-timers saw it as a sign, redemption from the greenhouse effect. "This is the way it used to be," they said, "before the world turned queer." They saw it as just retribution for all the newcomers who'd fled to Montana. Phil preferred to think of it as an anomaly, since he was still an outsider to the locals, something he hoped he and his wife Dolly would live down. He wanted to believe the next decade would offer short winters and warm springs. This spring, even the field mice were shocked back indoors, nesting in insulation. Dolly discovered the most recent brood in the drawer under the stove.

She'd heard the mice clatter pot covers in the night. To Phil's way of thinking, that was when Dolly first turned queer.

She was the steady one in their marriage. Even when Phil had taken early retirement from his accounting job at fifty-seven and a reduced pension to avoid layoff. Even when their only child, Lucy, married bad and moved to Brazil, her correspondence reduced to postcards with postscripts: "Roger's changed," or "He stopped drinking," or "Not fighting so much." Like they should be relieved.

It wasn't long before Phil realized the old-timers had it wrong—this weather did not signal redemption, but apocalypse. His first glimmering of it came at five in the morning, watching Dolly scrub out the stove drawer. She stood at the sink in her flannel gown and sheepskin mules. Her hair was braided down her back, her back wider than it had been as a young woman, but straighter. As straight as it had needed to become, given their history. Next to her, on the drainboard, was her favorite blue Delft plate. Arrayed in neat rows on the plate were five nubby newborn mice, pink. At a glance, they looked like a confectioner's mistake.

"Babies are not a pretty sight," she said, nodding over her shoulder at the plate. "They're still only half-baked, and anything else is a rationalization."

"Lucy was pretty enough," Phil said.

"You were biased." Dolly wiped out the drawer and slid it back in place. "You barely saw our baby, working as hard as you did. You hardly knew her." She picked up one of the infant mice. Between two fingers she rubbed its head across the plate with a squeak, as a child might wield an eraser on paper. She laid the broken one next to its siblings. "If we had it to do over again..." she said, and proceeded to kill the others in the same way.

"What?" Phil asked, focusing on the stove—its clamped doors, the elements cold and dark on its surface.

"We'd pay more *attention*," she said. "We'd see the way things were going, before they got so far." She lifted the plate. "Where are the parents?" she asked.

Phil sat quietly, his shoulders shrugging. What did he know of mice? He was only human. He was a man who had given the most part of his years to the process of addition and subtraction, balancing figures, facts provided and the formula known. He made coffee instead and fried long strips of bacon, eggs over easy, and buttered toast. Dolly set traps smeared with peanut butter. "Mice are relentless," she said. "They'll just start all over again." After breakfast, they took the babies outside, and under the lilac bushes, Dolly notched out a grave with a spoon.

It wasn't as if she went on a killing spree, but the weather stayed bad, and there were mice. In between the killing, Dolly kept her house in the order she'd always maintained. Clean enough to be healthy, messy enough to be a home. She was in the tail end of her latest hobby, one of many over the years. Their house was testimony to her infatuations—swarms of afghans, tôle painting, stained-glass sun catchers, decoupage, oil painting, ceramics. This time she'd taken up quilting, until the chairs were fat with pillows, the sofa a confusion of crazy quilt. Phil liked to think she was a woman driven to creating. He liked to believe he had some part in it, driving Dolly to craft stores, and he was never disappointed in the results, even when Dolly so clearly was.

He should have known she was on the edge of something new—the slowing treadle of the old sewing machine, the patches of flannel and flowered prints slumping on the closet floor. He should have read it like the weather. She made trips to the library, brought home the *Mammal Collectors' Manual*, the *Collection and Preservation of Animal Forms*. But no, he was busy sorting garden seeds, staking out rows in dirt too wet to turn, his only hobby of fifty-odd years, his only act of creation outside of his child, and that more an accident, a slip of the hand, as they'd never once in all those years said to each other, now we'll make a child, *this moment* we'll start a new life. And didn't that seem sad?—that the remainder of your lives is circumscribed by a moment of ignorance? A heedless orgasm? He knew the instant he put each seed in the ground. Knew the probability of success or failure.

The last mouse faced them off in the broom closet next to the dustpan and the Windex, the base of its tail clamped in the trap. The mouse stood on its hind legs, front legs striking out like a pugilist, tiny teeth bared. *It's the mother*, Dolly said, and Phil didn't know what she meant at first, the tiny mound of dirt dissolved weeks ago under the lilacs. Dolly pushed Phil back. "There's only room for us in here," she said gently. And then she lowered the mop down on the mouse, pinning it to the floor. She grasped its head between two fingers, just behind the ears and, with the other hand, released the trap. In the light of the kitchen, the mouse clawed at Dolly. She raised it to her face and stared into its eyes. She nodded as if those eyes told her what genitals and biological history could not. It was the mother, she was convinced. She placed it under the glass cheese bell on the kitchen table, then sat across from it and watched it run slow circles under the dome.

"This isn't healthy," Phil said.

"I'll scrub it out when I'm done," she answered, misinterpreting what he'd said. But he was grateful, not knowing after all how to pursue it or explain his fears.

"Do you want me to dispose of it?" he asked.

"No," she said. "You go about your business. We'll be fine." And he wanted enough to believe, or was coward enough, that he did. "If you're going out, take the umbrella," Dolly said. But he could not bring himself to do that. The locals didn't believe in umbrellas; he hadn't seen one in five years. Anyway, umbrellas were fixed in his mind with sunshine—a hot sunny day, and Dolly, young again and sweet with wine, sitting on the lawn, a red-plaid umbrella braced open over her shoulder to protect their child, asleep in her lap. It seemed all his past was like that now, a triggered picture, a smell, more real than the present sometimes. He supposed it was unfair, all the hard times brought to soft focus, a process of selective forgetting. But he still believed those were the best of times. Outside, the lawn was green as he never remembered it before, and longer, too wet to cut. The sky was squalid and pressed on the mountains. He paced out his rows, studied the drainage, charted the mounds for melons and squash, and through the long hours, the neighbor's horses tore out mouthfuls of pasture and chewed while they stood dreaming, their tails blunt clubs of mud.

He came back inside to warm the chill from his bones. He'd stoke up the woodstove, snug his back close to it, and bask in the steam rising from his wet pants. They'd share a cup of coffee, as if it were just another day. She would slice him a slab of pie and tease him about his weight, though in twenty years he'd never veered from the 240 pounds he carried so ably. She'd suggest a haircut, or she'd recommend a drawer that needed fixing, any number of small chores that needed his attention. It was what he found endearing about her, her gentle but competent relegation of tasks. But Dolly still sat at the kitchen table. There was a cutting board next to her, and her quilting scissors, needle and thread, a bottle of alcohol, a box of borax, a wad of cotton and a small pile of meat that was the mouse, its pelt stripped clean and turned inside out. There was an odor in the kitchen, shocking, sweetly fetid and too large, he thought, for the size of the carcass. He stood speechless, shifting from foot to foot.

Dolly scraped a pocket of fat off the skin with a fingernail, then dusted the skin with borax. She measured the wad of cotton against the skin inverted nose to tail, then slipped it over the cotton like a sock over a foot, turning it outside right in small increments, the nose, then the ears. The mouse unfolded under her hands, small legs dangling, wriggling with each tug as if alive. She tucked her finger inside, prodding the cotton into its head, its neck, then laughed as she tweaked the tail in place and danced the stuffed mouse about the tabletop like a finger puppet. "Can you do the Texas two-step?" she asked, and the mouse bowed.

"What in God's name—" Phil asked, his hand moving before he could think, snatching the thing off her finger, bending her finger in the process so that she sucked in her breath with an "oh." The fur flattened in his palm; the tail dangled through his clenched fingers. It felt warm in his hand, as if the skin hadn't had time to cool. "Can you *explain* this?" he asked, a plea and an accusation.

She looked at him as if it was their forty years together that needed explaining. "It's only taxidermy, Phil," and she peeled back his fingers. She placed the mouse on the table, straightening its limbs, propping it up on its tail. "Imagine this," she said. "Beads for eyes." Her fingers fussed at the air. "A nice piece of wood alongside." She extended the paws; she bumped the head up in a challenge. "*Voilà*," she said. "Mouse Rampant."

The first step. Cut the squirrel from the base of the neck down the center line to the vent. Be careful. Cut deep enough to sever the skin but not to puncture the abdomen. Lift the edge of the skin on each side of the incision and pull away from the body.

Dolly's fingers peeled with a delicate sureness. "*Un bel di*" from *Madama Butterfly* played on the stereo. She said opera was conducive to the meditation and patience required for taxidermy.

The squirrel was already dead when she'd found it a week ago. Until today, it had resided in a Ziploc bag in the freezer on top of two chicken pot pies and a roast, so that when Phil opened the door its milky eyes had stared back with matched distaste.

The thawed squirrel slumped in her hands. "You don't know what it died of," he warned.

"It's fresh," she said. She pulled on the skin. "No slippage. It's perfectly fine," she said, oblivious to the risks of disease—distemper, rabies, bubonic plague.

He could not watch what Dolly was doing, her fingers probing up under the pelt, severing the membranes connecting skin to muscle. He chose to look at her instead. This was what Lucy would look like when she got older, the same gray eyes that turned color with the clothes she wore or the sky she stood under. The same broad forehead and a tendency toward jowls. But she would never have her mother's serenity, and that unsteadiness was a dubious gift from him. Dolly and Lucy were as alike and unalike as mothers and daughters always were. That, he decided, was what had brought on this latest obsession.

Lucy had sent another postcard. She was still in Brazil, but she'd left Roger. "You can breathe easier now," she wrote. She was working as a waitress in a small restaurant. "I'm saving my tips to come home. Don't worry. Everything is under control." Phil wouldn't have worried, except for everything being under control. He imagined his Lucy teetering between tables. "Lady of Spain," the only Spanish tune he knew, was playing on a jukebox. He imagined a cluster of black-eyed men, fingers pinching out pennies for shots of mescal, anticipating the worm.

While Phil listed ways he could get some money, Dolly was pulling the squirrel out of the freezer.

"You could help," Dolly said. She was offering him the body of the squirrel, tail unraveled from its sheath, back legs snipped at the knee joint. "Just hold tight while I pull." And he found himself holding the clubbed legs. The pelvic joints popped, and the skin pulled up. Shouldn't there be blood, he wondered, his thumbs moving onto the abdomen for better purchase. The spine stretched with minute clicks and Madama Butterfly sang *"Tienti la tua paura, io con sicura fede l'aspetto."* Keep your fear to yourself, she cautioned, and sang on about faith and the lover who would return, while Dolly snagged the forelegs free with a crochet hook and crimped them with a pinking shears. Phil dropped the squirrel.

Rain beat his windshield in slugs. If he drove forty miles east, he might outrun the rain. If he drove four hundred miles west, the rain would turn warm. If he drove to Arizona, he could bask on a rock like a lizard. His skin would go floppy with dehydration, hang from his elbows in drapes. He cranked up the heater, and his glasses fogged.

Twenty miles south, Missoula had the only shopping mall within two hundred miles. It wasn't as if he liked malls, but as Dolly said, "It'll keep you off the streets," and in weather like this he wasn't about to take offense. He could buy garden tools and underwear and not get his feet wet. But once in town, the mall seemed too formidable, his needs insufficient. He stopped at the East Gate Lounge instead.

The bar was small, twelve stools and a television overhead. Four groups of tables backed by a row of poker machines. Off to a side was another room, bright with windows, paneling that might be found in a Legionnaire hall, more tables, and shuffleboard. Phil thought it a singular bar. There were no trophies, no shoulder-mount elks, deer racks, bobcats, hang-jawed moose, no Rocky Mountain goat under Plexiglas. He thought of all their dinners in restaurants whose walls were ornamented with taxidermied animals. From the start, Dolly had been intrigued. She would stare at them. He'd thought it was boredom. He was a poor conversationalist. But maybe it was the glass eyes that winked in candlelight. Or maybe it was the elk mount being groomed with a Dustbuster that first turned Dolly's head. What had been the first impulse? And why did she take such delight in it? He could not believe it was just another whim—there was an earnestness to it that had been lacking in her other hobbies, an intent he could see but not understand. She was blind to the results, the stiffening animals in mocking poses, as if she could, as if anyone could, transfigure death. He surveyed the beer signs on the walls. It was late afternoon. There were three people in the bar. Phil made four.

He sat next to a man, kept his distance from the large woman who crowded two stools. It wasn't as though he needed this, he thought, and took a chaste sip of beer. It wasn't as though he was running away, and he could picture the house slipping out of sight in the rearview mirror. But there were some things a man wasn't meant to hear. Like the sound a squirrel's head makes pinging off the sides of a boiling kettle of water. This was a mistake, Phil thought. The bar, the people in it, were depressing. But then, somehow, a stranger's depression seemed more palatable.

"How about them Lakers?" he asked the man next to him, then wished he hadn't—"California" being particularly taboo in a Montana bar. But the man took no offense, and so he too was an outsider, Phil figured.

"I don't watch the games," the man said. "I come for the noise."

Which prompted Phil to wonder about the man's life as Phil drank his beer and ordered another with a shot of Jack Daniel's on the side. The man was tidy. His clothes had the sorry look of a suit that's spent the day in an office: crimped at the waist, stretched across the back, the collar loosened so you could see the bite of chafing around the neck. Phil found himself almost homesick for it. What had five years of retirement given him but this vague dissatisfaction? It wasn't that he missed the work terribly. Though for the first two years he modestly missed his office mates. What he missed most was the appointed task—the preordained particulars of his day. He looked at the man seated next to him. He decided the man had no children. He decided the man had no wife to open his seams as he grew out and older, like Dolly did in the night while Phil was sleeping, easing seams strained beyond tolerance.

He ordered two more drinks. One for himself and one for the man who liked noise. And that reminded Phil. "You know what sound a squirrel's head makes boiling in a pot of water?"

The man turned to him. "This is a joke?" he asked.

Phil paused to consider that. "Only if it's not in your own kitchen," he said. "My wife's taken up taxidermy." He wanted sympathy.

"I hunt," the man said. "Can't seem to land a decent buck though. It's not the same when you mount a doe."

"She's got this mouse—"

"Just last fall I had one in my sights. I'd have had to take off the door to get it in the house. The sucker was that big."

"You're not listening," Phil said, and the man's arms swept out to show the scale of the rack. Phil downed the shot, ordered another.

"Lined up in my sights and some god-damned fool down on the highway—"

The woman down at the end of the bar was crooning to herself on the stool. Phil leaned forward to see better. Her breasts were ponderous, lying on the bar, and he imagined himself stretched out on the slab of them, blinking in the Arizona sun. A harmless dream, the warmth, the soft flesh, and then her hand lifted and he saw the hairy tumor growing out of the cleft of her blouse. Phil blinked. His chest squeezed and the Jack Daniel's rose at his shame. She crooned to it, stroked it sweetly, and it raised its head and meowed.

The man next to him was still telling his story, punctuating it with hands and energetic elbows, buffing Phil in the rib cage. Phil found himself moved, unexplainably to violence. He imagined grabbing the man's suit, bunching it in a fist around the man's throat. And then he imagined himself stuck there holding it, feeling foolish and at a loss for what to do next. The bartender stopped wiping the bar. "You need a drink?" he asked, and the woman tucked the kitten into her handbag and scooted off to the restroom. Phil pictured the man still hanging in his hands, his arms at his side, too small to be angry, even at an old man like Phil.

Phil backed off the stool. He left a two-dollar tip on the bar. He walked away quickly, feeling worse than when he'd come. If only he'd taken a swing at the man. If only the man had swung back. If only he'd never driven the twenty miles. If only he'd never married. At his back he heard the man ask, "Does she do fish?"

They traded their car in for an older pickup truck, sent the extra cash to Lucy. It was the best they could do, as Dolly had said no to a second mortgage. "We'd never be able to make the payments," she said. "We're too old." Dolly sold a quilt for one hundred dollars. She mailed it in a separate envelope to Lucy. It made him feel unaccomplished. He was being silly, he told himself. These were modern times, and no one expected the man to come to the rescue anymore. He should feel relieved.

Dolly mounted the squirrel on a sawed-off tree limb and fastened it to the wall. The squirrel was in the act of climbing, one foot raised for its next purchase. Its face was turned over its shoulder, looking down as if something were close behind. It looked frightened. It looked vaguely familiar. Phil praised her work, as he always had, and avoided that wall from then on.

Because Dolly never learned to drive, she sent Phil out looking for roadkills. "I have to get in practice for the season," she said, meaning hunting season, he supposed. She planned to advertise. Sure she was a beginner, but she would be cheap. He spent the next two weeks looking for a kill. She gave explicit instructions: nothing too old, nothing too damaged, no bloat or flies. He kept his eyes on the mountains. He watched the sky for redtails and osprey. The weather remained cruel, and the land looked blighted, the fields slathered with water. In the few hours of sunshine, he'd park the car, tramp into the nearest field, and lay his body in the soaking grass, until his back pinched with cold and his belly thrummed with sunlight. He stayed out long enough to convince her, and then he would return, empty-handed, apologetic. Smug.

The night the earthquake hit, they were in bed. They had not had sex in a while, and that was not uncommon either, excused by the grace of their years. But this evening was different. Phil had gone to bed singing that night. Dolly followed dutifully, as she had all their years together. They both knew Phil could not be burdened to sleep alone. It was not the time spent sleeping that was the actual burden, but the moment preceding, when his mind fretted, his eyelids fluttered, and his chest labored under the enormity of her quilts.

If animals can sense quakes before they hit, if something in the air riles their fur and starts the saliva flowing, perhaps that is what Phil sensed, too. The excitement. The expectation. Rain leached off the roof, and thunder cannonaded down the mountain ranges. The horses in the neighboring pasture ran in erratic circles, raising waves of mud with their hooves. Phil sang to Dolly. He sang like Louis Armstrong. "Well, hello, Dolly. It's so nice to have you back where you belong." And it was. For two weeks now there had been no viscera on the kitchen table, no skulls boiling in the kettles. The squirrel gathered dust. The mouse diminished in its pose. "Everybody's staying in out of the rain," he'd told Dolly. "Not a roadkill in miles." He turned the garden in spite of the mud, coerced her to join him. Wasn't this better? Wasn't the smell of dirt clean? So wasn't it understandable that on this night he thought of sex?

When he came to "Find her an empty lap, fellas," he offered

his own. He was passionate, as he hadn't felt since seventeen, when he broke his heart weekly, twice daily. Something of that came through to Dolly, as she rolled under him, her nipples full as squash blossoms. She encircled him with her legs, and she was a greedy young woman again. Lightning broadcast their movements with huge shadows wavering on the walls. There was the crack of light, the boom of thunder, Phil's heavy breathing, while outside the earth gathered in a long clench before the heave.

Dolly's fingers spread over his back, kneading deeper. Even in his excitement, Phil felt something disagreeable in it—her thumb easing up along his spine, her fingers punching into his muscles. He thought he could smell an odor. As if skin on skin struck its own atmosphere, like ozone off lightning. It was the smell of meat on meat. He reared back; he looked at her, at himself, at his penis holding its awkward pose, challenging and white. Mouse rampant, he thought, and felt it crouch and wither.

The bed shook, and Phil thought it was Dolly, but saw in her look it wasn't; the door slammed, and somewhere in the kitchen one of Dolly's hand-painted ceramic plates clattered from the wall and broke. There was a sound like thunder misplaced. Dolly reached up and Phil fended her off, breaking free, his skin intact, as the room quivered with relief and settled into quiet.

There was no damage to the roads. It was as if the earth had never shifted. Somehow, he'd expected to find a new mountain range formed, a lake where a creek used to wander. But the asphalt buzzed under his wheels, no ridges, no pitfalls, no cracks in the world. He watched the shoulder carefully.

Phil didn't like to think of last night's performance as a failure, but rather as an event decreed by nature. It had never happened before, but then he had never experienced an earthquake before either. Dolly was inclined to make more of it.

"Something's gone wrong between us," she said.

"An *earthquake* came between us." It was breakfast, and he watched her shell a hard-boiled egg. Earthquakes were unusual in this part of the country but not unknown. It had been a small temblor that raised thirty-six-point headlines in the newspaper. "Three people died in a mudslide, not ten miles down the road." Was there no respect for the forces of nature anymore? Was it so difficult to believe that an event of this scale could dampen an erection? How could she even think about that? Three people died.

"The way you looked at me, before the quake hit—"

"What do you mean?" And he was sincerely confounded, as though he had misplaced something. Perhaps the timing.

"Not just last night. You've been avoiding me."

She'd always been forthright and outspoken, which was a quality he tended to admire more in women he didn't have to live with. He turned the page, searching for the continuation of "Quake."

She skinned the white off the egg, rolled the yolk onto the far side of her plate, as she always did. It had never bothered him before. "Is it the taxidermy, Phil?"

"You'd like to believe that," he said, and could not, for the life of him, explain why he did.

"Is it Lucy then?" She pressed the tines into the yolk, flattening it, dusted it with salt and pepper. "Maybe you could get a small accounting job in Missoula. You know, just a few hours a day. Something to do?" She waited for an answer, then said softly, "You worry too much. She's gone. It was inevitable."

He stopped pretending to read. When he looked up, he barely recognized her. She was no one he knew anymore. A squat, tired, sour-smelling woman. She was cruel. Wasn't it tragic, to wait all these years just to sit across the table from a stranger in the morning? Tragic and ordinary. He stood. "You'll be wanting another dead animal," he said, and lifted the car keys off the hook.

Maybe there'd be an aftershock. Maybe he would feel it like a semi coming down the road. If it happened, he would ride it out, race the ripple clear into Arizona. Or Texas maybe, where he could pick up a hurricane and ride its backwash down to the bayous. Down to Mexico. After all, he'd never been there. What kind of a life was it, to have never been to Mexico?

You're all hot air, he told himself. *Lighter than air.*

Ahead, there was a bird on the shoulder. When he stopped, he could see it was a quail. She hadn't tried a bird yet, and then he saw the maggots. It was tempting. It was almost worth it, he thought, as he pulled away from the carcass.

He started looking with a new intensity. *Inevitable.* That was how Dolly saw it. As if he didn't know that. When had Lucy ever taken a step she didn't mean to? As a toddler, she'd been fearless. They'd put up rails everywhere because she'd walk off porches like she could fly. She looked for cliffs. Where had she gotten that fearlessness? What part of them had betrayed itself in her?

It was unfair, he thought. How few times he'd held his daughter, bandaged her scratches, listened to her stories. When had his scoldings ever been anything more than an afterthought? Dolly had always been the first one there. She'd had all the time in the world to let go. Maybe for her it was a relief.

He turned down the Bear Creek road. Something big would be nice. Something overwhelming. An eight-foot bed in a pickup could accommodate just about anything, he thought. There were rainwater pools in the road, and his truck raised a rooster tail of mud. Bushes were sodden with growth.

They should have had more children. That was the trouble with one, not enough distractions. It encouraged too clear a focus. To her credit, Lucy bore their attention well. In high school, she became a well-mannered child, her fearlessness became courage, her fierceness, loyalty. How to account for that? She terrified him with her capacity to love carelessly.

He turned onto the old two-lane highway, a road he'd avoided for weeks. Roadkill heaven. He'd pretty much figured out what he was looking for. He passed up the odd rabbit, prairie-dog road stew. It took him an hour and a half to find the right thing, and he smelled it before he saw it. A skunk off in the barrow ditch where it had dragged itself. He didn't so much gag as choke. It was still fresh, the air dense around the animal. It had been hit, deflected off a tire, maybe. Uncrushed. Ripe. He gathered it up on the end of a long stick, flipped it into the back of the pickup, and rode home, into the wind, with the windows open.

> *To deodorize a fur:*
> 4 lbs. finely chipped bar soap
> 2 gals. water
> 4 lbs. sal soda
> ¾ oz. borax
> ½ oz. oil of sassafras
>
> Boil together until soap and soda are dissolved. Add borax and oil of sassafras. Solution is ready to use when cooled. Rinse the pelt well before tanning.

He'd carried the skunk into the house, draped on the end of a stick. Dolly was in the living room, dusting. When the first whiff caught her, she staggered and turned. "What in God's name are you doing?" she yelled, and chased him from the house. "Have you lost your mind?" she shouted, standing ankle deep in the front lawn, the dust cloth held over her nose.

"Fresh off the wheel," he said, trying a joke. She was not amused. "Isn't it a beaut?" But he knew she saw through him. She knew intent when she saw it. He stood there, his arm tiring beneath the extended stick, so that the skunk trembled in the air as if rousing from sleep, only to find itself, once again, under the same unsurprising sky.

"It was this or nothing," he said, then started walking away.

"Where you going?"

He looked over his shoulder. "To get rid of it."

"No," she said. "Reasons aside, it's the right thing. I have to learn to deal with the worst of it. Might as well be now."

The skunk was a discarded piece of meat, the skin steeping like a tea bag in a bucket of deodorizing solvent. She'd busied Phil carrying a table and bench onto the lawn, setting up a small cook fire and putting the pot on to boil. The kettle rattled on the wire grate and the skull bobbed and bumped. Clouds were beginning to clot the sky.

Dolly was building an armature of wire and jute string. Phil stood aimlessly at her side, a consequence of mixed emotions—distaste and contrition.

"What should it look like?" she asked him. "What was its best moment?" She measured the length, crimped it shorter. "Do skunks sit up like squirrels?" He heard the excitement in her voice, but he was too tired to resent it. *Bring on the rain*, he thought, *smite the campfire. Bring on the earthquakes and the trumpets.*

Bring on the rapture. He was ready for a little rapture in his life. "You can bring the kettle over now," she said.

She picked the skull clean with her fingers, the meat slipping off the bone. "You may not want to watch this," she warned. She had a crochet hook in her hand. "Sometimes I wonder myself how I can do this." She fished the hook into the back of the skull, dragged it back and forth. She hauled the brain out in small bits and pieces. She held her breath. Her hair blew into her eyes, and she raised an arm to push it clear. Her hand shook. He lifted her hair back for her, clamped it in place with the drooping bobby pin. She was scraping out the eye sockets, so intent she didn't notice how his hand stayed on her hair, how he stood over her back, stunned with the feel of her hair in his hands.

"This is the worst of it," she said, cutting at the base of the jaw. She gripped the tongue with a tweezer and pulled. The tongue stretched and then the tweezer bit into the meat. "Too small," she said, and tried it again with a breaking tool, a pair of blunt-ended pliers she'd used in stained glass. The table was littered with all the pieces of her past—paintbrushes, quilting shears, needles and thread, clay—as if all the years had been a preamble to this, all the elements coming together for her. It was a hodgepodge, a sad collection of mismatched tools. *Heroic,* he thought.

"Oh," she said. "How could I forget." She looked over her shoulder to see him. "Lucy called, while you were out. She wanted to thank us for the money. She said we didn't have to do that, but she understood. She wants us to know she's happy. She's met someone. A Canadian exchange student at the university. They have lots in common. I asked her, what and she said, North America."

He should not have been amazed. It was so like Lucy. He looked at Dolly, then down at his hands. Lucy was the competent one.

"If we didn't mind too much, she'd like to use the money for a divorce."

"What did you tell her?" he asked.

"I told her she was welcome. She asked me to give you her love."

Dolly paused, and Phil waited. "Is that all?" he asked.

"She'll write a long letter, she promised."

"Another postcard." He smiled. "She'll find her way to Canada."

"Before she finds her way here," Dolly agreed.

Phil sat on the bench next to Dolly. "All of that came out of there?" he asked, pointing to the tongue that lay on the table.

"Surprising, isn't it," she said. "It was good to hear Lucy's voice. You should have been here. She sounded that well."

It started to rain, scattered drops that pelted the plank table. A cold drop spattered down Phil's neck, then another on his back. They struck like tiny blows. Their child was gone, one way or another. Here he was, sixty years old, in a place he had yet to learn to call home. His daughter was getting a divorce and in love with a Canadian in Brazil. His wife was building a skunk from the ground up, in the rain. As a young man, when he was still green and believed he could construct his own good life to a fitting resolution, did he ever dream it would be this? The rain began to fall in volleys.

Dolly was packing clay around the skull, building cheeks. "Isn't it strange. You strip it down, skin and muscle, just to build it up again." She smoothed the clay. "You have to remember it all. This is where the art is."

The fire guttered behind them with hisses. The smoke dark-ened like a smudge. What he wouldn't give for a week of sun, for the blessed days of Montana summers. Each day like the best days of summer he remembered as a child. Clear, hot days and cool nights. They were getting wet. Her face was shining with rain.

"We could take it inside," he said.

"You don't like my doing this in the house," she answered. Her fingers worked quickly.

"I'll survive," he offered.

"Yes," she said, and smiled. It wasn't the smile of the girl he'd married; it struck no chord from his youth. It was an earned smile, all the woman she was now. If she was very lucky, if she was half the woman her mother was, perhaps someday, Lucy would have that smile. "I'm almost done," she said, and continued to work.

He left her side, walked briskly to the house. In the living room, he stopped by the console TV where the mouse stood its post. He ran his finger down the groomed fur, brushed the whis-kers lightly with a nail. Its ears were fanned parchment. He bent close to the mouse, studying its face, the poised paws. It seemed as if the mouse could speak to him, chronicle the years, tell him all the things he'd failed to hear. But there was only the sound of the house, the odd bumps of wood and wind, his solitary breath-ing. He walked to the hall closet. It only took him moments to find what he was looking for. When he returned to the bench, she was still there, her blouse opened and tented over her hands, try-ing to keep the skull she worked on dry. Her breasts were ex-posed, soft and worn, the skin already loosening from her bones. He wanted to touch her. He wanted to gather her up and hold her close. He raised the umbrella over them. They sat side by side, the sound of the rain lively on the umbrella.

ELECTRIC

The last, fast thing about Haze was his quickly passing middle years. At fifty-six, it seemed as if he'd been catapulted through his life, only to come to this—a mostly unremarkable man of moderate means who no longer noticed going unnoticed in crowds. He was medium in height, managing to remain within fifteen pounds of what he'd always weighed, despite the expanded waist, the weight of which he believed had been offset by his shrinking rump and thinning hair. He sat across the desk from his boss, Ox Watson—owner of Hometown Electric and Lighting, largest supplier of fixtures west of the Rockies, east of Seattle, and north of the Great Salt Lake. Ox, an uncomely man, with a thatch of gray hair and the thick-shouldered appearance of a creature born to be yoked, was regionally famous for his billboards that graced the major highways across the better part of three states, in which he was pictured in suit and ball cap, asking: "Watt's your problem?" The store, though, was the real thing. Located on the strip at the edge of town, it was a gaudy palace of light, a jeweled aberration among the rank-and-file car lots, the fast-food drive-ins, the Christian bookstores, pawnshops, check-cashing joints, and cash-in-hand blood banks.

Ox was tilted back in his chair, feet up on the desk, the insides of his shoe soles oddly worn. He was telling Haze what had awakened him and his neighbors two nights previous—the very thing Haze had read about in the morning newspaper. "These sons of bitches," Ox said, gazing over Haze's head. "It's the middle of the night, 2:00 A.M., and these damn kids are driving down the highway, shooting cattle from their cars, like it's some kind of cheap penny arcade. I wake up to shots. I mean, who'd think it?" He shook his head. "Where's the respect? No. Never mind that, where's the common sense? Tell you what"—he dropped his gaze back on to Haze—"someone should hobble them out there with the cattle." His feet slid to the floor, and he tipped the chair back on all fours. "My neighbor Tim lost one of his steers. What if there'd been someone standing out there? Say, his wife?"

Haze was careful not to say anything. After all, what was the likelihood of someone's wife finding her way out among the cattle at two in the morning. But there was another reason for his silence as well, for, in some part, Haze believed he understood these boys—on the brink in a backwater way station and spinning wheels on the way to the real events of their lives. What else would you make of such an act? The cruelty, the heedless bravado. Burning their bridges, so to speak, in an effort to convince themselves and each other that they wouldn't be the ones left behind. As their fathers had been, who were, even now, shrinking in the eyes of the towering boys for having simply lived lives of small consequence: work and family, the odd night out at the church or bar. For having the shortfall of luck or the failure of nerve that left them indebted to prefab houses, and dreamless in beds they'd finally made peace with.

That was not to say Haze condoned the boys' actions, for there was nothing admirable about them. But still, he felt aligned with their despair, poised on the brink of sixty and at a transitional age himself. Sometimes you made mistakes, he thought. Sometimes you did the unthinkable, when what was called for was merely the remarkable.

The bell rang in the store, and while Haze knew that Buddy was on the floor, needing sales in a way Haze never seemed to, he used this as an excuse to leave.

He walked through the stockroom, past cabinet drawers filled with wire, plugs, harps, finials, wing nuts, switches, and lightbulbs. Past shelves sporting row on row of shades in the latest fabrics and saturated colors: burgundy, russet, green, and, for the dramatically inclined, black.

He walked through the warehouse and onto the showroom floor, where his mood lifted, beneath the prisms of crystal chandeliers, and the dim, stained glass, with its Tiffany knockoffs: glass dogwood, and wisteria. Past aisles of bathroom fixtures—all that crisp chrome and milky globes. Then into the central showroom, with its oversized wagon wheels and antlered concoctions so popular these days in the trendy log homes timbering the otherwise bare hills that surrounded this small central Idaho valley.

By the time he reached the front, Buddy had already nabbed the customer. He had her by the arm, the woman, Irene, the one

Haze had been helping this past week. *No big deal.* But somehow it had become just that, which was a genuine surprise—how disappointed he felt—and even more surprising, how he resented Buddy's having been in the right place, at the right time.

Haze was just turning away when he heard his name. *Mr. Doty. Please, Mr. Doty.* It was her. Calling to him. His heart began to trip-hammer, so that his hand rose, as if he was about to recite the pledge, and he turned to face her. She had a floor lamp in hand, a three-armed candelabra model she'd taken home the day before. A bit much to his tastes, but there was never any accounting for such things.

"I know I've been a pest," she said.

He waved off the notion. "Ms. Porter. How nice to see you," he said.

She set the lamp down, shade hovering at her shoulder, while her hands wandered upward, weightless with loss. "I'm at wit's end."

She was a little thing, a cap of short, dark hair, pert features. Not at all to his usual taste. Certainly unlike Carol, his wife of twenty-odd years, who was tall, and broad-shouldered, with a head of long, red hair that had begun fading to silver. He tried to shake it off, the electric thrill he felt merely by noting the differences—brown eyes to his wife's blue, the buffed complexion, not a freckle in sight.

"I'm at a loss what to do anymore…" She ducked her head, flinching.

"No trouble at all. Really." Haze patted her arm, startled by the heat under his palm. He took his hand away, tucked it awkwardly behind his back.

She was asking if they had a decorating service, or if he might recommend someone, but she didn't know that she could really afford a consultant anyway, "the move being so expensive and all," then she was saying what he'd half hoped to hear. "Perhaps you could stop by? Just for a moment. I know it's a terrible imposition—it's just that you know lighting…"

And, of course, she was right. He did know his stock, and, moreover, what was available. Twenty years, after all, was no small thing in the business of lighting.

He told her, he didn't know what help he could be. Perhaps her husband might be better suited? Or a girlfriend?

But she wasn't married. "Not anymore" she said, and again, there was that flinch. She'd just moved here, so there were no friends either, girl or otherwise. She was rushing onward, saying that, of course, she was asking too much. She apologized, backing away, said she'd give it another stab on her own, and then Haze was following, carrying the abandoned lamp in his hand, cord trailing.

When was it? Just short moments later as she'd turned to shake his hand, thanked him for his help, his constant patience, was it then he found himself saying, "I'll come by," and, "but I can't say exactly when…"

And then that smile that nearly lit him off his feet. "Anytime," she'd said. "Anytime at all. Just call." She pressed his hand with her own, and didn't it linger just a tad longer than necessary? Wasn't there a bit more warmth in the way her fingers pressed his palm? When she took her hand away, he saw she had pressed a piece of paper into it, as if she had had it ready all along. And then she strode away, a quick wave and smile over her shoulder, and Haze was left holding her address and phone number.

· · ·

After work, he drove his car straight home, not a turn or swerve from routine. He drove through the late-afternoon light with the window open, his elbow crooked across the frame, the heater fan blowing to counter the chill. Autumn. His favorite time of year, sad as it was, with lawns and sidewalks glowing under the fallen sycamore and maple leaves, and overhead, the first sketch of branches bared against the sky. He pulled up to his house and saw where the path of the morning street sweeper had curved around his wife's car curbside, the car not having moved all day. A nurse, she enjoyed the odd days at home, off from rotation at the hospital, pulling the occasional night shift. He sat a moment, enjoying the smell of clipped grass and burning leaves. His neighbor, stooping, waved and returned to swatting at the hot embers rising like bees off the smoking pile.

Even before Haze hit the porch, the scent of dinner was in the air, sweet and savory. Which should have been enough to speed him into the house. Instead, he opened the door and stood on the far side of the threshold. His home, a tidy two-story Cape Coddish affair that hadn't struck Haze as anything but comfortable, now seemed an ill fit—narrow rooms, overstuffed couch, the end tables with their baroque lamps it had taken him ten years to come to an accommodation with. The worst of it? Over the fireplace, the enormous oil painting, a seascape—the *dark, stormy night* kind of fare, ponderous with emotion. A wedding gift from her parents. More than a mild embarrassment to Haze—all the melodrama, and, insult to injury, the way Carol would stand before it, drawing on some past or imagined pain, tears freely flowing, not the least bit discomfited, claiming as she did that the world would be a better place if more people cried. "Cleans you out, like nothing else," she'd say. "You should try it sometime."

Which, of course, he never would, believing, as he did, that all too many people cried in the world already. Haze stepped into the room, hung his suit coat on the back of the Barcalounger. He followed his nose to the kitchen, where a dish of squash steamed on the stovetop. In the depths of the oven, from which Carol was lifting a braised chicken, he could see apples plumped in pans, baking on the lower shelf.

"Look good?" she asked, holding the chicken out, elbows cocked on her hips. She smiled.

Ten years ago, he might have thought it saucy. Now? It was just a thing they did, like asking about each other's day, or expressing an interest in the nightly news, or turning in when only one of them was sleepy. A life more habit than intent—the place you came to after twenty-odd years, when all that was left of marriage was the ordinary. He smiled back, then worried that she might see as he had, and so covered his mouth with his hand, a gesture unused since the buck-toothed days of childhood.

"Lovely," he said, and meaning to apologize for this small betrayal, he meant to plant a kiss, but, all brisk business, she whisked the chicken to a tray on the counter, and with spoons wide as paddles, probed the carcass to scoop stuffing from its cavity.

"Smell this," she said, lifting a spoonful to his nose. "Is that heaven, or what?" And then, before he could actually bring himself to sniff the offering, she lowered the spoon, knocked it clean into the bowl. "Dinner's almost on. Why don't you wash up?"

They ate with short asides to ask about each other's day, or to relay the latest gossip. Haze mentioned the news about the kids shooting cattle. Carol told him of the phone call she'd had from their son, Ryan, who'd gone east, to Michigan, for college.

"He sounded so good. You should have heard him."

And yes, Haze thought, he probably should have. But it would not occur to Ryan to wait and call at an hour when Haze would be home. It probably would not even occur to Ryan that it might matter to Haze. His part in the boy's life having been re-cast as the bottomless pocket. The man with the bucks. *Just tell me how much?*

"Is he short of cash?" Haze asked.

Carol laughed. "What boy isn't? And it's not that he didn't want to ask you himself, but…"

Haze frowned down at his plate, the scraping of bone and squash. Carol was going on about what a good son he was, what a good young man he was turning out to be, as if Haze didn't know, hadn't been there all the years it took. And then it was the other boys he thought of, the ones stalled here, driving the night-time highways, taking shots, pegging cattle, this one or that, and he thought of the unwitting animals slumbering amid slopes of sage and fescue. Felled in dreams, caught dead to sights in the or-dinary act of living. And he felt, as he had earlier, that curious sensation of his home life having grown too small.

"I'm happy for him," Haze said. "Our boy."

Carol stopped eating, looked across the table. "Well, of course you are, dear. We both are. Does that mean you'll send him some?"

"What?"

"Money. Not much. But enough to tide him over."

Haze sighed. He pushed the squash away. Bundled on the far side of the plate were thighbones and leg bones. Gristle and carti-lage knobbed the joints. At the end of such a meal, his own father would have taken the bone in hand and gnawed on those chewy bits. Haze had always thought it appalling, how his father would worry the bone, the top of the knuckle polished clean as pulley tracks. "That's the way you do it, boy," he'd say. "Clean as a whistle. Here, you want to try?" And he'd offer the other drumstick, with its shreds of ligament, meat, and veins flagging in his hand.

It's a wonder Haze ever ate meat again; and then he thought of Ryan, and the tender stomach he'd had as a child; the innumerable dinners Haze had coaxed him through, one item at a time. A far cry from the bone-cracking father Haze had lived across the table from. Michigan. What had been Ryan's reason to leave, to journey so far? *A little freedom, Dad, that's all. Some time to try the world on my own.* Hah. His own father had been enough to send a child running an extra two thousand miles. New York, maybe. But he hadn't, had he? No. Haze had stayed right here.

"All right, what's wrong?"

Haze looked up. Carol was setting a dessert dish alongside his dinner plate so that the apple slumped in heavy cream next to chicken parts, squash, and potatoes. "I don't think I can eat this," he said.

"Unheard of," she answered, and looking down at the sweet concoction, said, "Make an effort, dear." She patted him on the back, returned to her seat. After a bite or two, she looked up, fork wandering in midair. "You don't look sick. Are you sick?"

What if he said, yes. Sick. Utterly sick.

Then he'd have to say, of what it was he was sick. Damned if he knew. Damned if he understood how a man could walk out of the house one morning, ordinary as any other, and by evening, arrive back unsettled in his own skin. He could not say sick, but he might say, disillusioned. Disenchanted. Disheartened. And none of those entirely dishonest.

He could say, Irene.

Carol was studying him. "Well, you are a bit flushed. Do you feel hot?"

And then he knew; he could never pull it off. She would read his sin as surely as she read the weather: partly cloudy this morning, by late afternoon, clearing, with a chance in hell of infidelity. And just as well, wasn't he appalled that he had even thought of it?

He set down the fork, planted his hand in his lap. He had the whole night to get through yet. This night, the next. He stared at his plate, imagined the remaining lifetime of nights he had yet to get through, a sad retinue of routine conversations, lengthening silences, and diminishing sex. He sighed.

Carol began to fill the sink with soapy water. He looked out the kitchen window, to the deepening gloom where the hills were folding away for the night. He felt his blood silting down through his legs, leaving him lumpish in the chair, sodden clear to his soles. Carol filled the sink with dishes. The clock over the stove wound down, and his baked apple shriveled in its skin.

It wasn't as if he had a penchant for the illicit. No particular talent for lies, great or small, though there had been the little thefts as a kid: a Coke he'd snatched at the corner store, a pen from his teacher's desk. As a teen he'd had his share of foolish nights behind the wheel, and on the highway. There had been the odd drunken night with friends. And a hit-and-run—nothing tragic, mind you—a parked car on a deserted street, no victims, really, though, to this day, when he bothered to think of it, he had to quell the impulse to write a check to someone, anyone, in exoneration.

So it was three days before he found it in him to do a drive-by. It turned out Irene lived up on Coyote Ridge. A posh neighborhood, where the owners so prized their individuality that no two houses had much of anything to do with the other—a coincidental hodgepodge of Mediterranean, next to English, next to French, next to Italian Villa, Traditional Farm, and so on, that produced a collective of homes wholly dissimilar, united by the thinnest threads of size—minimum eight thousand square feet—and a required palate—off-white, gray, beige, and deeper beige—the chief aesthetic value being that they made no one house stand apart from another.

He drove to the end of the block, a cul-de-sac overlooking the valley, with a backdrop of umber hills, and below the hills, the confluence of two rivers in bright lines of reflected sky. And there was the town, and all about the town, flanked by trees, was the last of the autumn color glowing like embers banked for the night. Haze rested his elbow on the doorframe and his chin on his arm, stared out at the place before him, and, for this brief while, he did not think about the things he'd thought about the last three days. He let go of the worry, and the guilt he was rapidly accruing—the way he'd found it necessary to dodge his wife's eyes, the moments he'd stolen while pretending to be asleep or fiddling with chores. Those secret times he'd spent imagining Irene, imagining himself here, visiting her, at her home.

Looking down into the valley, he saw what was his block, a short walk from the community college his son did not choose to attend. And beyond that, the redbrick edifice of the small, Catholic hospital where his wife was at work. He sat transfixed, unsure as to why he was actually here, as surprised as if he had been jerked up out of his life and dropped whole onto this street, in much the way Irene had, by walking into his store one short week ago, lifted him wholesale out of reason. He sat upright, pulled his elbow into the car, and rolled up the window.

In twenty-seven years of marriage, he had never strayed. Not that that was cause for self-congratulation; but it had been some comfort, all those years, to be able to consider himself a decent man, a good husband and father. While other households came undone, drifting husbands and compliant wives, uncloaked politicians and defrocked preachers, he could look at the world from a place outside that turmoil. He was a respected salesman and an upstanding member of the community, a Rotarian, for God's sake. A secret Santa. He turned the key in the ignition, checked the rearview mirror, looked over each of his shoulders and out the side windows before pulling away from the curb. He meant to drive right past. Four houses away. Three, two, one, but then he was in front of her house, the car stopped and idling curbside. A small dog with crusty eyes wandered down the side-walk, lifted an aging leg on a sculpted yew. Haze could hear the dog tags chiming as it circled the bush, lifting a leg again, a dribble here, there. He watched the dog sniff what he'd left be-hind, and then, satisfied, amble back down across the lawns and out of sight into a backyard three houses away. He looked at the sad yew, then he looked across the lawn, at the locked house, its closed door, drawn drapes. It seemed omen enough. He slipped his engine in gear and pulled away.

He's young when this happens. He's a teenager hopped up on beer and hormones, in the backseat of Jim Jenson's 1969 Road-runner. He's kneeling on the seat, torso out the open window, while Jimmy drives, and Kurt Barber, that giddy youngster every-one loves but knows will amount to nothing, holds on to Haze's belt: counterbalance to the weight of booze, youthful immortal-ity, and the baseball bat Haze holds in hand. The car's hurtling through the night, trees ripping past, and there's Haze poised in the rush of air, mailboxes springing up as sudden as lust in the headlights. It all ends very badly, of course, these nighttime forays, this precursor of T-ball. It ends in an oversized hollow-bodied box, a box large enough to hold the JCPenney catalogue, the latest Book-of-the-Month Club selection, assorted magazines, and the cement pole that runs up the center. It's the last mailbox of the night, and the soon-to-be-last hit he will ever make. And it's a home-run effort. His upper torso suspends out the window, higher and farther than before. He levels the bat overhead, already battling air, the currents that twist the stick in his hands, the rush of wind that fills his eyes and cheeks. He is wiping his eye on a shoulder when he sees it, white and lumbering like Moby Dick arising out of the dark sea, it comes in a wash of headlights, and then Jim's yelling something about *the mother of all*—but Haze doesn't hear the rest, for the box is winging at him, now, like a fastball, low and to the right. He leans, swings. It's a hit.

The bat disintegrates in his hand, shatters, an explosion of wood flinging outward, shards flipping past his face like low-flying birds, while smaller shreds tangle in hair and on his clothing, and he's pinwheeling out there, driven off-balance by the concussion, and Kurt's tugging like a terrier, trying to draw him back into the car. It is then that the aftershock hits, the one that runs up his arm, and through his shoulder, his scapula, his neck, and lighting at last in his brain with something akin to St. Elmo's fire, all green and electric.

There is the long drive down the country roads, Jimmy Jensen driving with hearselike speed now, trying to convince Haze his pain is nothing more than passing, that it's no big deal, arguing that if they go to the hospital, someone's bound to put two and two together, if not tonight, tomorrow.

And hours later, his father, arriving at the emergency room to find Haze's arm already being bound in a cast. Green fracture to the arm, chips in the wrist, three broken fingers, and a dislocated thumb.

And Haze's father to the doctor: "Yes, but will he play piano again?"

Buddy had him paged on the floor, asked him to come to the service counter. Haze made his way to the store's center, right next to the stairway and indoor track lighting, where the service counter sat, and the women took catalogue orders, did billing, and cashed customers out. It was a small area, with barely enough room for a couple of desks, a table, and the countertop manned by the three perpetually smiling women. Haze walked into the ambient air of designer candles and brewed coffee.

"You had a phone call. It was a woman," said Buddy. "She couldn't wait, but she gave me this number for you." He held out a memo pad. "She mentioned in-home consultations? What's this about?" He looked over at Ox, who was leafing through catalogues. "How long have we been doing that?"

Haze lifted the paper clear. "It's just this one time," Haze said. "She's got one of those big houses up on the ridge. Needs more light and doesn't know how to go about it. That's all."

"Uh-huh," Buddy said. He glanced over at the women, then back at Haze. "Right. Right you are. Well," he slapped Haze on the back. "Good for you! Good for you." And then he walked off, a goofy smile stuck on his face.

Haze sighed.

The women looked away, down at the order forms, or at their manicures. Ox set the catalogue aside, and, in passing, asked, "You got a moment? Thought I'd show you something over this way. Some new fixtures that just came in."

"Sure, Ox." Haze pocketed the memo.

They crossed through the showroom, beneath the deerskin shade shaped like a suspended drum, wrought-iron arrows crosswise on four corners. Ox shook his head. "Who the hell would put something like that up in a house? Can you imagine? I mean, the room would have to be big as a hotel lobby." And, of course, those were precisely the kinds of home this fixture had immense popularity in. The new West with all its pricey icons, spurs and arrows, drums and cavalry trumpets. Acres of Cordoba leather. He stood under it, fingering the ironwork, the welded frame. "Good craftsmanship though, don't you think?"

Haze nodded, wondering what it was Ox wanted him to see.

"Takes years to pull this sort of thing off. You know, all that technical stuff, the structural needs, the weight, and metal chemistry. Takes an honest-to-God artisan." He stepped away, waved Haze forward. "So, how's it going with you? You doing all right? Carol well?"

Haze nodded. "Yeah, she's good." He glanced over his shoulder, at the women behind the counter. He thought of the looks they'd given him at the desk, Buddy's pat on the back, and now Ox asking about Carol. "She's working. Keeping busy. You know."

"Good, good," Ox said. "And your boy, Ryan. He good as well?"

"Yeah. Heard from him a couple days ago. Says he needs money again—the usual."

"Boys in college." Ox sighed. "You know I just wanted to talk with you about this thing...this, this job up on Coyote Ridge. You all right with going up there?" Ox stopped, knotted his hands behind his back, rocked on his heels. "I admire your willingness to go the extra mile, but"—and he rocked forward—"I'm not asking this of any of my people. In-home consultations...No, I won't stop you, if you think you want to do this"—he shook his head—"but, tell you what, you want me to—I could go with you on this..."

Ox, the eminently moral man. Haze wondered how must *this* look to him. But then, what precisely was *this*? A woman asks for help with lighting, and right away everybody's jumping to some dour conclusion about his life, his marriage. His state of mind. Haze was backing away, waving his hand. "It isn't like that—"

"No, no, I'm sure it isn't," Ox said. "But just thought I ought to offer. Sometimes people get the wrong ideas—sometimes you get talked into things you'd like to be talked out of."

"It isn't like that," Haze said. But he couldn't look at his boss any longer. He could hardly stand to be here, under the bare light of kitchen lamps. He could barely contain the shame as he fingered the paper in his pocket.

It was late by the time he got home, having stayed to help with inventory then his detour afterward, up Coyote Ridge again. But when he'd gotten in, Carol was sitting on the sofa, watching some series in which average women in average households had gone off the deep end. He wondered how Carol could watch that tripe, having always thought better of her. So he removed himself, forgoing the usual evening of television to read in the new guest room, where the shades of Ryan's former school pennants haunted the worn paint. He tried to read, but his attention kept wandering. In this room, this place where his son had lived the better part of his life, he could not bring himself to imagine her here, so he took himself to bed instead.

He buried himself under the quilts. Thought about his drive

up Coyote Ridge, and how he'd parked at the end of the block to call Irene on his cell phone. He could still hear her voice.

"Yes?" she'd said, and, "Hello?"

He'd apologized to her then, for calling so late tonight, for not calling days earlier. He was ready with the excuses he'd rehearsed, but she'd hear none of it. Said she was just so pleased he called. Said she understood he was a busy man. Understood there were demands on his time. It was enough that he'd called.

"When can you come?" she'd asked.

And how he'd wanted to say, *right now.*

So, what stopped him? He had her voice in his ear, the house in sight, the sidewalk leading to her porch a bright crisp path of new cement. He'd rolled down the window, leaned his head on the doorframe; the cell phone perched on his ear like a small bird. He'd felt something akin to what he'd once known as a young man. Back when the terms of his life were still undefined, his course yet to be determined. He sat there, with his head crooked on the cold metal doorframe, and just a few hundred feet away, she was waiting.

She would welcome him, wouldn't she? He was certain of that, wasn't he? Though there was no one thing he could attribute his belief to. The way she sought him at the store, the way her hand fluttered against his on occasion. How close she'd leaned as he'd leafed through the catalogues at the store with her. How alone she was, and how apparent.

And then he'd heard her voice again, saying, "How about tomorrow?" and the pause, before saying, "Tomorrow would be best. Would tomorrow evening do?"

"Sweetie, are you all right?"

Haze bolted to a sitting position. It was Carol, walking in on them. No. It only felt that way. He oriented himself, his room, his bed. Half-asleep was all. He waved off her concern. "I'm fine. Just snoozing."

She lowered herself to the side of the bed, put a hand on his forehead.

"I'm fine, Carol. Just tired."

"And off your feed, and staying late at work." She drew her legs up onto the bed, stretched herself out next to him, said, "That does feel good." She yawned. "So, what's up with you? In bed by ten. Tell me it's nothing serious. Trouble at work? It's Ox, isn't it, working you too hard."

"You guessed it, babe," he said. "Just too much work."

"Well, that's all right then," she said, flopping over on her back. "For a while, you had me nervous. Thinking the worst—a midlife crisis, something like that. You wouldn't do that, would you? I just don't think I'm up for something like that now." And she tucked herself against his back. "Good night, dear," she said. Kissed him on the neck. "It'll be better in the morning." She turned out the light. "I promise."

He is thirteen years old when this happens. He goes with his father on their once-monthly all-male grocery trip. Haze teases his mother, "You could come along, Mom," and his father says, "Yeah, Mom, you could come along." They laugh when she rolls her eyes, runs from the room.

His father calls it male bonding, walking down the aisles, filling a shopping cart: disposable razors, shaving cream, foot powder, liniment, Dr. Scholl's shoe inserts, and a deodorant designed specifically for the chemistry of men. His father picks up a slim packet from a shelf. "You know what this is, boy?" he asks, waves it quickly before his son's eyes, and when Haze shakes his head, his father says, "Good. Keep it that way." Sets it back on the shelf and, laughing, hurries the boy away by an elbow.

There's beer and soda, pork rinds and pretzels, popcorn, chips, and Cheese Whiz to go around. They stroll the aisles, taking their time, checking in on what Haze thinks of school, friends, and sports. His father asks, "You got a girlfriend yet? No? How old are you? Nah, you don't say—thirteen? Well, then it's just as well, hey?" And on and on, down the separate aisles, until the cart is full, until they can't think of another thing they can bring home to disgust his mother, or another thing that needs to be said.

The checker is young. A blond-haired, wispy-featured young woman whom Haze recognizes. He likes her because she has become part of this ritual, almost always the one who checks them through with a joke.

She moves the notions down the conveyor belt, comes to the pork rinds and lifts the plastic bag by a corner, says to Haze, "Must be breakfast, huh?"

He flushes, pleased to be the brunt of her good humor. He glances down in the basket, suddenly shy. Can't believe how his mouth has dried up. His stomach, gone pleasantly tight. He shakes his head. Looks over at his dad, and finds himself transfixed.

His father is transformed—the routine father, with his worn flannel shirt, sagging blue jeans, and tired smile has been replaced. The clothing the same, but somehow the man inside has gotten taller, or stands straighter, has a shyness about him as raw and new as Haze himself. It's the way his cheeks dimple deeply, his eyes flitting down just before they rise, and when they do, rise that is, it is with a shine that Haze cannot remember having ever seen before. More curious yet is the subtle way his father's face changes, becoming as foreign to Haze as it is familiar—a preternatural recognition of the boy his father had once been, of the way he must have looked in love, as a young man. In the same way that Haze knows this, he also knows that if his mother has ever seen that smile, it was a long time ago. Just as he knows it is a thing she will likely never see again.

He finds himself holding on to the cart, an ache settling into his chest. They pay, bundle grocery sacks in hand and under arm, and with Haze following his father, they trudge out of the store, neither remarking on what the one has seen in the other.

In the coming years, Haze will think less often of this day, though on the rare occasions when he does, what he will recall is his father's eyes, the way they shone, the way they winced beneath the shock of love.

It had been a long day at work, the time lagging even though Haze kept himself busy on the floor, or stocking shelves during breaks, even skipping lunch. At the end of the day, he'd slipped out the back door and swung home, where he'd showered, shaved, changed into clean clothes. He'd checked the fridge and the note, "casserole in the oven, sweetie," from Carol, who was working the late-night shift at the hospital. By the time he got into his car, dusk was right around the corner. He'd arrived at her house with the last light of day brimming the hills. But light fell quickly this far west, this time of year, so that even though the dark had deepened by the time he left Irene's house, the hour was still fairly early.

It had been a less-than-eventful evening, and when he pulled away from her house he tried not to look back, still feeling strangely mangled. He drove with the windows open, needing the fresh air. He drove, not as he had done as a younger man, back when everything was still available, and all it took was time, but rather he drove as a man on the cusp of sixty, fully aware there wasn't time enough in the world anymore.

He steered up the two-thousand-foot grade out of the valley, sped the sloping road on the straights, slowing into the switchbacks, up and up and up, and finally over the rim, to where the prairie stretched flat. Up there, he drove past the darkened acres, with their small spreads, homes and barns tucked into coves of windbreak trees; he drove tight-fisted, the accelerator at an inconstant plus or minus ten of the limit.

He thought about how she'd met him at the door, in a short black skirt, white blouse he could see through. How his mouth had dried while he stood there on the threshold, the bag of catalogues—closest thing he had to a briefcase—nearly dropping to the porch. She'd led him into the house, her arm linked in his, friendly enough, a crisp smile, a touch distant in the eyes, but who was paying attention to those details.

The moon crested, and still he drove, past the small university town with its hip coffee shops, college bars, and thrift stores, past the neighboring town with its grange hall, its feed store, and hamburger stand. He drove past the latest cult church, a strangely cubist-gothic structure, scale outlandish, set as it was across from a Dairy Queen stand, and thought it reminiscent of her house, with its cathedral ceilings throughout, including the guest rooms and her bedroom. Dwarfing. Or perhaps it had only seemed that way because she was so short, and so obviously alone. When she'd led him back to the family room, he'd begun to think it was going to be all right after all. He'd give it over to fate, content to be the passenger.

He felt another sting of embarrassment, and accelerated out of town, through the last stoplight on the highway, and out into the lightless deeps, with gravel shoulders brighter than the worn centerline. He watched for deer, the occasional coyote, his headlights catching the intermittent dash of mice across asphalt.

His speed fluctuated between fast and faster, according to the level of sting, the particular barb he inserted. His own hubris. How he must have looked, a rube on the doorstep, his hair still wet from the shower. The cologne that now gained in intensity proportionate to body heat in the confines of a closed car. And the additional barbs: her reckless disregard for how he *must* see this invitation. The way she rocked from foot to foot as he eyed the ceilings. The way she kept checking her watch. The final blow: "Will this take long?"

And then she explained. She was so sorry, but something had come up. "It won't take long, right?" The way she kept looking over her shoulder, at the hallway, the one that led to the front door and his exit.

But he'd seen enough by then. Hadn't he? The briskness with which she led him back out of the house, standing on the doorstep, waving good-bye in his face. "I'll call you tomorrow. I'll come by the store."

"Yes," he'd said. "Fine," he'd said. "We'll work something out," he'd said.

Like hell. The heat rose in his neck, the flush burned on his cheek. "Stupid," he said out loud. "Just pretty damn stupid." He looked up into the dark mirror. Say it. A young girl like that. "You old fool."

He was cruising back toward town now, the city lights a glow brimming over the valley rim. Behind him, a set of headlights rushed up, swerved in his mirror. The brights flashed on, off, on and then the vehicle was swinging wide. A pickup. Three young boys in the cab. They pulled even, and he saw the gun mount in the back window. And then they were drifting past in a rush of wind, laughter. A shouted something, something or other. And then they were gone, dipping down the grade, racing down the slippery slope toward the valley floor, all youth and daring, not a lick of sense among them.

Haze thought of the gun mount. Certain he knew what they were up to. He could see them already rounding the first hairpin below, straying wide on the inside curves, banking close on the outside, flying round and down the narrow two-lane road, leading far and farther away, gaining speed like a fall through space that Haze could never hope to match. He gave up trying, picked his steady way down the hills, past the tiny pioneer cemetery with its five headstones and wrought-iron fence. Past the homes scattered on the grade, and finally hitting the valley floor, but turning on the bottom, away from the lights, out toward the dark of the up-river ranches, where he was certain the young boys were headed. "Those sons of a bitch," he said. "Those god-damned sons of bitches." For he saw he was not like them. No confederate in their heedless lives, witless and winsome, rather, he was consequence, the toll of years, the inevitable reckoning delayed but never finally denied.

He sped along the canyon floor, down the ever-narrower two-lane road alongside the river. He watched for the hint of red lights around the next turn, or over the next rise, and then, where the basalt walls cinched close, and the road wound tighter, he was forced to slow, cautious in the dark that had fallen absolute on the canyon bottom. Finally, wearying of the chase, he pulled onto a turnout and stared upriver at the blackness that wound before him. He eased his hands from the steering wheel, turned off the headlights, and let his eyes adjust. Across the road, on the canyon side, and up the sloping hills were cattle—Charolais—the color of clotted cream against the darkened grasses. Most were scattered over the hillside, but a few nearest the road were standing with heads turned toward the river. To his right was a smaller clutch, some kneeling. Some few of them, prone. Dead, he thought, seeing them flat on the ground. Victims of that brutal youth.

Angry, he climbed out of the car, jogged across the road, and into the field with the animals, meaning to help, to staunch the bleeding, say, or comfort them in their dying. He was running over the broken ground, stumbling on the clump grass, and pitching to his hands in gopher holes. The standing cattle scattered, tails flagging above their lifting rumps, their startled lows sparking across the grass, so that the kneeling cattle rocked from their nests, and even the prone animals, as if raised from the dead, startled from what he now knew to be slumber, launched themselves up the side of the hill, until Haze was left standing, alone. Yet again, a victim of his own expectations, for the second time in a single night. Neither cad nor hero. What was he to make of that? And then he was laughing and lowering himself to his knees, until he was sitting, and the laughs turned small and deeply ironic.

He wondered if this was how his father had managed it, these midlife years? Part and parcel of his own periodic downfall, or the willing passenger, grateful, if only intermittently, to be made the fool? He wondered if once was lesson enough, or if this was but a glimpse into the folly of years to come.

This was dark territory, this tough perch on the side of a hill, this starlit introspection among cattle, which were, even now, being fatted for slaughter. When had the world gone so dark, he wondered.

The only movements on the hill were the wind in grasses and a few cattle moving back down the slope. They grazed and stopped, studied him a long while before returning to browse.

And then he was struck, by the solemnity of their stride, the efficient way they grazed the terrain, the grace with which they folded to their knees in fragrant beds of grass.

He sighed, looked out across the field, across the river to a brake of pines between river and road. After a while, a car moved down the far side, its headlights threading the way with light, zipping the dark shut as it passed. It might be the young boys, reckless with fear and cruising the road. He looked about him, at the cattle that had congregated nearby, and then down at his own shirt, at the startling whiteness. A certain target for whatever urge found its way down these narrowing canyon walls, and he understood that he should leave, but could not, feeling suspended, as he was, and given over to this dreaming landscape. He thought about the woman, Irene, and the ambitious house she was trying to make a home, and found he was suddenly grateful, for his own home, with its odd bits and pieces, its knickknacks and photos, furniture and china, like a manifest history of their lives together—his and Carol's, and, for that brief, electric time, when they were all young together, their son Ryan's—housed under the simple roof. He gazed out across the road, to where the river coursed blackly through the hills, and overhead, to the stars, an ambient reach that made the heavens seem impossibly near, and above and below this the generous hills, with its spattering of cattle, luminous against the dark, holding firm, like a constellation of flesh in this tough firmament.

TAP

Dance Happy

Helen's the instigator in getting the women to sign up for the dance class, as she is in most of the factory-floor amusements—the betting pool, the self-adhesive glue applied to the men's toilet seats, and the accompanying tweaking of private hairs announced by a sudden bawling behind closed doors. Small payback for the way the men forage the emptied glue barrels—the tacky adhesive of self-sealing envelopes—wad the remnants into gooey gobs they fling down arms in faux sneezes, or drape from zippers.

At Bledsoe Envelope and Stationery employees stay beyond their training periods, settle in jobs, girth, and progeny. The company's initiated a new program—erected a weight room in the factory's unlikely basement, pays a dance instructor off premises to exercise those employees less inclined to heft steel.

Helen's a contemplative forty, small, speaks softly and wears her brown hair in a pageboy, just as she did in high school, twenty-two years ago. She drives the first night, and all five women crowd into her Toyota. Heavyset Flora, a grandmother in her late fifties, takes the front bucket seat. This leaves the other three to fidget it out in back: Mary Jane, thirty and trim, Louisa, forty-seven with a midlife spread, and Rachael, the youngest at eighteen and all angles.

The studio is downtown Mill Valley, four miles from the sawmill—a town niched between the high-rising cliffs of the Camas and Palouse prairies of central Idaho. The studio's a long shed sporting a corrugated tin roof and aggregate siding a shade paler than the gray house it's attached to. The curtain, a scattering of lilies with red-tipped vulval lips, is closed on the large picture window. Over the front door hangs a sign—IDABOB DOPPUS DANCE HAPPY STUDIO.

Helen leads the group into the dark interior, where chairs fan out before a curtained stage. Like schoolchildren, they take their seats in back, are just settling in when a voice crackles over the loudspeaker. "Come up front. You may be all I have."

Flora whispers into Helen's ear, "What have you gotten us into?"

"Trust me," Helen says. She herds them front and center.

At five minutes to seven, in walks Clyde Woods, a day-shift janitor, a young fifty with a full head of sandy hair, pallid, smelling of industrial cleaners—a bleached man. His hands usually appended to a broom or toilet brush now cram deep in his pockets. He perches on a seat in back.

Helen scoots her chair back to glimpse this unlikely sixth member. Clyde, the mystery janitor. Not jovial like Hank Santini, the swarthy Mediterranean who sings tidbits of *Turandot ... O divina bellezza! O meraviglia! O sogno!* Oh, heavenly beauty! Oh, wondrous sight! Oh, dream! as he mops his way past women, singing to the clip, clip, snap, of the press, the kumble, kumble, chop of the folding machines. Nor is he moribund like Stan Callis, who wears his chores like a hair shirt. Clyde sports no wedding band, has a pinched look that suggests his heart has long ago been robbed. He arrives at work on time, departs on time. Lunches alone. Who'd think it? Clyde Wood.

There's a punch behind the curtain; the velvet wallows out like a breath and opens. A blue spotlight nails center stage and "Cool" from *West Side Story*, pipes through small wall-mounted speakers.

Idabob Doppus makes her entrance. What a surprise. A delight. Helen claps her hand over Flora's. Idabob's dressed in a tuxedo jacket, shirt, black fishnet tights, and black patent tap shoes. Her legs are shapely, her chunky waist cinched, white hair frizzing under a bowler.

"Cripes," Mary Jane says, "she's ancient." Louisa counters with, "I should look so good at her age." Flora says, "I should live so long."

Helen shushes them, peeks over at Rachael to see how she is taking it, and finds the young girl enraptured, lips parted as if for a kiss. It's painfully sweet, almost an embarrassment. Would Helen's own seventeen-year-old daughter Meghan see this with the same adoring eyes? She thinks not. A rude, worldly child—who would wave the magic off, slip out for a cigarette. Helen was sure she smoked. A wearisome child. Too damned independent and a questionable influence on her fourteen-year-old brother Chester.

Good God. What were they *thinking*? How could they have named him Chester?

But Idabob's high-stepping under the light, back and forth, back, back into the shadows, then into the illumination once again, her feet winking in and out, picking up speed, tick, tick, tack, shush, shush, tick, and Helen's caught, openmouthed, as foolish as Rachael, and grateful for it. A bluesy trumpet glides in, a sixties guitar, a bass viol. "Cool" dissolves into Dixieland, slide trombones, a chorus of saintly trumpets, and banjos. Idabob struts, her feet as inexhaustible as the smile on her sagging face.

Flora leans in. "I'm getting chest pains just watching."

Louisa reaches over Flora with a plump arm, prods Helen's shoulder and nods in Clyde's direction.

His face is wide and smooth, a moon beaming from the dark. He looks, how can she say it, transported. Cherubic. A faint, offbeat tapping comes from the back row. They could swivel their chairs to face him, and he'd take no notice, so caught up is he. Mary Jane snorts into her hand, and Louisa thumps her in the ribs. The spell is broken for Rachael, and Helen feels a twinge of grief, for now the young girl is emulating the adults, who are behaving like errant children.

Hadn't her husband Chet warned her of this? And, of course, that was why they'd called their son Chester, after his father, though Chester is stuck with Chester because it proves too confusing with two Chets in the house. "Five women, five *grown* women taking tap?" Chet had asked.

These days the world seems old. Especially Chet, who as a young man courted her with such invention, such—reckless loveliness. The midnight picnic on the gabled roof of his grandmother's Victorian house, where they made love dizzy on the peak, hoisting her drawers onto the lightning rod like a pirate's flag. This same man who now thinks tap dance classes mean trouble. The whole world *is* getting old, playing it safe. All but Meghan. "No," Helen told her last week at the mall, a TV monitor foisting MTV into JCPenney's aisles. "Pierced ears, yes. But no lips, nose, eyebrows, tongue, navel, or nipples."

So Meghan shaved her head instead.

The houselights come up, and Idabob reappears, dabbing her face with a towel. "Welcome. Welcome," she says, arms spread. Her voice is a crisp contralto. Late sixties, Helen guesses, maybe older without makeup.

They all put chairs away. Clyde looks worldly in this task, but once it's done, he stands orphaned. Idabob throws open a trunk filled with tap shoes. Flora, Helen, and Louisa find shoes that fit. Mary Jane says she'll purchase her own *if she stays*. Idabob grasps Mary Jane's chin in two fingers. "Doubting Thomas," she says. "You'll stay." She sweeps her eyes over the group. "Hard-bottomed shoes. Mickey on Tenth can put taps on if you can't invest just yet." She takes Clyde's hands in hers, and as he flushes a bright red, she turns to the women. "All the best tap dancers were men, you know." Helen waits for her to name them, a litany of saints, all the young men now gone slow with age, or dearly departed, but Idabob dismisses the subject.

"In seven weeks," she boasts, "you'll perform, *in recital*. Mark your calendars, people."

"Fat chance," says Mary Jane. Louisa looks game, already tallying up whom to invite.

Ball Change

Decidedly, the best part of dance class is afterward, the quiet hour or so when they wind down with refreshments. This week it's at Flora's home, a quaint little Victorian cottage replete with twin love seats and overstuffed chairs.

Louisa helps herself to a third brownie. "Isn't exercise supposed to help you lose weight?"

"Try exercising willpower," Mary Jane says. She has on a new leotard, looks good, but then Mary Jane has a body built for tight apparel. Helen's beginning to wish she hadn't invited Mary Jane along. At the plant, Mary Jane's an executive secretary who works, by her own admission, to have something to do during the days while her lawyer husband brings home the bacon, the pâté, the artichoke hearts.

Louisa rolls one thigh over the other. "Two husbands and seven children. Tell me, please, about willpower. Didn't think folks my age still had it in them, did you? Ha." She speaks to Rachael, but looks at Mary Jane. "Can't have enough children." Her head cocks to a side. "Given a chance, I'd have another. It goes so *quickly,* you know." She looks dreamy a moment.

Flora laughs. "There's always grandchildren. I've got three; none of them as annoying as their parents were."

Helen feels she's swooning with wine and brownies and good tired muscles in the soft couch. She finds Louisa's admission daunting. Another child. In her midforties? God spare her. She doubts her marriage would last long enough to raise another. It's a doubt that creeps in often these days, unexpectedly. She's not sure where it comes from—Chet, herself, the idea of slogging through another seventeen years. The conversation stills. Helen says, "Surprised to see Clyde again. Took courage to come a first time, more to come back."

"He's a creep," Mary Jane says.

"Mary Jane, you're such a bitch," Louisa says. She snatches brownie crumbs from her chest and pops them in her mouth. "It's why we love you." She pries her feet out of her shoes.

The room goes quiet once again. It's so cozy here, Helen

wishes she could slump off to sleep where she sits, but soon she'll be home with Chet, who's absorbed in late-night reading. He's taken to biographies: Mary Queen of Scots, Amelia Earhart, Eleanor Roosevelt, a formidable troupe of grande dames that drives Helen to fold more envelopes than anyone else on the day shift. So what if she's not like them? So what if she can't fly, let alone keep the damn steps to "Cool" straight? Though everyone else seems to be catching on. She just knows Flora practices each night while Anna reads. Louisa, too, lining her children up to applaud. Rachael's a natural. Mary Jane doesn't have to be good to look good. And what about Clyde. *All the best were men.*

The women bid Flora and Anna good night, head out into the crisp autumn evening. Mary Jane drives her new Aerostar van and cracks the driver's window, *because it's such a lovely evening,* she says, though Helen suspects it's so the smell of sweat doesn't mar the aroma of new vinyl.

"I could have stayed there forever," Louisa says, so she, too, noticed how comfortable the women were together.

"Imagine," Helen says. "A house where the toilet seat is always down."

Rachael turns from the front seat. She opens her mouth as if to speak, pauses, closes her mouth, and turns forward again.

"Nothing worse than two women in a kitchen," Mary Jane says.

"I'd miss sex," Louisa says.

"You would," Mary Jane says.

But Louisa smiles pleasantly, pinches the bridge of her nose, and says, "I think we should pair up Clyde and Flora."

Rachael's head snaps around. "He's *not* her type," she insists. All the women turn to her. "I mean, Flora and Anna, I think they're...lovers."

Mary Jane pulls up to Louisa's house, a rambling two-story

structure with whirligigs poked in the lawn, their blades spinning, and leaves scuffing up off in the breeze so that it looks as if all her yard's in motion. Warm lights are on in the main floor, the upstairs dark with its seven dreaming children.

"Don't be silly," Mary Jane says, "she's a grandmother."

Helen can't resist. "So she's a grandmother? What's that prove? We all make mistakes. Maybe hers lasted thirty years and produced children."

Louisa's tongue is roving in her mouth, as though she's tasting something. "Do you really think so? Lovers, yes. I believe you're right." She pauses. "That's charming, so much more interesting, don't you think?" She looks out the window. "Herbert's waiting—a late-night snack, then off to bed. Be good," she says, and she's out the door and up the sidewalk. On the porch, in the spot of porch light, she treats them to a shuffle, ball change, then closes the front door behind her.

The women sit in silence a while, and when Mary Jane cranks the ignition, it squeals. The engine is still running. They drop Rachael two miles from Louisa's, a small home with a derelict yard. The "Beware of" dog has been dead longer than Rachael can remember. She lives alone with her mother, when her mother isn't inviting boyfriends to move in. On those occasions, Rachael moves to her sister's on the uphill side of town. Her mother's between suitors now.

Helen slides in next to Mary Jane, wonders if Chet is waiting up. Probably not, she decides, to keep from being disappointed.

"What possesses some women?" Mary Jane asks, "to love women."

"Beats me," Helen says.

Mary Jane taps the steering wheel. "I want to think I'm progressive, that I'm keeping current—it's so easy to become backward here." She glances over. "I'm not sure what I think of all this...this woman woman thing. *It is illegal,* you know."

Helen just wants to be home, though she's not sure why. Habit maybe.

"But then, in Idaho," Mary Jane continues, "anything besides the missionary position with intent of children is illegal."

Helen's encouraged by the unexpected bit of humor. "Why don't you reserve judgment. Get to know them first, then decide."

"Yes," Mary Jane says, though she sounds skeptical. She slows for Helen's drive, hits the curb. "I'll do that," she says, and it seems to Helen that Mary Jane's relieved to have had the decision taken from her for the time being.

Helen looks over at her lawn, at the darkened house. Though, at least the porch light is on. Helen feels limp, and the brownies aren't sitting well. Mary Jane touches Helen's hand. "You don't think less of me, do you? Think of me as small-minded?" She looks wounded in the dashboard's light, her eyes punched.

Helen feels like a louse, gives Mary Jane a quick hug, but Mary Jane's not sure what to do with it, and now Helen's left feeling like an awkward louse. "I'll see you at work," she says, and hurries up the walk.

Cool

Helen, Louisa, and Rachael eat lunch in the break room, toting paper sacks larded with sandwiches, apples, celery, leftover fried chicken, which they offer in trade—a pickle for a cookie, tuna on rye for a breast of Kentucky Colonel. Now Mary Jane joins them, as does, more recently, Clyde Woods. There's a tape player bolted to the top of the lockers. Carl Sharpley arrived first, and so the lunchroom crowd has endured thirty-five minutes of Dwight

Yoakam. Flora shakes her head, hennaed hair braided, coiled, and pinned firmly at the neck. Two years ago, Heddy Tyler was scalped by the folder. "Why not Patsy Cline," Flora bemoans. "Hank Williams—the real one—or Bob Wills—my husband used to love him." She tells them that Anna prefers jazz: Coltrane, Miles, Monk. "Where do they come up with those names?"

Their third dance class is that evening, so they huddle around the table cramming, instruction sheets weighted down by pop cans. "Once more," Mary Jane says, and clips out a steady four-four with a pencil. On the count of three there's a tap, tap, shoop, tap, shoop, a scuff, and fumbling.

Louisa confesses. "It always looks so easy on Fred Astaire movies."

"It's the damn instruction sheets," Mary Jane says. "If that woman could spell half as well as she can dance."

Clyde pauses, meat-loaf sandwich halfway to his lips. "She's an artist," he says, and takes a bite. He's prone to comments like this, a word or two, a non sequitur and silence. It keeps him a mystery. Rachael's convinced he's done time, a botched robbery maybe—not armed she assures them—just some unfortunate late-night teenage prank at a 7-Eleven that landed him in jail and uncommunicative for the next forty years. The older women might have scoffed, but Rachael had been right about Flora, because, as Helen admitted, she's seen Flora and Anna kissing—in the car, after work, at an intersection.

"Ick," Mary Jane said.

"Not at all," Helen replied. "It was chaste. Not as disgusting as some kid pawing his date at a red light." And even as she says it, Helen wishes Chet would be a little *less* chaste, would paw her in the front seat of their car again, or the backseat, the hood, their bed, wherever. It isn't that he doesn't touch her, but no, he never

paws her anymore, and sometimes she wants it to be purely...
purely carnal.

Flora breaks the silence. "Cheer up. We've had two lessons,
and she hasn't kicked us out yet. Whose house tonight, after
class?" She nails Clyde with a look, but Louisa jumps in, offers her
house, invites Anna as well. She gives Flora's hand a squeeze. "I've
told Herbert all about you two—he's very open-minded."

There's an embarrassed silence. It's still all speculation.
Clyde's slowly chewing meatballs and bread. Louisa plunges on.
"Herbert's discovered gourmet-flavored popcorn." Mary Jane rolls
her eyes. "No. No," Louisa says, "fifteen ethnic flavors: Sri Lankan,
Chinese, Australian, Swedish, Wisconsin, a bunch more."

Flora's feet tap and shuffle under the table. "We'd love to
come. Anna will be so pleased." There are relieved sighs all
around, and Flora seems pleased with herself and them. As they
break up for work, Clyde asks, "Can we invite Idabob, too?"
None of them seem excited by this prospect. They offer various
versions of, I don't think she'd want to. Clyde takes this in stride,
nods once, his hands already looking huge and curiously mis-
shapen without a sandwich or broom handle to wrap around as
he hurries back to work ahead of them.

Rachael is the star of the evening's class, dazzling them with a
flawless grapevine, ball change, reverse, even though it means
stepping around Louisa who's caught in a ball change, ball
change, like a stammer. Everyone's jealous and pleased at the
same time, except Helen, who feels defeated. It's been a Waterloo
kind of week, what with Chet reading *Desirée*, the story of
Napoleon's lover. She can't seem to ease past him anymore without his piping up, "Listen to this! 'Through the worst and best pe-

riod in European civilization, through discontent and conquest, Desirée took it in stride.' "

It was the best of times, it was the worst of times, yadda yadda yadda, Helen thinks. "Very nice, Chet," she says.

To top it all off, Meghan is sneaking out, disappears, ten minutes, thirty minutes after dinner though no one sees her leave or hears the door close. She refuses to tell them where she goes, whom she's with. Chet tries to appease Helen. "She's just trying her wings. Like Earhart. She's spirited," he says, and adds, "but smart," so Helen suspects he's just as befuddled but braving it out. It's the first serious fight they've had in years and ends in Helen alone, cruising in the car down the streets at night. She pops in a practice tape of "Cool" to keep calm. Idabob's voice floats out the window: "Ball change, step right, step left." The streets are transformed. The Idaho hamlet stretches and yaws with concrete, school grounds become chain-link gang yards where kids snap fingers, flash knives, run in choreographed packs, and Meghan is out there. Out here. And no, it's not Russ Tamblyn or George Chakaris, but mill workers, loggers, and farm kids with large hands who don't know their own strength.

When Helen gets back, Meghan's already in bed asleep. Helen's anger is terrible, so Chet talks her down and, of course, he's right, but by God a little anger feels well deserved right now.

It ends unexpectedly. Chester and Meghan both sneak out. Two nights of this and Helen wheedles Meghan's secret life out of him. A movie. A visit with a girlfriend, coffee at the all-night diner after wandering the aisles of the IGA with a wish list of junk foods, and now Meghan seems to have expended herself, spends nights at home closeted in her room or Chester's, where they play Monopoly or The Game of Life. Chet nears the finish of *Desirée.* It can't happen soon enough.

The class is ending, and Rachael is gracious, claims she owes it all to the other members of the class who work with her during lunch hour. Helen looks on Rachael with wonder. How can her home life be so wrong and she turn out so right? It's a quandary she doesn't feel up to, and of course, how could you hope to explicate the workings of the heart?

Murder on Dixieland

They're fifteen minutes late for the fourth class because Louisa's car keeps stalling. It's a manual, so the four women get out and push while Louisa jump-starts the engine. When they get to the class, they're all sweating, except Louisa, who's composed and impervious to threats about the ride home. Clyde is sweating, too, center floor, struggling on his infamous grapevine. Idabob is looking distracted. On the front table is a bouquet of flowers: a swatch of roses, a horror of carnations and one royal lily that looms over the concoction. Rachael hangs their coats in the cloak-room. On the way back she scans the note spiked through one of the ferns. Helen moves to Rachael's side as they begin their stretching exercises. Rachael purses her lips, says, "Later."

Mary Jane gives a sterling performance. Maybe it's the new shoes mail-ordered through Taps Unlimited out of Chicago: black patent, rhinestones glittering along the side. She's wearing red tights and leotard, and her blond hair is pulled back into a girlish ponytail. She's beautiful. Louisa tries to emulate the way Mary Jane's hips sway in the mambo combination. She fails miserably, but seems genuinely happy for Mary Jane, and Helen wonders if there's a sour bone in Louisa. Must be the seven children—twenty-seven years of diapers. Humbling. Enough to purge anyone of self-delusion.

After class they go to Whiskey Sam's. It's Clyde's turn, and he steers them here. "I live alone," he says. "Not a pretty sight"—as close as he's come to a joke. He invites Idabob, who orders an Irish coffee. Louisa's into creamed drinks—grasshoppers, white Russians. Mary Jane orders a martini, Rachael a hot chocolate, Flora an old-fashioned, and Helen a bloody Mary. Clyde's camped next to Idabob but seems incapable of speech, so Helen tries.

"How long have you been dancing, Idabob?"

She sighs and looks at her fingers. "Professionally since I was seven. You know the old movie, *Murder on Dixieland Street*? Where the black kid dances down the alley past the dead body? That's me. Stained brown. I had to say 'Sho 'nuff, it's a daid body,' then dance all the way to the police station. My claim to fame. After that I worked in small dance productions, theater, a little off-Broadway."

"How'd you end up in Idaho?" Mary Jane asks. Rachel asks, "Were you ever married?"

"Yes and because," Idabob says. "Married Emery and moved here. He worked all his life in the mill, sawyer on the head rig, never had an accident. One night, he slips in the bathtub, wham, bang, and he's dead."

"Did he dance?" Helen tries to imagine Idabob dancing with her husband, but all she can see is a skinny-shanked old man, naked and stepping into the tub. *Wham, bang.*

"As if I could marry a man who didn't."

Clyde stirs his coffee. He looks pensive.

"And after he died…where would I go, at my age?" She stares at Clyde, and he smiles back; it's pained and sweet, all at the same time. Helen suddenly knows where the flowers came from. Idabob must have been a beauty once; her eyes—periwinkle blue—haven't faded. Idabob finishes her coffee and when she stands, Clyde offers to drive her home.

The door closes behind the two. Helen and Rachael exchange knowing nods, and Flora says, "That's the sweetest thing I have ever seen. It gives me faith in men again."

There's a sudden dawning in Louisa's face. "Do you think so?"

"*What?*" Mary Jane asks.

Rachael nods. Helen says, "Without a doubt," and Louisa fusses with her cocktail napkin as if it was a Christmas present.

"What?" Mary Jane asks louder.

Helen nods at the door, wings an eyebrow upward. "Idabob and Clyde," she whispers.

Mary Jane looks at the martini as if it's cod liver oil. "Oh my God. She's *ancient*. Must be ten, twelve years older than him."

Flora pats Mary Jane's hand. "The shocks just keep coming, don't they dear?"

"So am I the only one here who doesn't think *any* of this is normal?"

Flora fishes the cherry out of her drink. "He'll have a hard time of it. Poor man. It *does* make a difference, you know. A woman can be younger, better-looking, and still a man will believe she's lucky to have him." She shushes Mary Jane. "And when he's old, she'll take care of him, and he'll take it for granted because it's what men have been raised to accept. To be mothered. But a woman?"

The women sit looking at their empty glasses. "It's depressing," Louisa finally says. "Let's order another?" They signal for the bartender.

Helen's quiet. She's staring into a fresh bloody Mary, drawing circles on the table with the limp celery. "I think they need our help," she says.

Tats and Testaments

Rachael moves in with her sister again, though Rachael's mother says, *You'll like Mikey.* Rachael confides to Helen, she doesn't want to like him. She's too old now for a father, and when she hadn't been too old—all those she liked moved on, or were moved out. And truthfully, it wouldn't be so bad staying at her sister's, except that Rachael's sister extracts rent for babysitting. She's single with two children. Twins. Monsters, Rachael calls them, says, "If they were hamsters, *they'd* have eaten their mother."

Helen suggests Rachael find her own place and a roommate, considers handing over Meghan, but she's been a model daughter for almost a week now—helps cook, cleans her room, mothers Chester. Chet's taking the credit, not out loud, of course, but with doting smiles. He's a regular *Father Knows Best.* He's not reading anything right now. He started reading the Billie Holiday biography but put it aside. "Too depressing," he said. And Helen's grateful. She loves Billie, doesn't want him ruining that for her.

"It won't last," Rachael says of her mother's new relationship. "She has no staying power." Helen wants to comfort Rachael but isn't sure how she'd take it. For a young girl, she's seen and heard more than she probably should have already. And really, what's it about? Long-term relationships—a long-distance marathon? Choose your partner and remember to breathe. No. Surely it's more than that.

"You being a bit hard on your mother?" Helen says.

"I'm never going to fall in love," Rachael says. "Love is such an embarrassment, don't you think?"

Helen wonders exactly what Rachael *has* seen. A mother who falls and falls and falls. And truthfully, doesn't Meghan see Helen as an embarrassment? Wasn't Helen the same about her parents? And still, she fell in love. He was *different* then, exciting. How is it she can picture Chet so clearly as a young man and not as he is now? "You're still young," she says, and hates herself for this little pat on the head. Rachael deserves better. But at this point in her marriage, Helen's not the one to provide it.

The fifth dance class marks the appearance of a dapper Clyde Woods in charcoal pants, a pink shirt, and gray cardigan sweater. Louisa's proclaimed him a "Winter" and discreetly offered suggestions. During class, it does seem Idabob watches him more closely. Sometimes she confuses the shuffle with a ball change. Tonight Clyde executes the grapevine with panache. This is Mary Jane's doing—five full lunch hours with him in the storage room at work. She's gotten into the spirit of it, and boasts, "His crossover will undo Idabob."

The women leave class early, claiming chores, duties, irreconcilable differences at home. When they leave, Clyde's warming up for the mambo combination. Idabob looks like a trapped rabbit.

They're supposed to go to Helen's but decide at the last minute that Whiskey Sam's is more in order. A little celebration. Besides, though Helen won't admit this, Chet will be home, and Meghan and Chester, and for the first time in her married life, she's found something she's not sure she wants to share. Chet would pilot his La-Z-Boy, be attentive, all in all be a gracious host and loving husband. And what's so bad about that? Nothing, except Helen's not sure he means it. There would be, after all, not an Amelia Earhart among them.

They're nearing the bottom of their first round when Clyde hunches in alone. He orders a double Jack Daniel's and takes a swig. They avoid conversation, then they just avoid talking about

Idabob. Instead, they speak of work accidents—the forklift operator who toppled a pallet of envelopes into the watercooler yesterday. The stories degenerate: Mallory, her hand snagged in the
folding machine; assorted acquaintances, any number of fingers
nicked or chopped by the cropping blade, and ultimately the man
who caught his privates in the binding unit. They reserve a moment of silence. *It could be worse,* Louisa says. *We could be working at
the mill,* and unspoken, there are the mill-working spouses and
friends—aged, maimed, departed—and along with them, Emery
Doppus, the esteemed tap-dancing band-saw operator dead in
the bathtub.

They order doubles, hand Rachael the car keys. By the second drink Helen is tipsy. "So what the hell does she want?" she
asks, turns to Clyde. "You were a star tonight. A *star.*"

Rachael offers, "You did look wonderful tonight, Clyde."

"Winter," Louisa affirms.

"And his grapevine and mambo combination," Mary Jane
says. She orders a third round.

Clyde shrugs. The jukebox grinds on: truck convoys, wanton
women, lust, booze, love, heartbreak, dead dogs, and pride in
America. The table is cleared of empties, but there are wet
bull's-eyes where the phantom drinks have sweated. Customers
come and go, a few friends stop, but there's a vengeance about
this table's drinking, and so none of them stay. "I should call
Anna," Flora says, but remains seated.

There's no point in calling Chet, Helen knows. Long asleep,
no doubt, and when it comes right down to it, she really doesn't
want to. It's a new life, a new Helen. She's flying higher than
Earhart, only better—Helen won't lose her way home.

Rachael's beginning to slump, waves off another pop. "You
can drink only so many of these." She belches discreetly.

They decide on a little fresh air. Flora leads, down Main Street to Clark, then Lewis. In the distance the mill's a crucible of vapor and light, with its stacks, vats, cauldrons, and seeping pools. The air's sour, slightly acidic; it's the beginning of the inversion season, when the winds still and the woodsmoke and chemicals hang in a sodden heaven you can almost touch, so that people loom in the streets, the hills are diminished, and the universe becomes a very much smaller thing. As small as this street, Helen thinks, or these people. Above the chatter of Rachael and Louisa, Helen can hear the howl of the mill's central stack, flames flaring upwards of thirty feet. She wonders if Chet hears it in his sleep, as he's heard it every day for the last twenty working years: clean up, pulling chain, working forklifts, the saws. It took him twelve years to land day shift. By that time Meghan must have believed Chet was a snoring, rooting noise behind the bedroom door during the day. Helen had half believed that herself.

They're walking up Lewis, along the old riverfront, and past the log yards. The air is a curious mix of pitch and diesel. The railroad tracks spur, crisscross and dead-end. Pigeons coo in the dark. There's a row of buildings: pawnshop, gun shop, tobacconist, and one with its lights still on.

"I've got it," Mary Jane yells. It's unlike her, the circumspect one. "You need a gesture. A sign of commitment."

"Like a ring," Rachael suggests.

"A ring can be taken back," Mary Jane says, and it sounds like experience. *"Voilà."* She crooks a thumb at the one lit storefront, Tats and Testaments, combination tattoo parlor and Bible bookstore.

"I don't know," says Clyde.

"Do you love her or not?" Mary Jane leans into his face.

He nods, grim.

They march in, single file. There are cantilevered shelves of Bibles and religious texts: Mormon, Jehovah's Witness, King James, Adventist, and even a few with the Imprimatur. Before the window are a couple chairs and on the far side is *the chair* facing a large beveled mirror flanked by charts and illustrations—the artist's specialties: the bleeding heart of Jesus, crucifixes, scourge marks, Christ in profile, three-quarters, face on. The transfigured Christ and cherubs. Clyde looks appalled.

The artist looks up from the newspaper. "Secular section's in back," he says, nods to a smaller niche in the rear with the standard fare: skull and crossbones, a sinking *Titanic*, naked women, pirates, knives, crossed swords, snakes. The artist, a grandfatherly man with skin so thin his veins look like ink, swivels toward them. "Anything you name, I can draw. Letters, too. It'll hurt like hell, but some things can't be helped." He flips the paper back up and reads while they browse.

Louisa's taken with the tattoo of a sleeping baby. "It's Margaret," she says. "My oldest when she was brand-new."

Mary Jane says, "Crossed swords with *Idabob Forever* would be nice," but Clyde's looking at a snake, holding his arm up against the illustration to estimate the duration of pain.

Rachael hands a drawing to Mary Jane. "It's you," she says. They crowd around a sketch of a small ornate Spanish galleon. "Do you think so?" Mary Jane holds it against the crown of her right buttock.

Helen's getting drunker but is too complacent to consider that odd. She puts out a hand to steady herself, nails a pert armadillo with her finger, and it feels like the hand of Providence. Outrageous, silly on a woman her age—what will Meghan say? And what will Chet think? He'll look at her as if he doesn't recognize her. But Helen's suddenly tired of being accountable to her family. "I'll take this one," she says.

They all look at her as if they don't recognize her. She finds that reassuring. As if there's something in her still to discover.

When it's done, it hardly hurts—the small inscription on her right shoulder—but then again, Helen's not sure she's felt her feet for the last hour either. The room is rosy, and all the bleeding faces of Jesus look benevolently down from the wall. Louisa's in the chair, her left breast is bared and surgically draped. Willie the artist, that's his name, Willie, and Helen wishes his name were Art or Vincent or Maurice, but no, it *is* Willie, and he's quick and there are needles dangling tubes of colors that he snicks up and out of their holder like a dentist, and the same small droning noises, then there's a sleeping child on Louisa's breast, and Helen believes she will cry. She lightly touches the armadillo fresh on her arm, and thinks, my firstborn, Meghan, all shell and reckless abandon—courting trucks on the interstate.

Flora's next. Nothing ornate for her. "Can't you just see it, she says, "a basket of flowers wilting in wrinkles?" She chooses a simple "AnnA," and it graces her wingbone as though it could fly. It takes only minutes.

Willie doesn't say much more than, "What? Where? How big?" But he does talk about the Bibles. "Some people think it's not proper, tattoos and testaments. But I never seen people more in need of salvation than some I get in here late at night." The women intone *Amen.*

The chair reclines, and Mary Jane snoozes in it, facedown, drooling onto a pillow. Willie plumps the buttock, drapes it modestly before tackling the Spanish galleon complete with rigging.

Rachael begs off, and no one argues. It's unspoken, but none of them wants to see her young flesh marked with an indelible imprint that her heart's too young to recognize.

And so Clyde is last. He's selected a banner to wrap across his chest with ends like scalloped ribbons, a scattering of flowers and hearts, and he talks Willie into concealing a snake among the leaves. The banner reads: "Idabob." It takes most of the night, what's left of it, and the women alternate between the floor, the window seat, and the two free chairs. They're beginning to sober in little jerks and starts. Mary Jane favors her right cheek, says, "My Tom won't believe it. He'd never think it of me. Hell, doesn't think much of me period. He thinks of the law, his clients. He thinks and thinks...I think he thinks of other women," and no-body's heard it but Helen because the others have dozed off, and Clyde's lost in the hive of buzzing needles.

After a while, Helen says, "I know what you mean." But Mary Jane has drifted back to sleep, and Clyde's declaration of love is all but signed.

Mambo

This week, Chet's waiting up when Helen gets home. For six weeks she's wanted him awake after class. Now she wonders why. She's tired, tired unto exhaustion. *Not tonight, honey, my feet are killing me.* But he's hardly amorous, just sitting there in bed, no book in hand, with the bedside lamps lit. He asks how it went, and she chatters as she undresses, tells him about Clyde's improvement. Talks about what good friends Louisa and Flora have become, but at this point she's brushing her teeth and it comes out mostly garbled. She does not tell him about the week-old tattoo hiding beneath the Band-Aid on her shoulder. It's scabbed, itches as if the armadillo's feet are clutching her arm. She slips a nightgown over her head and walks past Chet. He's quiet.

She makes a final check of the kids. Meghan's asleep, one leg over the side of the bed as if ready to bolt. Her hair is coming back in, fine as the black cap she sprouted as a newborn. She's so beautiful, this almost-woman. Helen suffers a sudden insight of walking into this room in the future and finding the bed empty. She backs out and crosses the hall to Chester's room, but she won't try to navigate it in the dark. It's mined with pliers, screwdrivers, electronic bits and pieces from a secondhand stereo he bought for parts. He's snoring.

In their bedroom, Chet's still upright. She folds into bed next to him. "Any problems?" she asks.

"Hum? No. No."

She drops her head onto the pillow, but the lamp stays lit. She tries to drift off, though she's never been able to sleep with a light on so she gives in, turns toward him, tries to remember how he acted earlier, before she left for class. But it was so hectic. Making dinner, a last-minute run to the store, getting dressed. "How was your day?" she asks.

He turns off the light. Settles onto the pillow next to her. Facing her.

"Great," he says. His voice is flat. She wishes the light were back on. "Rumor's out they're going to sell the mill. We're sitting around at lunch, listening to Joe yelling at Earl about the band saw, saying the God-damned saw sounds wrong. Says the pitch is off, and he ain't going to run it again until they check it. And Earl's yelling they can't afford the backup, that they inspected it last week and it was fine and he can just put his lardy ass back into the booth and do his work or others will. But we all know they'll break the saw down again and that means downtime and one more reason than the company needs to sell the damn place and us up the creek. And I'm listening and thinking I wish Joe'd keep his fat mouth shut, and I stand up, ready to shut it for him."

He sighs, flops an arm over his forehead. He smells of Lava soap and sawdust. "And I start walking over there, but when I get close, it's like I see him for the first time. This sad piece of shit. Who's still got all ten fingers, and so have I, and you can't say that for many others in this town. So I go out to the floor and pull green chain with some kid who I suddenly take it into my head looks like Chester. Lunch break ends, and I walk. Right out the door." He's quiet. "Son of a bitch, they hurt." He holds his hands up. "I've gotten soft."

Helen's legs are sore from dance class. She doesn't want to get out of bed again, but she does. Hobbles into the bathroom, turns on the light, and flinches. She searches the cabinet. Her legs cramp and she's angry with him and just as quickly ashamed of herself. She thinks of him—leaving the work floor to go stand outside, and the gate there beckoning with its street that winds up and out of town, over the prairies, east, west, north, south. She doesn't have to ask if he went back to work. Knows he did. Always did, always would. She takes the bag balm with her, refuses to look in the mirror, turns off the light and feels her way back to the bed. He's still waiting there, with his hands out in the dark.

The Recital

It seems their whole lives of the past seven weeks have been aimed at this moment. New black leotards with sequins sewn around the necklines, Clyde in simple black pants and jersey. They've tucked a bouquet away for Idabob. Clyde's surprise is still tucked safely beneath his jersey. This past week at work, each of the women have come across him stroking his chest; maybe it's the tender skin or the scab's peeling itch, but when they meet his eyes it's as if something precious is couched there, beneath his hands.

All the others, except Helen, have shown their spouses the tattoos, with varying degrees of success. "Herbert found it strange at first," Louisa says. "Nuzzling up to a sleeping baby. But I think he's getting used to it, though he does tend to favor the right to the left now."

Mary Jane's Tom finds it *very* sexy. She blushes and worries about what she'll do when he gets used to it.

Anna cried, Flora says, called it no better than branding cattle, wanted it removed. "I told her love me, love my tattoo." Anna's finally adjusting to it, and Flora admits the grandkids think it's awesome. Helen wonders for the umpteenth time how Flora could have taken such a turn in her life. From a wife, to a grandma with a woman for a lover. "You've known Anna long?" she finally asks.

Flora nods, the machine clips the edge on a stack of envelopes, ca-chunk, and slides the next stack forward. Her hands dodge in, straighten the stack, and out, drops the lever, ca-chunk. This is their day: cropping envelopes before the final fold and glue. The women work alongside each other, as they have for the last three years, and this is the first time Helen has thought to ask a personal question, and isn't that a marvel?

"Since we were girls. Anna never married—for obvious reasons now, but not then—after Ed died, she moved in. It worked out."

Helen's not sure how to ask the next. "So, about you and Anna—"

Flora grunts. "We lived together. Touching just seemed natu-

ral. Isn't that the way it happens? You just want to be touched.
We're happy. There's a lot to be said for that."

Backstage, Helen fingers the hidden tattoo as she's taken to
doing in odd moments. She still hasn't shown it to Chet. She can't
imagine what she will say to the kids. Daytime, she wears long-
sleeved shirts, sweaters. Wears flannel pajamas to bed and gets
away with it because it's turned cold, with snow on the high
prairies, though in the valley it still rains. The chairs are set up,
and the stage is black, curtain drawn. There are whispers and gig-
gles. More chairs bang open. Idabob predicts a full house, and
they silently hope this won't be true, though they've all seen the
announcements Idabob mailed to the company. Rachael peeks
out the curtain, says, "Oh, my God."

The left front row holds Louisa's seven children and husband.
Tom sits directly behind them, next to Chet, Meghan, and
Chester, who range in looks: interested, doomed, bored. The right
side of the room is a hodgepodge of day-shift workers, their kids,
a few bosses and the company owner sitting center seat, front row.

Idabob says, "Have faith."

They clatter to the rear of the stage, their taps garish. "Deep
breath now," Idabob says. "Wait for the curtain, the spots—second
stanza, ta dum, ta dum, ta da, da, da."

There's the barest twinkling of sequins, some heavy breathing. They can hear Idabob, the coughing and whispers die. The
opening strains of "Cool" begin, and Helen looks over the disheartened lineup. She braces her shoulders. The spotlight dazzles.

What spectacle. The bank of blue lights shine on the se-
quined figures, and the cardboard urban skyline, tortured in per-
spective, seems right somehow. The static is gone—Idabob uses
the performance record, clean and unmarred—nearly unhinging
the dancers, but it's only a momentary distraction, and art trans-

forms them. Helen feels as if her body is not her own, and when her feet move, and she hears the taps, she's pleasantly surprised. She tries not to think of Chet, who must see her as ridiculous, a middle-aged woman in a tap-dance recital; instead, she concentrates on Flora and Louisa on either side, listens to the music, and imagines the noisy practice recording, comforting because of its flaws.

But it's a smooth opening, and a flawless refrain. They begin to loosen up. "There's Anna," whispers Flora. Then another name, and another, is whispered across the stage: Santini, Boyd, Karen, Chuck, Valerie. Faces in the audience float in and out as they move front and back, turn right or left. In the far reaches there's blackness.

The music shifts to "Fascinating Rhythm." Clyde takes center stage for the mambo combination. The women form a chorus line. When he misses a beat, the chorus taps fill in. There's a shouted bravo. "Santini," Flora whispers, and the women smile.

But when "The Saints Come Marching In" starts up, the audience breaks loose. There are hoots and claps, a few shouted amens. The air is brassy with trumpets and under the spots the light of sequins becomes as sharp as the sound of taps. The music's cranked loud for the finale and to cover their heavy breathing. Helen's legs feel like sausages. *No cramps*, she prays, and up and down the line she can see them winded and tiring, all except for Rachael. And Helen can't bear the thought of their evenings together concluding, though she knows they will, as they always do, and so she won't let it end badly. She wills a second wind, and there it is. One by one they gain new vigor and with it comes the final flurry, the last grueling minute and a half of hard taps; there's not a beat missed.

The music stops, the lights rear up, and the audience is on its feet. The dancers are stooped over and clutching their knees. No one seems to notice. They smile at one another and when they're able to straighten again, they hug, careful of each other's wounded skin; they're that intimate—the plump breast, the muscled arm, aging wingbone, shining buttocks, shaved chest.

They present Idabob with the flowers. More applause, then the families crowd on stage. Meghan tries on Rachael's tap shoes. Idabob is shaking hands with the company executives. The refreshments table is crowded. Chet finds his way to Helen's side.

"You were beautiful," he says, and embraces her. "I'm so proud."

Helen is stunned. He's sincere. The armadillo on her arm itches. She feels confused, half-resentful and terribly in love again and knows it's the excitement, the letdown, the town and friends gathered, the applause and sequins, and the thought comes to her like a small but pleasurable pain that this is how we fall in love, again, and again. There's something absurdly arbitrary about it, a missed step, an old friend, a new one, a guarded look or tattoo. And maybe that's love's attraction—the happenstance encounter—a revelation in the odd moments of the day, like a blessing unannounced. He grins, and there's something of the pirate in his look.

After the people leave, the troupe remains to tidy up. Idabob is clutching sign-up sheets. When she goes to the stage, Clyde follows. Helen is the only one privy to what comes next. She's standing to the side and sees Clyde lift his jersey for a shrinking Idabob, who looks flustered, on the point of calling for help, but then his tattoo is unveiled. Idabob purses her lips, shakes her head, then smiles, and it's still the same old Idabob. But Clyde is undaunted, and Helen is reassured that his love is, above all else, determined. Idabob says, "Sign up for the advanced class."

When they get home, Meghan and Chester barrel out, but

when Helen moves to open the car door, Chet stops her. He tells the two teens to get in the house, lock the doors and go to bed. Says they'll be back in a little while. Helen thinks to object, but finds she can't—she's too wound up. Chet drives with uncommon patience, no tailgating, rolling stops, or running ambers—lets the roads unfold at their own pace. He takes a long, involved route out of town, off onto the bench roads that spiral up and away from the mill's burning stacks. They climb higher, and trees drop away to where the fields level out and when they reach the crown of prairie the land is quick with snow. Chet is humming "Fascinating Rhythm," and Helen laughs and taps her feet on the car floor. She thinks of unveiling the tattoo, but knows now how he will take it—a kiss, a shake of the head, grace and humor. They perch on the lookout, high above the river where they can see the bank of mill clouds below, muddy with the town's light. In all the valley, there's only this tenuous illumination. She finds herself gripping Chet's hand. Somewhere in the valley, weighted down with the immensity of this night, are her friends, risking more than anyone can dare to lose, tendering their hearts to the dark.

TRASH

John Pratt scraped breakfast leftovers into the pail that was tucked under the kitchen sink, remnants of eggs, bacon, gravy biscuits—a heart attack special, his wife cautioned, but he'd been finding sustenance in the providence of God's good graces and his own honest work all his sixty-odd years, and who was he to question it now. His wife, Tillie, called that "comfortable thinking," and brought home boxes of cereals that were promptly stacked and ignored in the pantry. He could hear her now, singing down in the root cellar. She was slightly off-key, and he found it comforting.

"Tillie," he called down, and waited.

She came to the bottom of the stairs, assorted jars tucked under her arms, carrots suspended in a sling of newspaper. "Coming," she said, looking small, gray in the basement twilight.

At the top of the stairs, he took the carrots from her, held them over the sink, and pinched their black tips. "Want me to take these to the compost?" he asked.

Tillie shook her head. "I'll take care of them later," she said, and she lifted her face to him for a kiss as she had done every morning of their forty-three years together.

John brushed her lips, stood back. "We're getting too old for this." Then he put on the John Deere cap and wool coat she held out to him.

"We were already too old for it a good five years ago, but that never stopped us, did it?" She laughed as she opened the door. "You go on, and let me get to work. Soup for lunch."

It would be a good day, he thought. The fallen leaves sugaring the air with decay, the ground still pliant beneath his feet. John walked his fields, following the same route he'd walked or tended all the years of his stewardship, a discipline he exacted on himself: sick or healthy, clement weather or not—it had to do with responsibility. Respect. It had to do with what was delivered a man to do in his lifetime. He kept to the tree line bordering the southernmost pasture from the highway, concealing most of the subdivision that had risen like a blister on the far side of the road. He glanced over at what he could see of the raw ground and boards. Felt a righteous anger for having kept his land. And why not? The temptation of easy money held little sway for those who recognized the good life when they lived it.

He turned his focus instead on his fields, the crop, a skiff of leaves underfoot. He loved autumn—it was the green of summer well used and spent, a time when the year's labor accounted for itself. He squinted into the thin sunlight, opened the top button of his jacket to the breeze. He felt hale and strode off with a firm step.

He came upon raccoon damage in the field corn, several rows laid flat, the ears stripped to waste. But overall, the field would yield a respectable crop, and as his father had liked to say: "Take whatever good's to be found as blessing, and you'll never have a poor year." John looked over the corn, and although he was not a steady churchgoing man, he liked to believe he knew God's favor when he saw it.

He heard the commotion before he spotted it—a dog. Up ahead, in the ditch. A large dog struggling with an industrial-sized trash bag, the black plastic stretched thin in its jaws. And then he saw, at a short distance from the larger dog, a small one lying in the cover of the trees, its head cocked, watching the struggle.

John rolled his hands into fists, angry with the road trash that couldn't keep their garbage home. As if his land, the land of his father, was just a dumping place. He searched out a large stick and, raising it in the air, waved it at the dogs: "Go on, get!" He swung the stick in circles. He figured them to be vacation dogs, shagged from the backseat of a family car at the end of summer, their useful tenure completed, relegated to a nuisance that must make it on its own in a world the animal was no more prepared for than they themselves would be, tossed out naked and hungry on the side of a road. The smaller dog slunk back, tail ratty between its legs. The other, a larger longer-haired breed, held its ground, trying to pull the bag with it. Whatever was in there was heavy, the dog moving it in jerking starts and stops.

John picked up a rock and nailed the animal in the ribs with a "plock." The dog yelped, and the bag fell from its teeth. It moved as if to grab the bag again, and John stepped forward, "Git," he shouted. The dog scuttled into the leaves, looked over its shoulder, then hit the dirt running for the highway, while the smaller remained seated in the wood line. John neared the bag— the white plastic tie had slipped off in the dirt. He glanced at what had slid partially out of the bag.

It looked like the leg of a brown Swiss calf. Such a waste of good meat. He shook his head, keeping an eye on the remaining dog. He stepped closer, the leg's odd angle niggling at him, and then he saw what had disturbed him. It was no animal's leg after all, but a man's leg, with its fuzz of soft blond hair still curled tightly against the white skin. He stopped where he stood, looked down at his own squat legs as if to discover one of them missing.

When he looked back at the bag, it was still there, in the dirt, and on the skin a fly had landed, and was opening its wings to the sun. John lifted the plastic with thumb and forefinger, braced himself to look into the dark, at a jumble of body parts, seeing what might be an elbow, a knee. He dropped the bag, and the leg slid back down the dark gullet. The fly buzzed inside the bag.

John straightened. His arms hung slack at his side. In the field, the corn clattered in the breeze, and from the trees a magpie screamed. The air smelled of meat. Of meat gone bad. A car drove by on the highway, then another, and then none. He reached down, knotted the bag closed before pacing off a short distance. He stood to the left of the dog, in the tree line, staring. After a long while John left his place in the sheltering trees to return to the trodden grass and the bag in its center.

Something must explain this. He believed there must be some one thing that would come clear. If he only gave it time.

He looked around him, expecting to find the world had shifted somehow, everything gone out of true, no one thing defined or absolute. Even the air gone strange and perilous with the stink. But for that lapse, it seemed the day continued on out there, as any ordinary morning with slats of light falling through the corn, a rooster pheasant startling into the air, its cry a shrill aah, ahh, ahh. The skinny dog lay panting in the dirt. He should call the police. He moved as if to step away, and the dog's ears lifted.

It was clear John couldn't leave the bag. He looked up and down the length of highway, feeling strangely culpable, almost guilty, then he carefully hefted the bag. It hung at his side in odd bumps and sags. He turned toward the house, each step awkward, off-gaited. The dog trailed at a distance. "Go on, get!" he yelled. It backed up, trotted to a safer distance. John put the bag down, looked around the fields for an answer, then, hunching his shoulder, swung the bag around and over. He flinched as it thudded against his back, but it rode easier up high on his shoulder. It had the weight of a good-sized bale of hay, or better yet, a young calf.

Why, he used to carry his son this way, and he nearly dropped the bag with that thought. He looked over his shoulder, saw that the dog had disappeared into the rows of corn.

He stopped to gather his breath, hoping he might see Ben or Ben's son Luke in the neighboring field. They could stop. Talk. They would believe, as he had, that this was just another day, like any other. That there wasn't a thing in this acreage that wouldn't be known. He could show *them* a thing or two.

Back in his yard, John swung the bag into the burn barrel—a rusted oil drum next to the garage. The bag bumped against the metal, ponging softly, as John eased it down, settled it in the soot of old newspapers, cardboard and wax, milk cartons. Ash drifted up to powder his arms and chest.

He stumbled up the porch steps and into the kitchen, where

the radio played, and Tillie was at the cutting board. John hung his jacket on the peg behind.

Tillie looked up, surprised. "Well, you're back early. Hey, remember Carmen Miranda?" she asked. She held an onion by the stem, placed it behind her ear so that the pearly globe dangled like an earring.

He pushed past her, bellied up to the sink. He turned the water on hot, scraped bar soap up under his nails. The water steamed out of the faucet and stung his knuckles. An old song he could almost remember played on the radio, and out the window, across the yard, the burn barrel sat as it always had, in the lee of the barn, in a ring of trampled dirt, and it was hard to believe, even now with the feel of the bag still imprinted on his shoulder, that it held anything more than the everyday leftovers of their lives.

Tillie came up behind him, tucked her hands under his arms. "A penny for your thoughts," she spoke into his ear.

He wiped his hands and turned to her. Her eyes were the same blue as when he'd left that morning. Her hair was still gray, the kitchen still clean. But all he could smell was meat. He shook his head. "It don't matter," he said.

"John?"

"I found something. I got to call the police."

"What?" Tillie's voice rose. "What's happened?"

"Found a bag. It's in the burn barrel." He hesitated. "It's full of body parts. You want to see?" And even as he asked, he wondered if it was right to show a woman a thing like that. Particularly Tillie, a gentle soul who in all their years on the farm, still agonized about raising animals for anything but pets. And yet it seemed the years spent at her side gave him the right to ask it of her. "It's just out there." It became important that she see it, too.

Tillie backed away. "No," she said, crossed to the stove. "I don't understand." She wrung her hands in the apron. "I don't understand what you're saying."

John followed her across the kitchen, turning aside at the stove, where he lit a fire under the coffeepot. "It's just out there," he repeated, waving a hand at the window. He waited until moisture hissed from the pot, then he walked into the living room and called the police.

John sat across the kitchen table from their son, Karl. Dishes rattled in the sink as Tillie washed the cups the police had used earlier. Under the sounds of tap water and china, he could hear Karl's pregnant wife snoring on the living-room couch.

"This county's always been a dumping ground," Karl said, ground out a cigarette.

A cup banged on the sideboard. The overhead light was yellow on Karl's face, and he looked fleshy in a starched white shirt—like a banker. John looked down to his hands in embarrassment.

Karl's voice dropped. "Probably drug-related."

Tillie turned from the sink, wiping soap from her hands. "That's enough," she said.

"Dad should be on the eleven o'clock news." Karl walked into the living room.

The TV clicked on, and John stood from the table. "You going to come see?" he asked Tillie.

"I got dishes to finish," she said. And John thought that was so like her—the composure, her tidiness—a woman who knew what belonged to each part of the day, and these dishes just another part of another day, washing them as after a family dinner, a harvest feast, instead of a hive of detectives and police. Though he could see she moved with singular purpose this evening, cups clinking onto the drying rack, at risk of breaking. "I'll be right in," she added, but remained at the sink with her back to him.

In the living room, Karl sat on the floor in front of his wife, his head resting against her belly. She raised her head, the sofa pillow damp with a small dark stain of saliva where her mouth had been. John sat in his easy chair.

They were the first item of footage on the news. And there it was, his home, a quick pan of the barn—empty of livestock this past three years when it had gotten too much for him to manage alone—and a close-up of the burn barrel. The reporter faced into a breeze, his coat flapping like a scarecrow's.

"You're going to miss it, Ma," Karl called. "There's Dad."

And there John was on camera.

"You look good, Dad," his daughter-in-law said.

No. He looked thick. The weather-scrubbed barn behind him, which he'd always admired for being burnished down to the heart of the wood, looked shabby on the small screen. Everything on the small screen transfigured, his home, his barn, his life made small and squat. The sheriff appeared briefly, while behind him two men hefted the black plastic bag onto the coroner's stretcher. John had meant to tell the men they wouldn't need that—the stretcher—the weight sitting easily enough on your shoulder if you leaned forward a bit. But he hadn't said that. No, he hadn't said that, or much of anything for that matter. For what was there to say? Really? And there he was again, on TV, looking startled, saying what he'd supposed they'd wanted to hear. "Yeah. Quite a surprise."

John stood and looked away from the TV, knowing now that a person could not always believe what he saw, all of it appearing so matter-of-factly, just another workday for the cops, the newspeople, a small-time farmer. Tillie stood in the doorway between the kitchen and living room, studying him. He passed her on his way out the back door.

Outside, he stood in the cold and shoved his hands into his pant pockets. Moonlight congealed on the elderberry bushes, and the vague remains of Karl's old play fort canted into shadows. He started walking away, and when he heard the storm door bang shut behind him, he looked back to see Tillie pulling a sweater over her shoulders and stepping down into the yard after him. They went out through the orchard, his steps turning on fallen apples that had bruised and slumped into the ground. They passed the storage shed and empty cow barn, through rows of field corn, leaves flagging in the breeze, until he came out on the far northern field and stood on a hill, his breath churning the chill air. Tillie pressed a sweater over his shoulders.

He looked south. "You see," he said, "from over there." He fingered the headlights moving down the highway. "Can you imagine? All the way here to put such a thing on my land." Tillie leaned into him, but he felt separate, as if the act of walking out into his fields this morning had left her far behind. He stared into the night.

She ducked her head, and whispered, "Don't think about it," and snugged the sweater tighter around him.

John turned to her. "So you tell me. How do I walk my own fields again?"

Tillie hugged herself.

"How do I do that?" he asked, his voice trailing off, then, staring out over the fields, he asked, "Why me? What did I do?"

·   ·   ·

The next morning a hard frost scabbed the remaining squash in the garden. By ten o'clock the clouds had broken, the frost melted, and John found himself walking to the south field, not first, as he normally did, but last, as a thing worked up to. He'd started finding his way there since breakfast, where he sat longer than usual, drinking *two* cups of coffee and reading the newspaper. Slowly—a thing normally reserved for Sunday after church. The story was front-page: LOCAL MAN FINDS BODY. Inside were pictures: police with shovels, dog teams scouring the fields. He sat with the paper in hand, breathing through his nose.

After a sip of coffee and the first column read, he said, "Karl might have been right. Police think it might be drug-related. Maybe organized crime."

"Out here? For God's sake, why?" Tillie asked, a slice of toast cooling in her hand.

John cleared his throat, spoke each word as if he were counting change. "The head and hands were missing."

Tillie settled the butter knife onto the table, dropped the toast onto a plate, and looked out the window.

"Funny. I didn't notice them missing," he said quietly.

Tillie sat back, stared at him. "You looked?"

John felt the weight of her horror. Felt his shoulders flinch.

She looked shocked at her own thoughtlessness. "I'm sorry. Of course," she offered, "it would be the natural thing to do—"

He nodded. "I thought it was just meat, something off the rendering truck maybe, I don't know, but then I saw it was human, and I looked."

Tillie stared at her hands. John sensed her backing away as she had yesterday. He waited for her to scold him. Or better yet to ask: *What did you see? How did it feel looking into that bag?* And then perhaps, *How can you sleep, having seen that?* And he'd have to admit he'd slept well enough—after a while. But Tillie remained silent. "I should go now," he said, hoping she would argue with him. Tell him to stay. Give him an excuse to stay in like a school-child on a sick day. He spread both hands on the table, then pushed his chair clear.

Tillie shook her head. "I saw my father with his arm in the thresher. I've seen body parts. It's nothing new." She paused. "But this ... I wasn't much help yesterday, was I?"

John rubbed a hand over his eyes.

"You want me to come along?" she asked, and he shook his head. The only way he knew to answer. But as Tillie lifted her face for the morning kiss, he turned away, leaving a space between them. He left the house and walked to the north field as it had been his job to do each day of his adult life. Because the fields were his. That simple. They were given into his care, and he'd never taken that obligation lightly. Walking in the morning chill, he told himself, it was just garbage—that thing he'd found—trash like the roadside cartons tossed from fast-food joints. The beer cans and piss bottles. Or the litters of kittens abandoned in ditches. He wondered what his father would have thought of it all, the improbable waste. John walked down the crest of a small hill overlooking the fields, studying the rows of blank-faced houses in the near distance—stick homes, curbs, gutters, drive-ways, and roads. The good land, the practical dirt, buried in wood, mortar, and asphalt. Waste. But then his father would never have conceived of this either. His time here being long be-fore the highway and the trash it spawned.

John walked the plowed field. Maybe next year he'd lease it out. Ben could use the extra hay. I am getting *too old* for this, he thought. He ran his fingers through his thin hair and looked to the ditch alongside the highway where he'd found the bag. A car was parked on the side of the road. A young man stood on the gravel shoulder.

John hurried, his feet sinking into the soil. There were others in the car. John slowed as he approached. The man had a sweater tied in a bright yellow knot around his waist. His hair was burnished copper in sunlight. Laughter came from inside the car, and a door opened. Another car passed slowly on the road. John could see an arm pointing to him, to his fields.

He stepped into the ditch. "You got business here?" he shouted.

"Just looking." The man squinted over at John.

John stopped to pick up a wad of paper and a pop can. He pressed the paper into his jacket pocket. "This is my land," he said.

"Hey, mister, we're not bothering anything. It's a nice day."

"It was." John held out the pop can.

"This is a public road."

"That's the road"—John pointed to where a car drove by—"and that's public road"—he pointed to the sloping shoulder—"but this is *mine*." He pointed to the ditch.

The young man backed into the opened car door. "Fuck you, you crazy old man."

John fingered the can in his hand, threw it as the car pulled away, gravel popping from the tires. The shouts of the young people trailed like exhaust, then the car winked out into a curve, and John turned, facing the road that wound through the rolling countryside and eventually leveled out in the path of subdivisions, strip malls, trailer parks, and cities. "Go ahead," he said, wiping his hands on his pants and confronting the faultless blue of the sky. "You bring Your garbage here."

. . .

Frankie Aldtenburg's All Concertina Band played every Friday night at the Elk's Club. Although Tillie had often asked John to go, this was the first time he'd suggested it. The idea had come to him as he'd pulled off his work boots, then his white cotton socks—still clean after a full day—and looked down to see his leg hairs curling dark against the pale skin. He pulled at the hair, watched the skin pimple up and snap back when released. It was at that moment, with his eyes tearing, and his breath squeezed in his throat, that he'd thought of it.

In the club's Bull Elk Room, Frankie Aldtenburg sat in a wooden folding chair, center stage, his metal walking cane propped companionably alongside. The drummer brushed a slow shuffle on the snare, while his foot kept the one beat on the bass, and the high hat floated in the yellow stage light. The other concertina player sat to the right and slightly behind Frankie, squeezing rhythm in chords.

As John and Tillie walked by, fellow Elks and neighbors nodded, said, "A little dancing, hey, John?" and "How's by you?"

Their table was near the three-piece band. Frankie played polkas and waltzes and limping two-steps. Tillie ordered a Manhattan. John drank highballs.

In the space between songs, time and again, John leaned toward his wife as though to speak, only to fall silent. He wanted to explain how he'd found himself here, wanted to draw a connection between taking off his boots and the bright dance floor where old man Aldtenburg wheezed out melodies on the concertina, knowing only that it had something to do with simply finding your legs under you. During one break their neighbor Ben stopped by the table, his head politely inclined. He rested a hand briefly on John's shoulder, his voice funereal. "How's it been, John?"

John eased back in his chair, looked at Ben through the rim of his raised highball. It made his face look water-streaked and ruined. And it was as if at that moment, he could read the mind of his neighbor, knew that what Ben was feeling was relief, that it wasn't found on his property, a short fifty yards away—that thing, like an accusation from God Himself. "Fair to middlin'," John replied, and smiled. "Corn's looking good. Bumper crop. Hear you had some bad luck with that new soybean, though." He tsked, wagged his head in pity.

Ben leaned back, looked at the ceiling a moment, then back at John. "Have to say, I've had better years." He nodded to Tillie, then to John, and strode off across the dance floor.

At the end of two hours and five highballs, John let it all drift. He raised his face to the shine of stage lights, and as Frankie trailed out of a waltz and into a schottisch, John asked Tillie to dance. On the floor they stood next to each other, John's hand riding her hip. Of all the dances, this was his favorite, with its shuffling step and skip, its determined movement forward.

His mother had taught him as a child, out on the dirt of the chicken-pecked backyard, humming the oom-pa-pa under her breath, the hens racketing out of their way. His father watched, shaking his head at such nonsense. Given the opportunity, his father would walk him through the fields instead, tell him, "You put yourself down, and stay long enough to see what God provides."

"And what's that?" John would ask.

And his father would open his arms, as if gathering in all the crops and years in a gesture. "A life," he'd say.

John felt himself stumble, but Tillie held firm, kept dancing. He threw his head back far on his neck, and shouted, "My father named me John Root."

"Yes?" she asked.

He circled the dance floor, planting each step carefully, his body bearing down as if to pack the earth beneath them.

For a week, John lingered over breakfast, ate each item slowly before walking out to the fields with the same dogged deliberation. Things seemed normal enough, the fields in place, the sky holding overhead, as though the sin in that bag had never been committed, or his discovery of the bag had been only a glancing blow after all. If he tended to fall asleep a little later, or startle awake in the dead of the night, he told himself it was no worse than when he'd worried about musk in the corn or when Karl had sickened with chicken pox as an infant. Still, Tillie watched him from the corner of her eye.

On the eighth morning he came back from town and the barber with the back of his neck clean-shaven, and the tips of his ears white where his field tan never reached. Tillie was packing squash into scalded jars, wringing the lids tight. She lifted each jar to the light before immersing it in the hot bath. On the sill behind her, already finished jars pinged and chimed as they sealed tight.

"They stop talking when they see me," he said.

"Who?" she asked.

"Everyone. It's like I told them some secret they don't want to hear."

"Everyone's just a little spooked," she said. "It could have been any one of them." She turned down the heat under the canning kettle. "The same highway runs along many a one of their farms. They just don't want to know it could have been them." She put her hand on his arm. "Listen to me. You got to listen. You're a good man. You've spent your life working to feed others—"

He shook his head, swayed on his feet. "I truck my grain to the elevator, sell it cheap as dirt. If my father grew wheat that year, he saw the bread, knew the bakers and the families who ate it. What do I see? Do I see the bread my grain makes? No. I got to take it on *faith*. But I *know* some middleman is stealing from the broker to sell to some company baker, who's stealing from the workers, and the chain grocers are piling food in Dumpsters because it's two days past shelf life in some city, and people don't buy it because they're buying booze or drugs or lottery tickets. And then they come out here to take a crap *on my land,* almost like they knew who they were coming home to."

Tillie slapped her hand down on the table. Her body settled like dust into the chair. "It was trash, coming down the highway—it stopped at the dark bend in the road. There was no *knowing* behind it, John. It was the luck of the draw. Chance. A likely spot in the road." And as much as he willed himself to believe that, even as he knelt in front of her, and she held him in her arms, some part of him doubted still.

Later that evening, on their way to Edgar and Anna's for their regular monthly card game, John drove the road as he thought a stranger might. He counted the dark stretches of unlit fields, one after another, refusing to name the owners or acknowledge their histories. They were numbers, one after another, after another, until the fields became random and the dark accidental. He breathed deeply, reassured, and when he smiled to himself, it was as if he felt his skin stretch.

At Edgar's home, around the dining-room table, six men sat, each one alternately sitting out a hand. They played five-card stud, high and low, and aces and jokers wild, while Ernest always added a bump and a wiggle. They drank beer from amber bottles that Anna carried to the table, waved their hand-rolled cigarettes, and spat small bits of tobacco from the tips of their tongues.

After a few hands, John took a long pull at his beer, looked into the bottle, and asked, "What do you get when you mix beer cans and mobsters?"

The others fell silent.

"A Chicago landfill," he answered.

The men laughed uneasily at first, then loosened up with Charlie's belly laugh.

"I don't know if we should be joking..." Anna said, and faltered. Tillie looked at John in surprise. He basked in the men's approval. Their relief.

"They should all do each other in," Ben said, and the group looked to John.

"Garbage," John said, looking away from Tillie. He leaned over Ben's hand. "More garbage," he said, his laughter coming like a bark.

"I didn't deal it." Ben scowled.

John sat out the next hand, and relaxed, thinking that perhaps it didn't matter after all. And what of it? Even if it was an accounting, as his father had promised, and if God had given him this, then hadn't John looked deep and not found *himself* wanting, but rather the greater world? And what, really, did he have to do with that? He'd been right from the start. Trash. Just trash.

Ben excused himself from the table.

Charlie raised his voice over the general laughter. "Speaking of that. I heard from Clifton that his department thinks it might have been sexual. He got a report some guy's been missing since a week ago Saturday."

"Sexual?" Hank asked.

Charlie nodded. "As in *homo*sexual."

John set his cards down.

"Said he was canvassing for AIDS or something."

"You calling?" Edgar asked John.

John folded. Edgar split the pot with Charlie, and Ernest dealt the next hand. John sat quietly. The cards hit the table with a soft sound like slapped flesh. Their voices hummed in his head and he sat with his cards flat on the table. He didn't understand what it was—how the word sexual had *changed* things, or why it had done so. He felt his breathing grow shallow. But it had. He remembered lifting the bag, how it hit his back, that fleshy contact, even through plastic, that he could not allow himself to believe at the time.

John stared at the cards spread facedown in front of him.

Edgar spoke up. "Well it don't matter. Still garbage, ain'a, John?"

John straightened in the chair, looking around the circle of men to where Tillie sat with her eyes down on her hands. "Garbage," he said.

Ben entered the room from the kitchen, a black plastic trash bag in his hands. He dropped it on the table in front of John. "Must be for you," he said, and laughed.

John's face whitened as if slapped. He sat looking at the bag as Ben turned to see how the others enjoyed the joke.

"John." Tillie left her chair next to Anna, moved to his side.

He looked up, and the group fell silent. He glanced at Tillie, then down at the bag. Tillie moved her hand toward it, but John stopped her.

"No," he whispered, wanting to spare her what he wouldn't have a week ago. "Don't look."

Ben stepped forward. "Hey, hey, it's nothing," he said. His

laugh turned awkward. "Just a joke." He ripped into the bag, and sandwiches scattered out. "It didn't mean *nothing*," he said, and, grabbing a sandwich, bit down into the bread.

Later that evening, back home, John called Karl long distance. In the background he could hear Karl's wife, "Who is it? Who is it?"

"Sell the damn place," Karl said.

"It was supposed to be *yours*," John answered.

There was a long moment of breathing on the line, then, "I don't want it, Dad. I mean, look what it's gotten you."

And how did he argue that? He sent his love and hung up. He tried to watch television, and later, in bed, he tried to rub himself alive, and failing that, to press himself limp into Tillie. She tried to help, her hands stroking him, but he remained limp, all he could see in the moonlight was a piece of himself, a piece of her, and something of them—all their parts jumbled in the dark of the room.

He got up, dressed, and left the house. In the yard, he found himself walking to his tractor, an old Allis he'd bought almost new in '64. His hand ran along the dented right wheel cover, from back in '67. He swung himself onto the cast-iron seat that knew his spine better than he did. The engine stuttered as he choked it back to life. He pulled out into the yard, and the night fled, contracted down to two converging circles of light from the tractor's high beams. He backed over to the disker, its rows of metal plates buried in wilted ragweed. He hitched it to the tractor, belly down in the damp weeds. A stone for a mallet, he hammered in the cotter pin, then looped two lengths of chain over the hook on the back of the tractor. He hiked the disks lever, and the plates lifted up to the height of the trailer wheels. Standing in the dark, he admired the gleam of frosted metal—blades he still honed himself, just as his father had, in the off-season. The damp on his shirt was like a second skin, already stiffening in the cold. The porch light turned on as he pulled onto the dirt road, and he saw Tillie standing in the doorway.

He pulled out the side yard, down the tractor road. The moon was low on the horizon, a small sickle his grandfather had used as portent for harvest in a time, long ago, when this soil was clean. John could have driven with the lights off, but he kept them on to skitter over the road with each bump, and leap onto the trees like someone whose line of sight is jerked this way, then that, by the rush of objects thrown at him. He shifted down for the rise that led into the south field. The engine warmed; the exhaust cap popped with small, contained explosions, metal ringing each time it slapped back down. The wheels churned gravel, then he was over the hill and idling, looking at the vast prospect of corn marching in straight rows outside of the headlights' reach. Here and there, he could see the illuminated eyes of raccoons peeking through the rows.

He slipped into gear, rolled forward, and the corn rustled through the headlights, then snapped like teeth clamping shut beneath him. Over his shoulder, he could see the ten-foot-wide swathe he mowed flat, flush against the wall of corn on his left. He steadied his hands on the wheel, his heart banging in his chest like the roosting pheasants that shotgunned out of the corn, scattering into the dark. There was an excitement he'd not anticipated, an intense joy rising up from his stomach, and he shouted into the drone of engine and snapping corn, nearly rising from his seat to lean over the wheel, to see what the dark revealed.

Halfway back across the field, he saw Tillie crossing the ruined path. Her hair was loose down her back, and she hugged herself as she stumbled over the flattened crop. In the light, she looked small as the startled birds. He shifted to neutral and pulled the brake.

She had a hand shading her eyes against the light. "I can't see very well," she said, nearing the tractor.

"Over here," he said, and when she stepped to the side of the tractor, he offered her a hand. She climbed up onto the wheel fender. "John, think about it. Wait until morning..."

But he shook his head, engaged the gears. "I know this field," he shouted, "don't you worry about a thing." And he did know it. He knew this field better than his own body, he thought. Maybe even as well as he knew Tillie's. She nodded for him to go on then, her arm tight around his waist, her other hand gripping the wheel cover she perched on.

They mowed the next row, and the next, nearly a quarter of the field scraped flat, the remainder bristling at the edges of the light. Tillie slumped against John. He could feel her weariness, and the joy in him turned like winter storage, old, then soft and bad. He turned the tractor at row's end, driving on.

This was what it came to. The final leveling—his father's body leading a three-car cortege, John's son, Karl, an accountant, John's own life work, and all the things he'd believed in a lifetime of belief—just so much trash. *See what the Lord provides.* He felt the anger stewing in his stomach, like a long, slow cramp, and he shoved in the clutch, shut off the engine. He stepped down from the tractor, braced against the fender, breathing through his mouth. Tillie clambered down after him, then stood at his side, stroking his forehead, trying to shrug her sweater over his shoulders.

Out across the broken field a pair of eyes winked at ground level. John started to laugh, pointing them out to Tillie. "God-damn raccoons," he said. And then the eyes, burning in the light, floated effortlessly higher to a height even with John's knees, and then it moved into the broader sweep of headlights, and he saw it was a dog. His knees went limp, his back soft, and he let out a soft cry as he made out the shape of haunches and shoulders, the narrow head of the smaller dog he'd shagged off the property days ago. The animal was ribby, its sides stove in by hunger, rummaging about the ruined corn, feeding in silence. The air was dense with the smell of bruised corn, and he hid his shaking hands in his pockets.

"It's just a dog," Tillie said. "Here, boy," she called softly. "Come here."

John stood fixed at her side, watching the dog lower its head, studying the pair of them for intent, before it slid back into the safety of the shadows, where John could feel it waiting, watching.

John sighed, his breath gelling in the cool air. The earth sounded hollow beneath his feet; he judged the depth of frost at two inches.

She turned to John again. "I'm sorry for what happened at Edgar and Anna's. It was...an ugly thing for Ben to do. He didn't mean to hurt you—"

"No," he said, "he didn't." He turned off the tractor lights, hefted the disks back to trailer height. He walked clear of the tractor, leading the way, looking for the small stray. "Here, boy," he called, crossing the standing rows of corn until they came to a small creek skinned with ice. He could hear water rustling beneath. He squatted on his heels, broke the shelf of ice with his fingers, dipped a handful and pressed it to his cheeks. He could feel Tillie's hand on the back of his head.

"I'm so sorry," she said. "All these years. Shouldn't I know how to help you?"

He patted her hand with his own, and standing again, he led the way, down the creek and away from the road. Tillie's fingers rode soft on his arm.

"The dog," he said. "One of the two I ran off that morning."

She was silent, then she squeezed his hand with her fingers. "It's just a lost, starved thing."

"But when I first saw it," he said, shook his head. "The bag, and the thing spilling out of it, I thought, for just a moment, that it was my own legs someone had cut out from under me, and I just didn't know it yet." He stopped and peered down into Tillie's eyes. "Isn't that strange?"

Tillie's eyes were bright in the dark.

John straightened up, glanced over his shoulder back along the way they'd come, toward the highway. "All this time, I've been thinking it was some kind of judgment. That after all these years I'd reaped what I had never known I'd sown." He turned to her. "I mean, how was I supposed to take it? This thing dropped on my doorstep. Out of all these miles of road, all these acres of land, it's mine that was marked for this...this corruption. Know what I did? That next day, I was so damn mad, I stood in that road and dared anybody, God included, to go ahead bring me their garbage." He looked at Tillie. His laugh was shaky.

He looked up at the broad dome of sky overhead, the clouds wadded on the horizon, "Then, at Edgar's house—when Ben brought out the bag, I thought He'd answered, sent me the damned head and hands."

Tillie squeezed his arm.

How did he explain what had come to him in the field just now? That moment he'd seen the small dog, in the dark, and felt again what he'd felt deepest that day, not the horror of the discovery but rather the soft hit and roll of the bag on his shoulder when he bore it home. And the cost of placing that burden on his back, the feel of leg, and arm—that thing in the bag—the intimate humanity of it in even that most inhuman of circumstances. He shook his head. "Ah, Tillie," he looked over at the fence line. "I called it—*him*—I called him garbage. That young man. As if I hadn't *seen*."

John Root leaned into Tillie and pressed his chin against the top of her head. He listened to her breath, cavernous in her small body. Over the top of her head, he saw the dog, a lighter patch in the dark, biding its time, waiting on the edge of the field. He would call to it again. He would coax it home with them, give it food, and a name he could bear to hear in the mornings. He would wait out here with the animal, however long it took to win its trust, and so he closed his eyes, listening to the sound of wind in the corn and water moving over rocks. He imagined the creek wandering in a tangle, under fences and roads, moving into neighboring fields past the homes of friends, and beyond to where houses squatted in packs and dogs barked and ran the lengths of their chains. He imagined row on row of distant houses, and inside the houses, all the ordinary people who shed clothes, lifted tired legs into beds, drowning the noise of dogs, of the highway, of their everyday lives and their own slow dying in the muffle of quilts and the close comfort of flesh.

THE SAME SKY

When the pickup hit the horse, it was unlike anything she'd been told about accidents. Time did not slow down. There was no slow-motion parade of hooves and whitened eyes. She was driving down hardpan, the kicked-up dust fuming in a red wash of taillights before dissipating in the dark. Nighthawks. Miles of nighthawks startling up into her headlights like hands thrown up in the air. The high prairie roused awake at night, jackrabbits cutting a zigzag course alongside the truck. A burrow owl flushed out of the roadside, running head forward, tilted into the dark ahead of her lights, legs pumping like some skinny-shanked old man.

All of this was true. And this, too, that she was driving too fast for open range. There was a movement at the side of the pickup, a hard knock, then the truck was skidding sideways down the road, the ditch in the headlights and her head rocked forward into the steering wheel.

When she lifted her head, there was the screek of windshield wipers and the headlights hot in the weeds. The side of her face was warm and wet. When she looked up into the rearview mirror, there was a frieze of black lines, like summer lightning down her face. The large, side view mirror was twisted back on its frame, the glass webbed. She unstrapped the seat belt, opened the door, and slid out into the ditch. Both front tires were flat, the rims bent. She slapped her hand on the truck, heard the reverberation in her head moments before she bent over in the weeds. It wasn't until after she'd finished retching, her heart steadied, that she wondered what had happened. She stumbled out of the ditch and onto the road, waiting for her eyes to adjust from the glare of headlights in the weeds. Pieces of night came to her slowly—farther before nearer—the blue haze of moonlight on the breaks where the land buckled down into the Missouri River bed, scrub pines, jack pines, cedar, and juniper bristling along the rim, looking at this distance to be no more than a bramble of briars; then sage, black welts on hardpan and, finally, the road glowing with its own light. Standing to a side of the road was a horse with its feet splayed out like a foal finding its first balance.

She thought, Thank God it wasn't a person. But until that moment, hadn't realized the possibility had existed in the back of her mind. And who would she expect to be out here, on foot, at night? No one she'd want to meet. Still, there was the gratitude of relief, feeling indebted to the animal for being an animal. She approached the horse slowly, wiped blood from her eye with a sleeve. "Whoah," she said softly, as the horse pivoted, swinging its rear toward her as if to kick, but then standing there, swaying with the effort, its head hung low. It was not a large animal. Her husband would say fifteen hands and shallow in the brisket, and the horse would stand condemned. But Sara was no judge of horseflesh, and she ran her fingers over the trembling flanks.

There was no reason to believe it had actually happened, except that here was the horse, and there the truck in the ditch. She believed they'd gotten off lucky—the horse stunned, herself a cut on the forehead. "What the hell are you wandering around here alone at night for?" she said aloud. "Don't you have a stall or something?" She took the mane as the horse turned its face full to her, and then she saw the muscle swinging free on the far side of its face, the eye gone. She stood in the roadway, her fingers gripping the coarse hair. There was the soft plopping of drops, and small black craters formed in the dirt road.

The horse snorted against her jacket, its breathing furious with shock. "Easy, girl," she said, then loosened her fingers one at a time and backed up. The horse collected itself, plodded after her, sought out her belly again with the warm blowing muzzle, and she braced herself.

They stood in the road like a piece of the land jarred loose, tumbled up against each other while the truck engine ticked, cooling in the dark, and the crickets came alive. The horse's breath fluttered up Sara's belly. It smelled of sage and grass, of something sweet and iron, while the wet patch spread from the horse's muzzle, across Sara's stomach and groin. She looked back down the stretch of road, then ahead, where the road passed seamless into the pearling horizon.

No lights came down the road, nor were there likely to be, for hours, maybe days. It was the reason she drove them, these back roads, ranging from abandoned homesteads of the thirties, sixties, and now the nineties, because it was her and the truck moving forever, until *she* chose to stop.

She tried to remember if she'd driven this road before, but her head felt stobbed with cotton and the horse's face was flush on her stomach. Its soft grunts of pain rose like pinpricks on her skin. When she looked up into the sky, the stars blurred, and she was dizzy. She detached herself from the horse carefully and returned to the truck. She knew she should stay with the truck, but she wouldn't. The road would cut true north, then east toward Malta, and somewhere ahead was a ranch with people who would take her in, set her politely on the sofa, and pour her boiled coffee, who wouldn't ask questions while she telephoned her husband, their eyes averted. She also knew that by daybreak, everyone within a hundred miles would know how she had come to the door, injured and alone, lost for all means and purposes—everything they'd suspected proven out. She did not belong. She wrote a note and left it on the dashboard—I've started on foot. See you soon, love Sara.

Over her shoulder, she strapped the canteen of water Rob always kept full and clean in each of his vehicles. She looked at the shotgun in the rack over the back window. She took that, too. Rob would understand the wrecked truck but not a stolen gun. She pocketed three shells from the glove compartment. The horse was at the side of the truck bumping it softly as if it were another horse it could tuck up against, head over rump. She left the headlights on, in case someone did happen by. When she slammed the door and stumbled up the ditch, the horse watched uneasily with its one bright eye, then clambered after her.

She walked the road like she drove it, eager to put what she'd seen behind her, wanting, just ahead, some sight that would dazzle and terrify, make everything new. She was young, just twenty-two, and believed she still had time to make that happen. But on her own with the wounded horse plodding beside her and the land marching farther into the dark than her imagination would permit, she had her doubts.

"What do you know about living out there?" Her father had asked that. It was his weekly Sunday drive to "blow the carbon out." Sara sat next to him, as she always had, while her mother snoozed in the backseat, the only respectable choice for the Sabbath to her way of thinking. "What do you know about living out there?" he asked Sara.

"He's a good man."

"The road to hell is paved with good men."

"That's *intentions*, Dad."

"That's a naive interpretation. And you're a naive young girl who's never lived outside the four walls provided by family, surrounded by friends in a place you've always known."

"That supposed to be my fault?"

"Who's talking fault? I'm talking facts. We send you to college. To meet a cowboy? You've fallen in love with *yes, ma'am, no, sir, foot toeing the dirt, God-damn Gary Cooper*. You don't know what it's really like, and not likely to until you're too far in it to get out."

When the horse staggered or started blowing heavily, they rested. Its breathing made a high, keening noise, then it coughed, and its forelegs and the road darkened scattershot. She looked at the new freshet of blood and felt culpable, but with reluctance. Yes, *if she hadn't been here*, but then *if the horse hadn't been here*, and finally, *if this place wasn't what it is*.

The road was mostly level with long slow dips she only felt as a lagging in the muscles. She kept to the center, clear of the prickly pear and sage that lined the ditches. She watched her left for a break in the road ahead. The three-quarter moon stared over the blue-white hardpan, the sage and gramma grass in silver-and-gray relief. In the farthest distance, she thought she could make out the drop to the breaks, black and opening like a tear, and she imagined the Missouri as she'd seen it with Rob, churned muddy in daylight below crumbling, ochre cliffs. She could love this place, she thought, if it allowed.

There was the sound of hooves stumbling, sage snapping, and Sara turned to see the horse had angled down into the ditch. Crickets trickled out in the road from the crushed sage. The horse stumbled, went down on its front legs as if genuflecting to the ditch and the brittle crickets and the skin of hardpan under the wide black dome overhead. It is bigger than us all, she thought. Nothing and no one walks large in this place. She felt sweat cooling on her neck and looked back, over her shoulder, to where she'd come from, where the truck she could no longer see was still lodged in the ditch, headlights on. It would be safe. She could hole up like a settler in a sod house, under a roof, doors locked until someone came by to get her. Rob perhaps. Though in this minute, her skin as alive as the insects, she knew that wouldn't happen, convinced as he was that she was leaving him.

It had started months ago, with the beginning of summer after the roads had baked to brick from the gumbo of spring melt. "I need to get out sometimes," she'd said.

"Every day?" he asked, pulling on work jeans.

She sat on the bed, still amazed she could do this—watch a man draw his clothes on, study the tucks in his stomach as he bent over, the dark hair rising in a line up his belly while the sun cracked through the window, and dust skimmed the sill with the first light. The room smelled of them, from the way they slept tangled in each other.

"I just need to get out," she'd said.

"Go visit Maggie."

And she did that on occasion, visited Maggie, the wife of his uncle Art, who Rob worked for in hopes of earning shares in the childless couple's ranch. Rob's older brother, Greg, was partner in his father's ranch, struggling to sustain two families now. The economics of land acquisition weren't the same as back home. Here cattle had to range and be rotated from section to section for grazing. To sustain Art's herd, his ranch totaled thirty thousand acres, of which six thousand to seven thousand were deeded acres, the rest supplemented by leases from the Bureau of Land Management. It was not something a young couple, just starting out, could afford. You worked your way into it, earning shares and finally a partnership and maybe at the end you could afford to buy the remainder when the time came with corporate profits. Rob was on probation. He would make or break his uncle's trust within the first five years. She could be the daughter Maggie never had. It was unspoken, but it was there. Through family, you made your way in or out.

He pulled on his boots. "You're leaving. One hundred and fifty miles yesterday." He took her pillow from her arms, raised it to his face as if trying to remember the smell of her hair.

"I only left seventy-five. It took the other seventy-five miles to come back." She smiled.

He leaned over where he was sitting, her pillow in his lap, his breathing shallow. "How am I supposed to fence or work cattle knowing you're a hundred miles gone and still going?"

She felt like a child. After he left, she cleaned, the dust easing back in even as she worked from bedroom to living room to kitchen. It was a small two-bedroom house, owned by Art and Maggie, located on the far side of the spread, and took little enough of Sara's day to keep tidy. She made a casserole and stuck it in the refrigerator. She sat on the front porch, let a fine grit build on her legs while their dog Coot moved with the shrinking shade that slanted off the truck. Prairie hens buffed their breasts in the dirt, their wings snapping like shuffled cards. The land burned into a distance that quaked in waves, then damped, sweeping forward in a clean relief against the bright so that she could tell the shape of each cloud rolling overhead, and the sky was a wide magnifying glass blowing huge shadows around the timid house and truck.

She could do more, she knew, other things, bake bread, hoe the small garden, watch the TV she left on all day for the sound of voices. But she wouldn't. Her reasons had to do with living in a place where none of the old rules held true, where she had to learn everything over again. It had to do with sitting on a front porch and owning a dog she'd never watched grow up. She walked over to the truck, opened the door, and settled into cushions sagged by the shape of her own body. But Rob had taken the keys. It was the first and only time he'd done that.

The horse nudged her, and careful to keep to the undamaged side, Sara stroked its neck and rubbed behind the ear. "How you doing, girl?" She rested her cheek on the horse's withers, the pain in her head easing with the pressure. She could hear the horse's breathing, and beneath that the bones, like rocks knocked loose from sockets deep in riverbeds during spring melt, and the heart like a soft echo of the pounding she felt in her own head. And she thought, for a moment, she could feel the animal's pain, as though what she'd done to the horse, she'd done to herself, too, and it staggered her. She stood back and waited until her stomach eased. Then she unstrapped the canteen and poured water into her hand and raised it to the horse's muzzle. When she pulled her hand back, it was a dark smear, the pain in the horse's eye as tight as Sara's heart squeezing in her chest. They would fix the animal, and every step they took seemed to prove it could be done. As long as an animal was upright and moving, there was hope. Rob had told her that. She and Rob could buy it. It would be hers to care for. She would love it. How could she not? "We'll find help," she said. "People out here know about these things."

They'd been walking well over an hour, she guessed. The gun knocked into her back from the sling over her shoulder. It felt strange, like a reminder of something she should remember. Rob would be home now. He would have turned on the yard light as he did every evening—"It's like I own something," he'd once told her. "Even if it's only one small part of the dark." And though he'd have seen the truck gone from the yard, he'd check the house, go room by room. Coot would be lapping up the freshwater in his bowl, spilling as much as he drank, and Rob would absently clean it up. All the details she could imagine clearly. And that frightened her.

There was movement, out in the sage. At first she'd dismissed it as her own nervousness, seeing it, then not seeing it. But the third time she turned to stop and watch, she could make out the gray shifting on the blue hardpan. She saw it stop and fuse into the sage before trickling out again. And then there was another one, farther back and maybe more. She knew little enough about coyotes, except their thin barks heard through the bedroom window at night and the occasional coyote scuttling through the fences during the day. Then there was what the ranchers said. "Wolves. They want to bring back the son of a bitchin' wolves. As if the coyotes aren't bad enough." And although they might never look at her while speaking, she felt the conversation was pointed at her, as if she were emblematic of all the *wrongheaded newcomers* come west to Montana. Coyotes took their toll of newborns and the weak. "And now wolves—" They would nod, and the conversation would move on to bounties and jokes about wolf-pelt seat covers for the truck. They cataloged the three S's. Shoot, Shovel, and Shut Up. Subject closed, and who was to argue? She felt ignorant and young, robbed of seeing the things they had seen. She kept quiet.

Ahead, perhaps a quarter mile, she could make out the shape of a building, a square of dark rising on the land. She walked faster, her legs tiring and the shotgun digging a ditch down her spine. The horse kept pace, turning its head dully from time to time to see from its remaining eye what it could smell through its own blood—coyotes ranging in a loose string behind them.

The building was an old log cabin with a roof that slumped like a saddle and touched the ground on the far side where the back wall had imploded, over time and under weather, across the cabin floor. There was no front door, just the smaller hole opening onto the larger in the wall behind. She crossed the sill, her shoes gritting on bits of metal. Wedges of window glass winked from the pine floor that yielded under her feet like sponge. There were rustlings in the dark corners where small animals bullied their way through the debris. A dish shard gleamed white in the shadows. She called out, hello—an old courtesy retained from home where neighbors walked across lawns and stopped by to chat, or stepped out for a moment leaving doors open. Outside, the horse nickered, a bubbling spring welling out of the bed of lungs and bones through hollow reeds of cartilage, the sound fluctuating with the tidal heart. She returned to the porch and watched the horse. Its back was washed with moonlight, the ruined side of its face turned to her like a geologic fault, slumped free and eroding. The coyotes circled nearer, tails down, heads up. She threw what might have been an old tin can at the foremost coyote, but it fell short of the animal. Still, it dodged off in a sideways dance, tail down and ribs convex. The others stood still. She unslung the gun from her shoulder. She fingered the three shells loose in her pocket and withdrew one, studied it in the dark with shaky fingertips. She rubbed the dirt and lint from it.

She stepped off the porch, walked slowly past the horse, keeping an eye on the coyotes which backed off in a lope. "Easy, girl." she told the horse. "I'm a regular deadeye with one of these." She felt clumsy. Truth was, she'd never shot a gun until she'd married Rob. He'd taught her how to load and fire, but she was inconstant in her practice. He gave up. "Get close," he said. "This'll do the rest." How close was close? Fifty feet would do it. It was an old twelve-gauge Remington pump. She could feel the initials R.O.B., for Robert Otto Barnett, inscribed on the stock. The middle name Otto was his grandfather's but, even so, it was a name Rob rarely admitted to. She placed a shell in the chamber, heard it click into place, and began to feel better. She could do this. She braced the butt against her hip for leverage and pumped with her left hand. The horse had swung its ears back, its eye bright and turned on her. She raised the gun to her shoulder, the barrel seeming longer, heavier than her arm could manage. It swayed a bit and she planted her feet and tucked it tighter, putting her back into keeping it up and steady. Aim low for the kick that would follow. She remembered that. The coyotes waited in a loose pack. She squeezed the trigger and found it locked. "Shit," she said, and lowered the gun to thumb free the safety. She raised it again, snugged it tight, braced herself, closed her left eye, and squinted down the sight. She took a deep breath, held it, and fired. The gun kicked up and there was a brief flash and the bang racketing in her ears all at the same time.

One of the coyotes leaped, its rear end slewing out from under it, then scrabbled up onto all fours and limped off, the others chasing after, nipping at the wounded one. The horse bolted back toward the road. It hit the ditch, lost its footing and regained it, then slowed to what looked like a stumbling two-step. Sara followed, the gun swinging in her hand. After a few minutes, the horse stood in the road snorting, its ears twitching. She could see where fresh blood had spattered the chest.

There was no sign of the coyotes. She pulled at her earlobe to quiet the ringing in her head and felt a crust of blood. Her fingers traced the knot on her forehead, and her head throbbed with the excitement, the noise, the run. "You and me, girl," she said softly to the horse. "What a pair."

She felt stronger than she'd ever felt since coming west eight months ago. She wondered what her parents would think of her now. She traced the straight line of her nose, ran fingertips over her cheekbones as if expecting to find a whole new configuration of muscle and bone, the change inside as apparent as her face, this newfound certainty—she *could* do this. It was the West after all, the land declaring its own terms, the gun putting them in your favor.

She stepped off and, after a pause, the horse followed. As they walked, prairie hens startled awake in a quiver of wings; the wind stirred, and she opened her collar to the breeze; the moon paced them across the sky. She could not tell how far they'd come, all distances looking the same, the horizon no farther nor nearer, no landmarks to judge by but the tiring of her body. She imagined telling Rob about this evening. He'd be proud. She'd be one of them.

Not that her neighbors treated her with anything but kindness. They treated her as a guest. When she had been in Montana for one month, and true spring was still a month away, they'd been invited for dinner to their neighbor's house to "meet some folks." She was sitting in Janet's kitchen with the neighboring women, neighbors being a relative term when homesteads covered miles, ten or twenty between them—sometimes more, rarely less. Janet and her husband, Ted, were school friends of Rob's. And that Janet and Rob had had a history seemed obvious from the distance they carefully maintained.

Sara sat near the doorway in the kitchen, half-hearing the men and the women. It was like back home with the men gathered in the living room, smoking, sipping drinks, amid talk of work and friends and fools, while the women grouped in the kitchen at the cutting boards, the stove door opening and shutting on waves of heat as breads were shuffled out and pies in. Rhoda, a heavyset young woman armed with a limp swatter, slapped stock flies from the walls. Sara leaned her head against the doorframe, privileged to both conversations.

"From Wisconsin? Knew some folks from Illinois. Come out for elk," said a man's voice.

Another crack of the flyswatter. "Hate those bastards," Rhoda said, scooping the fly off the wall. There was a silence from the women, as though they hadn't heard Rhoda speak.

"Filthy things," she said. "I know where they've been. Wake up with them crawling on your face in the morning—" She smacked another one.

Another man's voice, "Told him where the damn cows were. Forgot to mention the horses." There was laughter.

Several children filed in through the kitchen door, talking and lifting hats from their heads. The screen door bounded shut behind each one. Janet's youngest son, Tyler, clomped in last. Janet hooked him with one arm. "Go back out, scrape off those boots."

"—read about it in a history book. So he's fixing to do it just like the Indians. Put the damn thing on, rack and all, right over his clothes." There was a snort and silence.

"He'll be a one to contend with, that one," Maggie said, her eyes fixed on the cutting board.

"Well, did it work?" a man's voice.

Janet nodded. "The girls are still better on horses though," she said, referring to her twins. "Gripes him to no end." Though Sara could not decipher what it was, something unspoken passed between two women, Janet's eyes lighting with a concealed pleasure and Maggie's hand tightening around the celery stalks.

"They're older," Maggie answered curtly. "Couple of years, he'll get some size on him. It all evens out in the end." Another slap from Rhoda's flyswatter.

The men paused for a sip of whiskey while building up to the next story and the next, until dinner was served. What was it Rob had said during the meal? "Best I've eaten in a while." The meat went tough in Sara's mouth. The women reproached him with silence, while the men looked amused. Throughout the dinner, it seemed to Sara there were levels of conversations she could not read. Sides taken, issues avoided. They spoke of old neighbors and friends accompanied by nods or a tight shake of the head, as if there were whole histories related as much by the silence as the talk. It was congenial. Careful. Polite.

. . .

She stopped in the road. The horse had dropped back about twenty feet and was standing still. She called, "Come on, girl." The horse stayed still. She walked back a few steps. "Not much farther now." She looked around for farm lights. No, she corrected herself. *Ranch* lights. How far had she come? How much farther did she have to go? She tried to find that certainty again, the confidence she'd felt those few miles back. How could it escape her so easily, like sweat wicking into the high plains air. She admitted it. She felt so God-damned alone. And maybe, she reasoned, you had to need solitude more than anything or anybody to make it out here. And maybe it was true. Maybe she *was* leaving him, heading east on foot with the horse at her side like the women before her who didn't make it.

It was a hard thing to give over what she believed, what she imagined to be so. This was not what she had wanted herself to be—scared and alone in a place that only served to remind her of all she did not know, of all she would never know. "So who needs it?" she asked, looking out over the land, turning to the horse. "Who needs it?"

The horse stood in the road with its feet splayed out the way she'd first seen it, its head wrenching queerly on its neck. Even from this distance, she could see how the muscles bunched and twitched as it dropped to its knees.

The horse fell to its side, its eye rolled back and the maimed side of its face ground into the dirt. She watched absorbed, more afraid of the horse now and the commotion that moved through its body—intestines coiling, heart cavitating, its brain electric.

She backed off. The seizure went on as a nighthawk whistled overhead. When it ended, the horse remained prone and disoriented. She talked to it, trying to soothe the animal, to make it recognize her again. After a while, it rolled to its knees, its muzzle resting on the dirt. It finally rose to its feet, stood stunned a moment, then lifted its head and blew its nostrils clear before moving off the road, striking across country, its head held high as if sustained in a singular vision.

Sara watched it leave. She called, but the horse kept going, intent on its own course, its head held like a compass against the stars. Lost on the road was one thing. Lost out there was another. The road was something she could know about. It connected things, homes, towns, people; there was a name for where it had been and where it was going. But out there, she would have no way of knowing. It was a warm evening, and the snakes would be active. It would be easier to spot them on the road. She was wearing tennis shoes, for Christ's sake, tennis shoes and blue jeans. Did snakes hear? The horse was moving away, and then none of that mattered, not the snakes or the tangle of land. All that seemed important was that the horse was leaving. She took a sip of water, loaded a shell, and stepped off the road. Grasshoppers snatched at her clothing, clinging and dropping. She brushed at them, then gave up and let them ride. The air was fragrant with bruised sage where the horse had walked.

When she was young and stubborn with the pleasure of wading chest deep in the smell of green, she'd trampled hayfields. Back home, she knew the stink of skunk cabbage that grew in the kettles and the wet smell of saw grass in the marshes. There was the sight of May apples like a clutter of parasols under the oaks in the deep woods. There were columbines, and shooting stars, wild cranesbill, and jack-in-the-pulpits. Her trees were aspen and oak, maples, ironwood, hickory and elm. Here it all looked the same to her, if not to Rob.

In the thirties, Rob had told her, they burned off the spines of prickly pear with handheld blowtorches so the cattle could eat

it. They had been walking the fence line on an early Sunday afternoon, late spring. The ground was just firming from the gumbo it
had been, and the smell was the sweet and tender sage just coming into its own. But there was no smell of dirt, and Sara thought,
who could have prepared her for this—spring without the smell of
black earth, until to breathe it was to eat it. They edged around
the alkali pools where cattle would drink through the summer,
water already beginning to shrink from the edges that would later
crack into plates, lift in slabs, and curl under the midsummer sun.
As they walked, Rob taught her incidentally—by anecdote—as if
what he knew came of a *need* to know, and anything gained otherwise was worthless.

"That's greasewood, an invasive plant. Poisonous to cattle in
some stages of growth."

"And that?"

"Cheat grass. Grows on broken land that's been let go. Bor-
ders a lot of the old homesteads. Makes decent forage when it's
new, but when it's dry the seeds are sharp and work into the
cow's face. Impactions and abscesses. Nests beneath the eyelids
like a clutch of eggs. Hell of a mess." He stepped back and
scanned the fence line.

"And this?" she asked.

"Silver sage." He shrugged.

"I thought that was sage." She pointed to a large silver-leafed
clump.

"It is. Big sage," he explained and stopped. She could see
how her frustration worked on him, how his hands hung at his
side, his back braced, his chin up. How he watched her for a clue.
"Same family, though," he said, trying to encourage her. And then
he tucked his hands in his rear pockets. "Give it time," he said. He
looked over her head, then down into her eyes. "We got a while,

don't you think?" And she thought she never loved anyone better than Rob at that moment, with his hands caught in his pockets and all his love perilous on his face.

The horse was weaving, its pace slowed to a stroll, its head rigid with purpose. The moon had slipped down near the horizon. In the distance, Sara thought she could make out the shape of cattle, and farther yet, a faint glow, a yard light, maybe, or house lights, but the horse angled clear of that, heading back into the darkness. She stayed with it, keeping a watch for snakes, hoping she would hear the rattle through the buzzing in her head. Her head felt numb, the knot on her head larger than when she'd last checked it. She wondered what it felt like to have a seizure, the brain firing a barrage of synaptic fireworks. Her mouth went dry, and she took a long drink of water. She thought of other things. Her old home. Her parents readying for bed. *She is eight years old and has snuck out in her pajamas and walked down to the lake. The evening is warm for late spring. She stands on the grassy shore and hears a multitude of bells, tiny and chiming in the water. She kneels down and sees ice reduced to nuggets, ringing on the water's surface. The houses around the lake are dark and fold into the trees and the trees into the sky that only begins where the stars end.*

Who or what, she wondered, could have prepared her for this—the necessity of familiarity? Big sage, she told herself, and touched the shrub. But who was to say if she was right. She tried to think of a plant from home that would be like sage. That could give her some comfort. It seemed she could not look at the present without looking back first—back home this, back home that, back home *we*—the past was more tangible than this place whose names remained elusive and unconvincing without experience.

Still, with the dirt solid under her feet and the sage crushed in her hand, she had to think, *but that she could remember it with such detail, her past might never have happened.* Who was to say if she still was who she had been? Sara looked at her hands. In what do you believe? She lifted her head. Orion's belt brighter than it had ever been back home. The North Star. Then she imagined Rob. *He is out on the porch, watching for truck lights, still wearing his work clothes, a tear in his jeans, high on the left thigh where a barb caught him. He holds his broad-brimmed hat in one hand, bumps it against his knee in a steady rhythm. He thinks about the length of fence he has tightened, certain it will hold now, thankful for how his hands ache from the work. He wonders if this will be the first night he will sleep alone again. He tries to imagine Sara behind the wheel of the truck, the direction she's taken, the distance she's covered. He thinks about the stretch of fence he has to check tomorrow. What more could he have done? The house is dark behind him, and Coot ranges in the yard, the tags on his collar chiming like tiny bells.*

The horse moved off. Later on, she would tell herself she always knew it, but, in truth, it had only come to her at that moment, standing there with the tiny clutching of grasshoppers and the smell of sage. Animals walk off to die alone. The horse dropped. It was that easy. From this distance, she could see the legs fold like wilted petals and hear the rush of air billowing out. It rolled onto its side with the ease of water, rolling and subsiding, its belly fluid and white. She stood with her arms at her side, the gun butt wedged in the dirt, the shell still chambered. She could see the horse's sides slump, the puff of dust settle from its last breath. And then, with its eye already milking white, its legs began to move, treading the air in a slow, ponderous gallop, as if its final resolve was a thing of flesh and will, fixed, like its eye, on the distance. The animal quieted, its body pooled into the sage and the sage into the land, and all of that into the horizon and on into the sky until, after a long while, Sara's eyes began to dry and each thing—the sky, the land, the sage, the chirr of crickets—became individual, as particular and purposeful as the ache behind her breast. On the horizon, heat lightning illuminated a bank of clouds green as new hay. She looked one last time at the horse, then turned away, walking back to where she believed a yard light burned a bright hole in the land under the wide dome of heaven, clear and pierced with starlight.